Small Secrets

Joan Jacobson

This is a work of fiction. The people and events are products of the author's imagination. Any similarities to real people and events are evidence of the veracity of literary archetypes and the unchanging nature of the human condition.

Bible quotations are from the *New Revised Standard Version* (NRSV) or the *Revised Standard Version* (RSV).

Design by Susan Tyler
Cover Photograph by Maksymowicz
ISBN-13: 978-0692976456
Published by WORDS & PAGES LLC

DEDICATION

For all writers and readers.
We couldn't survive without each other.

.

TABLE OF CONTENTS

PART ONE

The grave soul keeps its secrets, and takes its own punishment in silence.

Dorothy Dix

Halcyon, Minnesota

2016

1

WHAT DAY IS a good day to confess? To answer for the lie that's your life?

Raki's mentor lay in a casket, taking her secret to the grave. Whatever it was. Quite an accomplishment. Not one Raki wanted to emulate, but their circumstances were different. Miss Dolores Richter left no descendants. Raki had a daughter. Josephine deserved the truth.

How? When?

She sniffed. The piney fragrance of fresh lavender hung over the funeral like a pall. Appropriate. Dolores's garden had beaconed summer: 'It's that time of year again. I smell Miss Richter's lavender,' the people of Halcyon, Minnesota, used to say. Her porch railing, hung with sheaves of it, was the small-town landmark: 'Turn left at the lavender house,' was how they gave directions.

So it hadn't seemed particularly odd that the deceased left instructions for her casket to be packed with lavender. Raki didn't think so. Nobody did. Or maybe everybody did.

What was the deal with all the lavender? Forty-plus years, and I never even asked? Coward.

Whatever secret Dolores had buried, it was certainly no worse than her own. They could have had a mutual unburdening. Too late now.

Tears crawled down her cheeks. She felt a soft tissue urged into her palm. Nothing like a funeral to wring out regrets.

Then again, the lavender may have been nothing, a mere female fascination, like collecting birdhouses.

No way.

Raki swabbed away the tears and turned her attention to the eulogy.

A long-time employee of Miss Richter's newspaper was describing his boss's infamous fashion sense. Miss Richter preferred a wardrobe of black business suits, he reported, because of her small interest in laundry or dry-cleaning. "She told me, 'I can spill a whole spoonful of spaghetti sauce on myself at lunch, wipe it up and still be presentable for the editorial meeting,'" he quoted. The mourners chuckled softly.

Raki scoffed. Dolores didn't even like spaghetti. And why black? Red would camouflage tomato sauce just as well. And what about all the purple accessories? Always an amethyst brooch, a violet blouse or a flowery scarf. What about them? This man was one lousy reporter.

The words "Let us pray" interrupted Raki's judgment. After "Amen," the organ struck up the alleluia verse.

The minister intoned from the monumental Bible spread over the pulpit: "No one after lighting a lamp hides it under a jar, or puts it under a bed, but puts it on a lampstand, so that those who enter may see the light. For nothing is hidden that will not be disclosed, nor is anything secret that will not become known and come to light."

An ironic reading, considering that Miss Dolores Richter had worked so hard to hide her philanthropy. Some may have guessed where all the gifts from 'Anonymous' had come from through the years, but until it was revealed upon her death, nobody in Halcyon knew for sure.

In the Sixties, when Raki was a girl, the gifts had been small, like the wool coat a classmate got when the thermometer fell to thirty-below. By the Nineties the gifts had grown to tuition-size or down-payment-size, but were never publicly acknowledged. Unlike other scholarships and economic development grants, all duly heralded in Miss Richter's *Halcyon Times*.

That 'jar' from the scripture verse. It hid more than light. What had Dolores camouflaged with philanthropy?

The obituary folders turned into fans as the sermon dragged on and the air conditioner failed against the heavy heat. Then the final hymn boomed from the organ and they were excused to the fellowship hall.

SAM'S WARM BREATH whiffed Raki's ear as they exited down the aisle. "I think I'll bond with the boys over beer," he whispered. "If that's OK with you."

Such a helpful husband he'd been during the service, keeping her supplied with tissues. But he surely didn't need any more weak coffee and white cake. He got his fill of that on the job.

"Take a day off," she ordered. "I've got our daughter and my best friend to keep me company. Not to mention all these people whose names I've forgotten."

"I'll pass her a note when she doesn't know a name," said Margaret. "Like my students used to do in class."

"You're a good friend, Margaret," Sam laughed. "Josephine, keep that thank you speech short. No more than twenty minutes."

"Oh, Dad, a pastor like you gets twenty," said Joey. "Five minutes is all they'll stand from a politico."

The women waved him out the door as they turned up the stairs to the hall.

"Never mind names," Raki said to Margaret as they waited in the buffet line. "They can't expect me to remember everyone after all my years away."

Plates filled, they found three chairs at a table of townspeople already deep in reminiscence.

"Miss Richter didn't always wear black," recalled a white-haired gentleman. "She used to waltz in with that out-of-town boyfriend, back in the old days at the Bloody Bucket Saloon, wearing this skin-tight green dress."

A boyfriend? Who knew?

"Watered silk," said a woman who looked to be his wife, forking up some pasta salad. "It captured the light. And only tight on the bodice. The skirt was poufy—very fashionable back then. Remember those crinolines? Makes me itchy just thinking about it. Must have been 1950 or so."

Dolores Richter in a green dress? Swooping around a dance floor with a man? Raki couldn't imagine. Something major must have happened to turn her into a single-minded career woman.

The wife leaned over the table, lowering her voice, "I'm not sure when she went all black. She even wore bright colors during the Depression and World War II. The rest of us girls were so dowdy, but her father spared no expense."

"Old Judge Richter," agreed her husband. "He thought she was the prettiest *and* smartest girl ever born." He cast his eyes about the table, pointing his mayonnaise-spotted fork at Joey. "Did you know she clerked for the judge when she was still in high school? He was certain she was going to become the first woman on the Supreme Court."

"My inspiration, Sandra Day O'Connor, took that slot," said Joey, fishing a maraschino cherry from her fruit salad. "What made her switch to journalism?"

"Well, she never finished law school. Went for a year or so, I forget, and then took off for France to help some friend of hers working for the Red Cross. Armistice had happened quite a few years before, but I guess there was still lots of work because of the refugees."

Raki looked to Margaret, who shrugged. Had Dolores ever mentioned France? Not that she recalled. Table talk turned to speculation over why such a laudable detail hadn't made it into her obituary.

"It was less than a year she was over there. Then she came back and that's when she went into the newspaper thing," said the wife. Her silvery coif bobbed as she reached for the insulated coffee pot.

"Who knows what she was even doing in France?" said the white-haired gentleman. "Pushing papers? Picking through rubble? Probably nothing worth bragging about sixty-some years later."

"Nothing worth hiding either," muttered a different old woman. "You people are ridiculous. I lived next door to that woman and I can tell you, if there was ever anybody hiding something, she was. And it wasn't sweetness and light and good deeds she was keeping tight under wraps."

Raki flinched.

"Don't mind her, Raki," whispered Margaret. "Town gossipmonger is all she is."

"And the smell!" continued Gossipmonger.

"The smell?" Raki couldn't tell who said that, but everyone craned their necks for the answer.

"Those damned flowers of hers. There's too much of a good thing, you know."

"Whatever happened to Miss Richter's boyfriend?" Raki interjected, changing the subject.

The old man squinted at her as if he was trying to place her face, but could not quite remember. He mumbled to his silver-coifed wife, who responded in a whisper loud enough for the non-elderly to catch. "That girl with the funny name. Ran away with that pastor. You remember."

He turned back to Raki. "Never saw him again. Dropped off the face of the earth, he did."

Dropped off the face of the earth? What did that mean?

Margaret chimed in. "Can you imagine our Miss Richter dating? Getting married? Darning socks and that other nonsense we used to do? Not her style."

"Mrs. Michael Voll," said the old wife. "Surely you, of all women, have never darned a sock."

Margaret smiled. "I married into the fancy house; I didn't grow up in one." She mimicked stitching in the air. "I know how to patch a hole with needle and thread."

And so the people at the table prattled on about how times had changed. From the Fifties through the Sixties, Seventies and so on, changes reported in, and sometimes instigated by, Miss Richter's weekly newspaper.

"Remember that deplorable fire trap she got shut down? The one where they kept those unwed mothers locked up like criminals? Fifty years ago?"

"That paper of hers was mostly useful for finding out whose kids had piano recitals and what nonsense the school board was up to.

But she turned into Edward R. Murrow when she found out how those poor girls were treated."

"Muckraker," Gossipmonger mumbled. "Bastard children."

The old man ignored the interruption. "People said those girls got what they deserved. But there were never any boys there getting what they deserved. Takes two to tango. I know that from personal experience."

His wife pretended to blush.

"I'll never forget the hoopla." He shook his head. "People threatened to quit subscribing if she didn't retract the articles. She never did. They never did."

"Her paper was the only way to get the grocery coupons," explained his wife.

As the sandwiches and salads were replaced with white cake and whipped topping, a church woman hustled to the front, waving a microphone at the crowd, asking for tributes. Chatting drained away as the flower shop owner thanked the deceased for the down payment on her first greenhouse.

"I would've offered her free lavender for life, if I had known." The crowd chuckled. "Seriously, though, my baby grew up in that greenhouse. It was our life."

Two friends related how they met in the day care Miss Richter subsidized. A story was told about a used Cavalier gifted to a single mom so she could get to work. Back rent suddenly paid up. A pair of glasses for a preschooler. And so on.

Was there a pattern in all this? Some clue to Dolores's secret? Raki's sleuth training had ended with Nancy Drew in the fifth grade. But if she could discover her mentor's secret, perhaps that would give her courage to reveal her own.

Joey, or Josephine Bergstrom, Esq., Chief Counsel to the governor, as Raki was proud to hear her so grandly introduced, was the last to speak. She expressed gratitude for the scholarship that allowed her to attend the University of Minnesota Law School, the same school Miss Richter had attended then abandoned.

Raki hid troubled thoughts behind a proud smile.

How do I tell my daughter I'm not the person she thinks I am?

2

AS THE TRIBUTES ended and the clatter of cups and scrape of forks resumed, Raki picked up her annoyance with the gossipmonger's defamation of the deceased. Defamation, a word she had learned from Joey.

Gossip rankled hard. For all the decades she'd lived in Minneapolis, Raki still wondered what dirt they dished on her back here in Halcyon. 'Girl who ran away with the pastor' wasn't so bad, but what else did they whisper, more discreetly, when she wasn't sitting right here?

"What are you glaring at, Mom?"

"Not you," she mouthed, swallowing the last bite of cake.

"Good," said Joey, getting up from her folding chair. "I'm going to meet Dad and the guys." She pecked her mother's cheek. "Join us when you're ready."

When Joey was gone, Margaret echoed her question. "You didn't answer. Why are you glaring like that?"

Raki jerked her head toward the old gossipmonger, busy licking non-dairy whipped topping off her fork. Margaret lifted her hands palms up, peering over the top of her eyeglasses.

"Never mind," said Raki. In spite of her annoyance, she didn't want to speak against the old woman, who was only voicing the same suspicions she had always had.

Back in the Seventies, when Raki first met Miss Richter, it would have been disrespectful for her, then just a teenager, an unwed mother, to pry into the personal details of such an older and accomplished person.

She and Joey had been living—hiding out, really—with Margaret. And yet, this newspaper publisher, the most notable woman in Halcyon, befriended them. It seemed that no matter what time of day Raki strollered baby Joey to the playground, Miss Richter determined that time to be the perfect hour for a picnic lunch. Before Joey cut her teeth, Miss Richter always seemed to discover an extra banana to mash up. Once the baby's teeth were in, it was a cookie Miss Richter consistently found herself too full to enjoy. The newspaper lady would sit at the rough picnic table in her black suit, watching Joey fly in circles on the little merry-go-round, chubby legs stuck straight out in front, hands clutched fast to the metal handle, squealing glee. Miss Richter would close her eyes like an opera-lover rapt in a final aria. She never left ahead of Raki and Joey. Whether they stayed for an hour or two, she would still be sitting on the picnic bench when Raki put Joey back in the stroller for the walk back to the Voll mansion.

Margaret's whisper interrupted Raki's reverie. "Are you worried she talks about you, too?"

Raki shrugged.

"You're not wearing a scarlet letter, you know."

Margaret, still the English teacher.

"Thanks to Miss Richter's articles," she said, resuming a normal volume, "they imagine you're wearing a halo, Mrs. Reverend Samuel Bergstrom, CEO."

Very doubtful, but nice to hear. Time to change the subject. "When shall we start tomorrow?"

Dolores Richter had bequeathed Raki, Joey and Margaret (i.e. Rakella Bergstrom, Josephine Bergstrom and Margaret Voll, as properly set forth in the legal documents) the task of going through the personal effects left in the lavender-bedecked house. Joey was taking time off from her duties at the capitol in St. Paul. Raki had left her managers to supervise the bakers at Blessed Breads Co. Margaret was taking a break from her retirement project—reading all ninety-seven titles on the ALA banned classics list.

"It doesn't matter to me," Margaret answered over the squeal of her chair scraping the linoleum. "Check with Joey when you get back to your sister's house. Call me." She left, striding between rows of tables lined up straight as desks in a classroom or corn in a field.

RAKI THOUGHT IT WISE to leave as well, before anyone she didn't remember recognized her. That would require the embarrassingly vague response, "Oh, how nice to see *you* (no name inserted). After *all these years*." Raki gathered her purse and retreated to the restroom.

She took out a comb and used it in front of the mirror. Her sister Lija used to call her hair 'rhubarb-colored.' Their dad joked that red suited her personality. The steel gray replacement suited even better. Kinking every which-a-way and prone to escaping, yet capable of being brought under some control—given a bit of love and attention.

Like the love and attention she'd given her unruly baby nephews. The ones now drinking beer with Sam and Joey at the Walnut Room. Time to join them.

THE WALNUT ROOM had once been a place for white table cloths, finger bowls, linen napkins and candlelight, before its reputation fell apart in the Seventies. Like her own. Now resurrected as Halcyon's place to go for craft beers and artisanal liquor. Almost citified. Like herself.

Coming from bright sunshine into a dim bar made it difficult, but Raki spotted Sam right away. Four decades married and he was still the best-looking guy in any room. Even when he wore that ridiculous circular collar, which he had been glad to leave at home today.

Joey sat next to her dad, bantering with her cousins. The guys, dressed neatly, nails scrubbed clean, were having a grand time cutting her down to size.

"Just making sure Cuz here doesn't let that bastard she works for screw us farmers," said Jimmy, Jr., grinning and slapping Joey on the back. So close in age and remarkably alike. Same snub nose and hay-colored hair. But then half the people in Halcyon were blond, thanks to all those Scandinavian ancestors.

"Here, here," said Jimmy's three brothers, raising their glasses as Raki flagged over a waitress. She ordered a pinot as the men and Joey mixed farm jokes with state politics. Sam had limited knowledge of agriculture and politics, but he was listening, probably mining the conversation for sermon ideas.

The waitress slid a napkin on the table and set Raki's wine on top. These upstanding and jovial men enjoying their beers, her sister Lija's boys, gone broad in the middle, gray at the temples, were the babies she had bottle-fed, tucked in at night, kissed their boo-boos. Before their mother had made her disappear.

The memory of those lost years still stung, but just a little. Her reconciliation with Lija had salved the sting long ago.

When it became unwise to order another round, the guys excused themselves to their own farms, families and chores. Raki, Sam and Joey were expected at Lija's.

RAKI SPOTTED HER sister, tall and round, waiting behind the screen door. Mrs. Isaksen, widow of James Isaksen, proud owner of a thousand acres, wearing her trademark gathered skirt. When they were teenagers, Raki thought Lija dressed hopelessly square. Now her style looked classic, reassurance that not everything changed.

Lija thumped around her spacious kitchen, slicing tomatoes and cucumbers and peeking at the chicken browning in the oven. Raki wanted to help, but it was too late to start bread. Joey offered, but Lija shooed her away. "What does a lawyer know about cooking? I can probably trust you to set the table, though."

The pasta salad from the repast hadn't even digested yet, but Raki would not offend Lija by sitting out dinner. She nibbled, pushed the food about her plate and got the conversation going with the story about the green dress. Lija dug out a yellowed newspaper clipping, a picture of her young family building a snowman that Miss Richter had put on the front page. Then talk drifted to work, school, home improvement projects and the latest controversy on the internet.

Lija poured coffee. Joey volunteered for kitchen duty. "I clean up the governor's messes, so I can clean up yours." Sam retreated to the den. Raki took her cup into the living room. She held it to her nose, breathed deeply and looked about.

So much history within these walls. Growing up here, Raki had imagined what it was like in the era of hoop skirts and waltzes, back when the house was a show place for an immigrant family with money, the ancestors of Margaret Voll's husband. Or sometimes she had imagined flappers dancing the Charleston in the living room, because that was the era when her grandparents had somehow acquired the place. Then came miniskirts and rock and roll, which she didn't need to imagine, because she remembered.

Even that time had long passed. Raki sunk deeply into the plush sofa. Lija's interior design was all comfort and family. Big furniture accessorized with the detritus of grandchildren.

"When will you be going through Miss Richter's things?" Lija asked, settling into her recliner.

"Tomorrow. No time to waste."

"Won't it feel intrusive?" said Lija, "Pawing through someone else's, what's the proper term, personal effects?"

"I think of it as historical research. Perhaps we'll find souvenirs from Europe, old love letters, maybe even the green dress."

"She may have been a hoarder. I doubt anyone else has been in that house since her parents left it to her." Lija sipped her coffee. "She published the *Halcyon Times* forever. And bought a string of other papers besides. There could be piles of newsprint and file cabinets full of green accounting ledgers turning to dust." Lija shuddered. Her thin hair, permed into an impressive volume of white fluff, didn't budge. "I'm glad not to be a part of it."

"I'm looking forward to learning more about her, and what it was like back in the 'olden days,'" Joey chimed in, a dishtowel slung over her shoulder. "You know what my assistant said to me when I was getting ready to come down here? That she envied how 'smooth' women's lives used to be."

Raki spurted coffee on her hand. She licked it off.

Lija shook her head.

"She thinks she knows you all so well, she's given you nicknames," Joey continued. "Aunt Lija, you're 'the Matriarch.' Margaret is 'Lady of the Manor.' You, Mom, are the 'Do-Gooder.'"

"I'm just a pastor's wife who found a way to stay out of trouble," said Raki. "And was delighted to find out how much champagne and dessert are involved in do-gooding."

Joey wagged blonde bangs at her mother.

"Maybe it seemed Miss Richter had a 'smooth' life, but only because she was older, and had so much money she could give it away." Raki peered over the rim of the cup. "But I think she had the hardest time of all."

"Still obsessing about the alleged secret, Mother?"

"Everybody has a secret."

RAKI AROSE EARLY the next day to make fresh biscuits for breakfast. It seemed the least she could do in return for Lija's hospitality. After loading the dishwasher, Sam drove himself back to his church in Minneapolis. Raki and Joey borrowed Lija's car to drive to town. First stop, pick up Margaret. Second stop, retrieve the key from Miss Richter's attorney.

He explained, "My client asked me to read this." He cleared his throat, signaling the transition from his own words to hers: *Dearest friends. I apologize for the enormity of the task I have given to you. I have no right to ask anything of you, and no way of making sure you follow my instructions, but I trust you will. On my living room bookshelf is a box. Please read the contents before clearing everything away. I pray you will come to understand.*

He handed them the key.

MOST OF THE LAVENDER sheaves on the porch were desiccated and long void of scent. Raki found the freshest and lifted it to her nose. Scratchy, but the aroma of old friendship. She slid the key into the keyhole. The door swung smoothly. Deathly quiet.

To the left was the kitchen. Tidy, counters wiped clean. To the right was a large living room. Also in good order. Not a hoarder house. Margaret pulled open lavender drapes to 'shed some light on the subject.' The walls not dominated by mullioned windows were latticed with shelves crammed with books and mementos.

Raki ran her hands along the bookshelves. She found a few ancient law books, novels spanning Jane Austen to F. Scott Fitzgerald to Khaled Hosseini. Amidst the books was displayed a black and white photograph of a distinguished gentleman standing guard over a middle-aged woman and a beautiful ingénue. The Richter family, of course, when Dolores was young, posed on their porch in its pre-lavender days. A few mementos interrupted the rows of books. A silver spoon embossed with the imprint of a 'State Capitol' and engraved, 'Denver, Colo.'

No miniature brass Eiffel Tower? No spoon from Versailles? That old man said Miss Richter had spent time in France. Where were those souvenirs? No French-English dictionary. No empty wine bottles or stained corks. Not even a soaked-off label. It wasn't as if Dolores had been a teetotaler.

The box sat on the shelf as promised. They opened the flaps and peered inside. A fresh white envelope with a Florida return address perched on top a pile of decaying papers tied in bundles, all written by hand in black ink on featherweight paper, the blue stationery used only for sending letters via air mail. From the white envelope Joey extracted a computer-printed letter to Miss Richter.

Dear Dolores, Joey read aloud.

> *Your friend, our mother, Katherine, passed away a few months ago. We found these letters among her belongings. Because you authored them, we thought you might want to have them back. They may be of historical value. They appear to have been written to our mother when she worked for the Red Cross. We hope they will provide you with fond memories. Sincerely, the children of your friend Katherine.*

"Writing letters. Saving letters. Tying them up with ribbons. People don't do that anymore," said Joey.

"Hard to believe, but when I was in college, '68 to '72, that's how I communicated with my parents," said Margaret.

"Don't fool around," protested Joey. "I know when telephones were invented."

"But we had just one phone in the dorm hallway, and everybody could hear everything. Mostly we wrote letters."

"What about love letters? Did you get love letters you tied up with ribbon?" asked Joey.

"Maybe a 'Meet me for a burger after class' note from Mike, but nothing worth tying up with ribbon," said Margaret.

"Never," said Raki.

"Let's read aloud," said Margaret. "Do you have the time, Joey?"

What a ridiculous question. Joey was one of the most important women in the state. Of course she did not have the time.

"Sure," said Joey, contradicting her mother's thoughts. "The state is not going to shut down if I miss a few days. And old letters will certainly be more interesting than statutes."

Raki picked the oldest from the top of the sheaf. As delicate as phyllo, the paper crackled between her fingers. Patriotic red and navy slashes bordering a blue as pale as the sky. Miss Richter's Palmer penmanship. Faint odor of decay. The letters were like ghosts, sending messages from the past.

ॐ

May 8, 1949

Dear Katherine,

Happy VE Day! It is truly remarkable to consider that it has already been four years since we whooped it up in the streets at the news of victory. I am so proud of you for going over into that chaos to help innocent victims.

I cannot leave my parents to fend for themselves. I find my days here in Halcyon bereft of adventure.

Take today, for example. I am writing this missive as a means of distracting myself from my most fascinating task at hand. I am helping Judge Richter (aka Daddy) check citations in the briefs submitted by the lawyers for two neighbors squabbling over hay. Hay! It is hard to imagine people getting so worked up about horse feed. The seller of the hay claims the buyer took more bales than he paid for. The buyer insists the seller miscounted. Seller claims perfect skills in elementary school arithmetic. This case will be heard by a jury—provided they can stay awake. In the meantime, the lawyers have managed to fork all manner of legal precedents—am I boring you yet?

You see why I yearn to pick through the rubble with you? Or reunite refugees with their families, or whatever it is you are doing?

It will not be long before the heat and humidity and bugs arrive. Next week, I expect. In the meantime, I am writing this letter on our porch. The Spring breeze has an easy time picking up this light airmail paper, so I have had to weight it down with a book. Not a law book. Taylor Caldwell's latest novel.

I have just re-read what I wrote and can't imagine why you would want to read such drivel. However, since I used up a precious piece of airmail paper, I will send it in the hopes that all news from home is welcome no matter how tame.

Your Friend,

Dolores

P.S. By the by, are all victims innocent? What about the guilty victims? Do you help them, too, and how would you ever tell the difference? These are the types of questions that burden my mind when I am supposed to be concentrating on hay.

May 22, 1949

Dear Katherine,

I so enjoyed your last letter. Thank you for the fascinating stories! You are not missing much here.

Being the dutiful daughter is very tiring. Every weekend the pile of papers that Judge Richter (aka Daddy) wants me to read to him grows bigger. He tells me he merely enjoys hearing the sound of my voice, but it is clear he has a problem with his eyes. He has gotten new glasses several times, yet more than once has asked me to pass him the salt, when it is right in front of him! When I point it out, he laughs and says, "Oh! My! How did I ever miss that! Right in front of my nose! How funny!" Well, you know the Judge is not much for 'funning,' so I conclude something is very much not right.

Mother's back continues to plague her. She told me once that it was worse than giving birth. I don't know if she wants me to feel obliged to stick around; or to prevent me from ever marrying and having my own baby. Perhaps she was just stating fact.

Regardless, I'm much too busy taking care of them and chasing daddy's dream to think about anything romantic or infantile. I am preparing for the law school entrance exam. My professors are skeptical. They warn that it is extremely difficult for a woman to be accepted into any law school, regardless of grades and other credentials, especially now that the regents are so intent on keeping slots open for the veterans. I have never let on that my father is a judge, so perhaps they do not appreciate that I have a special advantage.

I really don't believe I'm deserving, but I could not bear to let Daddy down. When I make a cogent point about something legal, he calls me 'Doliver Wendell Holmes.'

So sorry for blathering on about my tedious life. You must want news from home. The crop has been planted; the mosquitoes are getting ready to attack; many people have been born and not as many have died, so our population is growing fast. If I had real money of my own, I would invest in a baby carriage company!

Your Friend,

Dolores

୭

TEDIOUS WAS RIGHT. Mosquitos? Dad jokes? Hay controversy? Why on earth had Miss Richter wanted them to read these old things? Raki suggested a break. She needed air, and sunshine. Joey set to checking her email. Margaret took out a novel from Dolores's bookshelf.

RAKI'S FEET TOOK her straight to the old playground. Forty years gone and she made not one false turn. It was not far. Nothing in Halcyon was far. One square mile surrounded by agriculture.

The trees at the park were different than she remembered. The big ones were gone and the little ones big. Saplings where no trees had been before. So much had changed, yet stayed the same. When Raki described her childhood, it came out sounding like a Norman Rockwell painting. But there was no such thing. Those are paintings.

Long gone was the merry-go-round where she used to push Joey. A faint circle marked where it used to whirl. She traced her finger along grooves carved into the old picnic table. Right where Miss Richter used to sit. Hard to see through all these layers of paint. C.J. plus D.R. inside a heart. Are C.J. and D.R. still together? Could D.R. be Dolores? Probably not.

What was Dolores's secret? It seemed the letters were her confession, the women her confessors. The mystery chafed Raki's mind like the old picnic bench chafed her bottom. Whatever her sin, Miss Richter repented of it every minute of every day. Not like Raki.

How many times had Raki asked herself, if she could go back in time, would she undo her own mistake? Not mistake. Sin. Lija forgave her long ago. But Raki had never repented. Never would. She had no regrets. If she had it to do all over again, she would change nothing. Not even to spare Lija, not even for her.

PART TWO

Home is . . . the streets and squares and monuments and shops that constitute one's first universe.

Henry Anatole Grunwald

Halcyon, Minnesota
1962 – 1965

3

THE DAY AFTER their mother's funeral, Lija ordered her sister out to the garden. Their relatives and friends had left. The kitchen counters were wiped down, the floor swept and the refrigerator crammed with noodle casseroles and fruit salads. The counter was piled with cakes. Their dad was back in the field.

Just four days before, sixteen-year-old Lija had become like a mother to little Raki, seven-going-on-eight. Lija vowed never to say the words, but felt no choice but to play the role. She was determined to do it well, her gift in memoriam.

Lija forced a lilt into her voice. "Raki, the garden needs weeding. Let's do it together."

Raki lay sprawled on the living room carpet, staring at the TV, watching Bill Cullen auction off vacations and cars on *The Price is Right*. Her eyes didn't move, either to follow the goings-on in the Hollywood studio, or to respond to the suggestion.

"Rakella Mary," Lija said, sterning up her voice. "The garden needs weeding."

"I don't like weeding."

"You don't like *The Price is Right*, either. So come with me. My goal is a grand champion purple-ribbon-winning cucumber for the county fair."

"Can't I bake something instead? Some bread or cookies or cake? It would be practice for my 4-H project."

"Little girl, this place reeks of sugar. We don't need more of that." Lija could still taste the guilt of her last bite of cake. People already called her 'sturdy.' Thought they were being polite. Gawd. But it was true, and her homemade skirts, gathered at the waist, only hid so much. Her sewing projects never sashayed on her like they did in the pictures on the pattern sleeves. She lectured herself: those tiny-waisted women are just sketches, not real.

The game show broke to a commercial for hair dye. At least her hair color didn't come out of a bottle. Lija tucked a loose strand of blonde hair into the barrette at the back of her neck. How many times had Mom advised her to put it up in curlers, give it some body, make it flip? She would give the sun and the moon to fight over that one more time. She touched the ends brushing against her shoulders. Like straw.

Not like Raki's. How would advertisers describe that mane? Luxurious tresses? In her mind's eye, Lija saw their mother plaiting Raki's long, auburn hair, tying it with colorful ribbons. That job fell to her now, or those thick waves would get wild and tangled. Raki would also need help picking out school clothes. Left to her own devices, Little Sister would wear jeans to school, and get sent home for violating the dress code.

School. The thought suffocated Lija, like a ton of corn pouring into a silo. She gasped, tears spilling out, yet again. She would not be taking English from her mother after all. Because of that boy, a boy her own age, barreling down Highway Forty straight into her mother's car. Lija had dreaded seeing her mom in class every day. The memory made the tears spill faster. She would give the stars to learn Shakespeare from Mom now.

Lija wiped her face, gathered her composure and looked past the TV, out the window. Dad was on the tractor, in the fields. Why was he out working, the day after burying his wife? He didn't even like field work. His heart was in his side business, advising their neighbors on business and taxes. He never missed an opportunity to inform people that he had two degrees. Business and accounting. Even at the funeral he had reminded Mom's teacher friends. Like they didn't know. He did taxes for some of them. At least he didn't make that tired old joke of his: 'It's what I do to avoid messing with manure.'

A half-section, three hundred twenty acres, of corn and soybeans was respectable enough, but the lack of cattle, pigs or chickens did set them apart.

Lija shook herself back to the task at hand. The garden. Pulling weeds. Finding a purple-ribbon-worthy cucumber. It would be good to get out of the house, good for both of them.

"Raki, I mean it!" Lija walked to the set and turned the knob with a taking-charge flourish, grabbed her sister by the wrist and pulled her upright.

The walk to the garden took almost five minutes. Through the wide green lawn, past the barn and the implement sheds and beyond. It was just a corner of the bean field their father plowed in the spring, where their mother had planted flowers for picking and a few rows of corn, green beans, cucumbers, potatoes and carrots. Just enough to keep a teacher busy during summer vacation. Lija had much bigger plans for next year.

RAKI STUCK HER lower lip out and stomped her feet on the way to the garden. It galled her that Lija didn't notice. Mom would never have made her do this. Raki pouted harder and louder, and still Lija kept her eyes forward.

When they arrived at the garden plot, Raki fought the urge to kick off her shoes. The clods of soil, turned over in furrows by her dad's big plow, looked like big chocolate marshmallows, soft and inviting, but that was a lie. A big person in heavy boots might crush them, like her dad, or maybe Lija, but Raki's little feet didn't stand a chance.

There was the one time she tried running barefoot through the field. Her feet had been plenty tough from running through the grass, up and down the concrete steps and even on the gravel. Still, she twisted her ankle on a dried clod. She had cried. Her mom had put ice on it. *Mommy.*

Raki kneaded her fists into her eyes and snorted fresh tears back up her nose. Then she plopped down next to Lija, sighed dramatically and started yanking. Elephant ears, cockleburs and lamb's quarters. Pigweed. Thistle. Volunteer corn and volunteer soybeans.

"Not like that," Lija lectured. "Grab the weed close to the ground and pull straight up, strong and firm." Lija demonstrated. "The way you're doing it, the tops will just snap off and they'll grow right back."

Raki's hands and fingernails were already turning black and green. She wiped her forehead with the back of her arm, careful not to smear dirt on her face. "Why can't we just let the weeds grow? Why can't the beans just get along with the elephant ears? Why does the sweet corn even care if there's some pigweed way down on the ground?"

When Lija didn't answer, Raki shut up. After a minute she sat back on her heels. "When I grow up I'm going to have a garden and just let it grow naturally and take what comes. And it will be just as delicious as yours." *Take that, big sister!*

"The weeds steal water from the good plants. They grow up and choke them off," said Lija. "If you don't pull them, they take over and smother what you are trying to grow."

"I just think that we don't appreciate weeds. Mommy said you can eat lamb's quarters. Like spinach."

"And people sometimes use elephant ears in place of toilet paper. Because the leaves are so big and soft."

Ewwwwww. Raki scrunched up her face. "That's ishy."

LATE THAT NIGHT, Raki awakened to Lija smoothing her hair and kissing her brow.

Raki rubbed her eyes and sniffled.

"You were crying in your sleep," Lija whispered. "It's all right. I'm here."

The following morning, after their father had eaten his eggs and bacon and left for the field, Lija led Raki by the hand into their parents' bedroom. She took down their mother's clothes and spread them across the bed. She opened their mother's dresser drawers.

"Take something to hold at night to remind you of Mom," she said. "Something that smells like her. Then take something to wear everyday like. Something that reminds you of everything she did for us. Then one of her nice things to save in your closet until you're older."

Raki fingered the school teacher suits, the flounced skirts for church, the new pencil skirt her mother had worn to the teachers' union cocktail party. She put her nose up against the blouses, inhaling the cherry almond scent of the lotion her mom had used. She carefully slid shut the drawers that held the lingerie.

"Try not to cry," said Lija. "Tears might stain the clothes."

"Everything is so beautiful," whispered Raki.

Her first pick was something Lija had not bothered to take out of the closet—the red velvet robe with the satin collar their mother left hanging on a hook. Raki caressed her cheek with the collar and buried her face in the downy velvet. "I want to sleep with this."

Then Raki picked up a cotton button-down shirt printed with pink and yellow flowers. She held it up against her small chest. It engulfed her.

"It's too big, but can I wear it around the house and in the yard?" she asked.

"Yes. And you'll grow into it."

Finally, she chose a dress of coffee-colored stretch lace with a lining of peach satin. A matching brown fabric flower was pinned beneath the shoulder.

WHILE HIS DAUGHTERS retrieved relics from his wife's closet, Lawrence mourned atop his tractor. In the privacy of the cab, like a monastery cell, he railed at the injustice of God, but did not pray. He wept, great masculine dollops that fell onto his lap. Tears Raki and Lija could never, ever see.

The mothering, that he would have to leave to Lija to do for Raki. He did not know the first thing about clothing and hairstyles. His wife always looked stunning in whatever she wore, an observation he knew in his logical mind could not possibly have been the case. Even if his daughters wore gunny sacks, they would still be the most beautiful girls in the world.

He vowed to his dead wife, over the roar of the tractor, that he would encourage good grades and higher education. He would praise

Lija's vegetables and Raki's bread. He would spend Decembers at their Christmas concerts and Augusts in the 4-H Hall at the county fair.

His heavy heart warned him he was doomed to fail. Guiding such different girls was like steering with front wheels pointed in opposite directions. Lija's workaday stride, practical outlook and straight-forward approach favored himself. Raki's sprite and curiosity favored Laura. Like her mother, Raki skipped, plucked wildflowers and questioned everything.

As for taking care of himself, he could always escape to the tractor or his ledgers, devoting himself to the therapy of straight rows. Or get a little crooked at the golf course bar, to forget what he had lost.

4

JAMES ISAKSEN SURVEYED the fields as he drove. Soybeans stretched ditch to ditch, deep green and uniform rows, like his mother's Grand Champion afghan at the county fair. Knit one, purl one, knit one, purl one, on and on for as long as it took to earn the oohs and aahs of the neighbors. The windows rolled down, he caught the scent of manure waxing and waning as he drove past hog barns, cattle yards and fertile fields.

The bean fields were at their most immaculate in early August, just after troops of teenagers finished combing the fields, pulling up every cocklebur and elephant ear, hoeing the pigweed and lamb's quarters. For this, farmers begged, berated and ordered their own children into the fields, recruiting town kids like James only when they didn't have enough of their own.

James could have earned easier money mowing lawns or flipping papa burgers at the A & W or teaching little kids to braid plastic lanyards at City Summer Activities. But like almost all his friends, he was suckered into the hot and dirty soybean fields every summer by the twin temptations that respectable farmers craving respectable fields dangled before him.

Money and skin.

They paid double minimum wage. Turned a bemused eye to the flirting, the boys shirtless in cut-offs, the girls in halter tops and short shorts. Handed out hoes at sunup. Called it off at noon when the sun had cooked away the last whiff of cool.

Girls loved nothing more than taking their bean walking tan lines to the lake in the afternoon. James had a car to drive them there, plus enough of his own bean walking money for movie tickets and popcorn in the evening. With a little charm a boy could earn a satisfying return on investment. Or so he'd heard.

Rolling past the fields outside Halcyon, impeccable rows brought to mind the farm kids who had taught him proper technique. Pull the cocklebur up from the roots and lean it against the bean row, root up to roast in the sun, so it won't replant itself overnight. Keep a keen lookout for every hidden elephant ear masquerading as a bean plant, because even the softest-leafed elephant ear is only days away from bursting forth into a six-foot behemoth capable of crippling a combine if not pulled up by the roots today. Farm boys enjoyed nothing more than pointing out when a town boy missed one. They were even happier to reach over and whack an overlooked weed for a pretty girl.

James shifted in the seat of his dinged-up Dodge Dart, picturing those pretty girls in his mind. The vinyl groaned beneath his thighs. He felt the familiar pressure against his zipper. On the one hand, it may be wrong to have these thoughts. On the other hand, he was a well-brought-up and well-mannered boy, young man, and what he thought about and what he did in the privacy of his own car was nobody else's business. Still, this would not do. He had a job interview to get to.

He turned his mind to the clean bean fields. They reminded him of a blanket again, a blanket with a girl underneath. So that did not work. The war! Guns and napalm over there in the jungle, guns and tear gas over here on campus. Well, that did the trick.

Now if he could just focus on this interview with Lawrence Pederson. A farmer with no sons and a reputation for an open mind. Possibly the solution to James's dilemma. More than anything, even more than making out with girls, maybe, James wanted to plow, plant and harvest fields just like these. But town boys don't become farmers. Walk the beans, sure, but no more than that.

How many times had he been reminded, farmers are grown from seeds planted by farmers. Farmers learn their profession on their daddy's laps, riding in huge machines that rip up black soil and force it to produce food. From the time they toddle, farm boys do 'chores.' James's only experience with chores was sweeping hair from his dad's barbershop floor, a skill that would barely qualify him for sweeping hay from the barn. In spite of everything everybody told him, James refused to accept that farming could not be taught, like anything else.

Social integration might be the bigger problem. James hadn't made his friends in 4-H Club and on the school bus. Town and farm communities weren't totally separate, for sure. Farmers went to town to get their hair cut, drink coffee at the cafe, and haul their harvest to the elevator. Some even went to church in town. But for all that, James wondered if the other farmers would ever welcome him into their clique. He had no way of knowing. No town boy he knew ever dared to infiltrate, if the thought even occurred to one.

The thought had occurred to James. All the time. Like an addiction. For which he had a fix. Hire on as a farm hand to catch up on all those years of learning. Not be a lifelong hired hand, one of those pitiable, sorry excuses. Own his own land someday. At nineteen, he already had a year of college at South Dakota State under his belt. Modern farming was as much business as lifestyle. He was convinced of it.

But neither the lifestyle nor the business was within his reach until he got himself a mentor. Mr. Pederson might just be his ticket. Two daughters. No sons.

The Dart crunched off the highway into the Pederson's graveled driveway. The large expanse of grass needed tidying. Beyond that stood a grove of pines, the traditional windbreak. A two-story farmhouse, probably built last century, looked remarkably grand. His engine sputtered as he slowed. A girl, ten or eleven maybe, stood next to a riding mower and a big gas tank on stilts.

"Your car sounds like it could use a drink," she shouted, waving the nozzle.

Must be the younger of the two daughters he had been told about. The ones whose mother got killed in that car crash several years back. The other one was supposed to be his own age.

"No, thanks."

The girl turned to hang the nozzle.

"My name is James Isaksen," he continued. "I have an appointment with Lawrence Pederson. Your father?"

"I'm Raki. I'll tell him you're here."

Her Keds kicked up dust on her way to the door, a too-big flowery cotton shirt puffing out around her waist as she ran. The screen hinges creaked as she reached her head inside the door, shouting, "Dad! Somebody here to see you." With one arm holding the screen open, the other holding the door jamb, leaning with one leg extended back, she looked like a sparrow taking flight. A moment passed and she returned to earth. "Go right in."

LAWRENCE PEDERSON SHOVED his adding machine back toward the wall. Rows of numbers on green-tinted paper grew neatly upon the burnished wood acreage he called his desk. He enjoyed the manorial atmosphere of this office, with its rich paneling and fireplace, empty today, of course, with temperatures in the nineties. A small fan oscillated in the corner. A few east-facing windows let in light; the west side cloaked in heavy curtains against the afternoon sun.

Lawrence rose, extending his big hand to the young man. "So, you heard I'm looking for help. James, right?" They shook formally. Lawrence assessed the young man's grip. Firm, good. He motioned the prospective farmhand to sit in the green office chair he kept for accounting clients. Himself he lowered into the sticky embrace of his high-backed black-leather executive chair.

"Yes, sir. I've been asking around for quite some time, looking for somebody who would take me on. As I explained on the telephone, I want nothing more than to become a farmer. I want my own farm someday, but my dad's a barber. I need somebody to take me under his wing. Give me an opportunity. Last year after high school I went to SDSU. Planning on a business and ag double major. I can tell you recognize that today's farming is a business. It's the business I want to be in." He nodded emphatically as the last words tumbled out.

Kid must have practiced that little speech a hundred times. "Take a breath, boy."

Lawrence perused James. Medium length hair, the color and texture of ditch grass in November. Recently trimmed, probably by his father. Traditional cut, nothing faddish. Shirt and pants and shoes shined enough to show respect, but not so much anyone would think the kid had gotten lost on the way to a bank interview.

"I need help during planting and harvest." Lawrence raised his voice to be heard over the whir from the fan and the thrumming from Raki's lawn mowing. "You're in college in the spring and the fall. I wouldn't want to be responsible for you dropping out. Staying in college would be a better bet for you."

"Of course," James responded. "If you hire me on, I will transfer closer, go full-time during winter semester, take fall and spring off and maybe pick up a night class during the summer. It doesn't really matter how long it takes or if I finish at all." He gestured out the window to the fields outside. "This is what I really want to do."

"Finish at all? No, you must finish. But why? Why do you want to farm?" Lawrence leaned back. The chair springs squeaked as he crossed his ankles, wrapping his arms across his chest. The feel of his biceps gave him a sense of authority, even if they weren't quite as impressive as they were back in his football or Army days.

The young man sat up straight, his leather shoes planted solidly on the floor. "Lots of reasons. I like working outside. I love the idea of growing food. This is so going to sound idealistic, but really, I want to feed people. That's what it's all about. Farmers feed people. Everybody needs to be fed. A lot of people don't get enough to eat. Agriculture is the answer. Modern agriculture."

"Good, god, take another breath. You young people—peace, love and all that." Lawrence paused before continuing. "Well, all right. Farming is what you think you want to do. You don't really know, because you've never done it. This is no nine-to-five operation. When you're not in the field you're worrying. Too much rain, not enough rain. What's the government up to? And so on. Not to mention that you could lose your deferment. You could get drafted. You won't learn farming in Vietnam."

"I won't be drafted. I'm Mennonite."

Lawrence raised an eyebrow.

The boy rushed to explain. "The regular kind. Not Amish or Hutterite or anything. I can drive. Cars, tractors, whatever."

"Best not to insult my intelligence, kid; I know the difference. But that explains why I haven't heard of you. You're from Menno Prairie, I assume?"

"That's right." James shifted in his seat and sat up even straighter. Lawrence liked that. It showed respect.

"I'll be blunt. Might as well get used to it. I wouldn't mention Menno Prairie around here. The Lutherans and the Catholics around Halcyon resent that you Mennonite kids get to stay out of Vietnam claiming conscientious objector when their own peace-loving boys get shipped over to the jungle."

Lawrence watched James squirm, but was having too much fun to stop. "Personally, I don't feel strongly about this war. I fought in World War II. That was different. But I can't afford to have you ticking off my friends and neighbors and my accounting clients because they think you think you're better than their sons because you're some certified card-carrying pacifist. Just on account of being born Mennonite."

"I don't want to tick anybody off. I just want to learn how to become a farmer, grow corn and soybeans and maybe some oats and alfalfa. That's all."

Lawrence tilted his head, listening ostentatiously, amused by James's desperate attempt to get the interview back on track. He even allowed a little smile to turn up the corners of his mouth.

"Hire me on a trial basis," James suggested. "If I work hard and learn quick, then I'll be more dependable than any other hired hand you've ever had or will have and we will both benefit. If I can't get the hang of anything, then you just point me down the driveway and replace me with somebody else. No risk. Someday I want to buy my own land, but first things first. Gotta start somewhere. Here."

"Oh, you won't let me have any fun, will you?" Lawrence bellowed. "I want to talk theology and politics and you turn it back to corn and soybeans. Some college boy you are. You want me to mentor you on modern agricultural practices? Fine, then humor me. Question. Mennonite pacifism, true or fake?"

❧

THIS INTERVIEW with farmer Pederson was not going at all as James expected. He had rehearsed over and over again a variety of different explanations for why a young man born and bred in a small town would want to live in the country and raise crops for a living. He had memorized a list of his best relevant qualities: strength, stamina, good sense, dependability, intelligence, aptitude for machinery, problem-solving skills, willingness to get up early and work late, everything he thought a farmer would want to know about a hired hand. Now this guy wanted to talk religion and politics.

"True or fake for whom?"

"OK. Now we're getting somewhere!" Mr. Pederson boomed, just as the mower shut down outside. "Thank god that girl ran out of gas. It's very hard to shout theology. Let's start with you. Is your pacifism true or fake?"

With no idea what the man wanted to hear, James resorted to honesty with a dash of Sunday School. "I grew up being taught that Jesus abhorred war. We are supposed to act like Jesus. Nobody is going to be able to do that, but some try. The men I grew up around planted trees and built roads during World War II. Alternative service. Did some of them wish that they could have had the chance to blow apart Hitler's brains instead? I bet some of them did, but I don't know because that's not something they would say out loud." He took a breath.

"Keep going." His prospective employer was leaning forward now, elbows resting on his thighs.

"Church-going people get into arguments with each other all the time," continued James, wishing he could be talking about anything else, but sensing the need to cater to this man's whim. "Those are kind of like tiny wars. It's hard to live out your convictions, but that doesn't mean you don't have them. War is complicated. Everybody hates it, but like with Hitler, what other realistic alternative can you come up with?"

"World War II is easy. What's your opinion of Vietnam?"

"The war in Vietnam is harder to justify. If I had to choose between going to Vietnam and going to prison, or Canada, I'm not sure what I would do. I guess the greatest gift I ever got was my pacifist upbringing, so that I don't have to make that choice. I believe I am a true pacifist, but there are probably guys over there fighting now who are just as pacifist as I am."

"And some of those guys are going to get blown to bits."

"That's true. It's not fair. But I'm not going to get drafted, unless you go and tattle to the draft board what I just told you." James flinched as soon as the unfortunate word 'tattle' left his mouth. Mr. Pederson didn't seem to notice.

"So, you want to save the world by growing corn and soybeans?"

"Something like that."

"If I hire you, I'll be considered the biggest fool in the county."

"Yes, sir."

"OK, just so we're clear about that." Mr. Pederson put his chin on his fist. Humidity seeped around the curtains, through the one open window, pooling with the sweat wicking through James's shirt. The little fan did almost nothing to budge the turgid air.

"Let me loan you some work clothes and show you around."

James shot out of his chair. "No need. I have some in the backseat."

An hour later, a thorough tour under his belt, with instructions to come back in the morning, James climbed back into his Dart. On the way out he spotted the girl called Raki trimming around some bushes with a small hand mower. He waved. Just as he turned right onto the county road, he spied some ditch roses just off to the side. High from the tour and hopeful for the future, he stepped on the brake, pulled over and hopped out. He gathered a bundle of the hot pink blossoms with the sunburst centers, jumped back in the car and reversed up the Pederson driveway. When he got to Raki he stuck the bundle out the window and called out, "Something for you!"

She walked over and took the little fistful of blossoms, looking confused. It was a silly gesture, but he didn't care. His future was on track.

"These reminded me of the flowers on your shirt. You can tuck them in your pocket like a corsage. See you tomorrow." The Dart's tires spit gravel as he left again.

&

LAWRENCE WATCHED JAMES drive away. That was the most fun he'd had in ages, grilling the little draft dodger. Not that he held that against the kid. Truth be told, for all the ribbons and medals squirreled away in the attic, he would have preferred planting trees to getting shot at.

He swiveled his chair and looked out the window, resting his forearm atop what he liked to call his 'sphericity.' What was that kid doing? Handing a bunch of weeds to Raki? Or are those flowers? He squinted. Well, now, that's interesting.

It would be smarter to take on an experienced hand, or a farm boy wanting to earn some money away from his dad, anybody who at least knew something. But Lawrence had let himself be seduced. To be this earnest young man's mentor. The idea was irresistible.

When Lawrence took over his father's farm, and spread the word that he was also qualified to provide financial advice and tax services on the side, the novelty of a working farmer with a college degree had earned him a handful of respect from his neighbors. When his girls were little, they idolized him. But now his neighbors saw him as just part of the landscape, and his girls had grown out of their adulation. He yearned for some renewed esteem. If this son-of-a-barber really wanted to learn farming from him, he would have to fork over a modicum of sycophancy as part of the bargain. James would listen to all of Lawrence's ideas for achieving better crop yield, but he would also have to humor him when he wanted to discuss science, world affairs or theology. If Lawrence felt like sharing the latest dirt he heard in the Halcyon Café, he could joke that gossip was just 'sociology 101 fieldwork,' and James would get it.

Another idea was growing in the back of Lawrence's head, an idea that did not fit at all well with his modern, progressive way of thinking. But there it was. Here was a way to preserve the family acreage. For another generation. Maybe more.

Lawrence always knew it was up to him to keep the farm going, GI Bill or no GI Bill. It was all about the land, which is why he had had no compunction about emptying the barns when his father retired. No need for hogs and cattle when his sole goals were to make a middle-class living—a late model car and an occasional glass of fine Scotch—and keep the acreage intact.

Laura had given him his two beautiful daughters before the car crash killed her. "Damn kid," Lawrence cursed to himself, as he did every time he thought about the crazed, hell-bent-for-leather speeding teenager who demolished his beautiful wife.

Back to the girls, he urged himself. It does no good to brood. Lovely, both of them. And neither one was going to take over the farm. When it came time, the land would be parceled out for sale.

Unless. He mused on that ditch rose bouquet. A little of the romantic streak women liked. Lija was nineteen, not too young anymore. Even after she moved into the dorms at Mankato State, she came home every weekend. Lija liked it out in the country. She would stay, if there was a way.

Raki was just a little girl, but he could already tell she had no aspirations for staying on the farm. She had no interest in gardening and did the lawn mowing with tremendous unenthusiasm. Raki told him she wanted to go to college, open a bakery and live in town, or better yet, a city.

James was never going to buy a farm. Even a barber's son knew that phrase was a joke. Tell the man trimming your hair that some guy "bought the farm," and he would know as well as anybody to check the obituaries and not the real estate transactions.

First you inherit a little land, then rent a little more, then you borrow to buy what you are renting and make payments till they bury you. But it all starts with that inheritance, something no town kid was ever going to get. Unless.

Lija was due home any minute from babysitting the neighbor children. As soon as she got home, she would pick the garden, fry some store-bought chicken, boil the vegetables, and boss Raki into setting the table. At dinner he would inquire about whether she had registered for classes. She claimed she wanted to teach kindergarten. Maybe, Lawrence thought, or maybe raise a bunch of kids here. On this farm.

Of course his older daughter could achieve her life goals entirely on her own merit. She was as pleasant a girl as he had ever met. That counted for so much. Still, his older daughter deserved all the loving help that her father could provide. James would start tomorrow.

NO ROMANTIC BOUQUETS were proffered when Lawrence introduced James to Lija the next morning. The young man did show sufficient friendly interest. Lawrence hovered as the two compared the attributes of their respective colleges. James inquired if she had any helpful "inside information" for a student, himself, who would be transferring to her campus in the winter. She tittered nervously.

"I guess if you get lost, you could ask me for directions," she stammered, "but of course I probably won't be there when you get lost." That inane exchange wouldn't make it into a Hollywood movie, was Lawrence's critique.

Nevertheless, he noticed that Lija found her prettiest barrette and wore her most flattering skirt when she came out to shoo them in for lunch. For his part, James complimented Lija on her cucumber salad. Even so, James appeared less interested in lunch than he was in getting back to the machine shed and then out into the fields.

Lawrence enjoyed his new hired hand's enthusiasm. For all his own hard work and astute management, Lawrence knew full well he lacked passion for agriculture. James certainly added zest to the tasks. He could learn the rudiments and probably even had the business sense to grow the acreage. *Lord help me if he wants animals, though.*

Having another man around to talk to was another benefit. The hands he'd brought on before just wanted to do what needed to be done and go home for a beer. James wasn't the beer type. Turned down Lawrence's offers of Scotch, too. Probably his upbringing. But he stuck around late, drinking his ice water. Seemed almost disappointed to be sent home. Good.

AFTER JAMES LEFT, swirling a little bronze shimmer inside his glass, Lawrence worried about rain and crop futures. As usual, or sometimes. More often about his girls. He only wanted the best for them. For them to have what he had lost. Or something like it.

Alone in his office, which he had not bothered to tidy up for the past three years, Lawrence conjured up the past. He and Laura were in their senior year at the university when he brought her home to meet his parents. As she and his mother cleared away the dishes, his father pulled him aside: "Buy that girl a ring. We'll move into the mother-in-law house across the road. You can take this place." They kept their word and mostly minded their own business until old age compelled them to a nursing home.

Laura, for all her sophistication, loved falling asleep in the country. Next to him. It never ceased to amaze him. But of course he hadn't expected her to stay home and pluck chickens. He was proud of the fact she taught high school literature. Before Lija was born and again after Raki started kindergarten. Good thing the house was an easy drive to town.

And an easy drive out for her parties. The ice tinkling in Lawrence's lonely glass was a faint echo of the festivities they once hosted in this house. He mused on the way Laura used to swirl ice with the tip of her fingernail, flirting with it—and him. He listened to the memory of his wife's guilty laugh as she swiped the first taste from a perfectly mounded dip bowl. He pictured their Annual Halcyon Education Association Back-to-School Extravaganza, when teachers on the arms of their husbands took a brief respite on his deep porch, tidying their hems and smoothing their lapels before ringing the bell.

He lifted his Scotch to his lips. Smoky, like his wife's bacon, fried up for her canapés. The ones she made for the Spring Fling, when his accounting clients, the most prosperous farmers, came over to nibble and drink beneath his and Laura's shimmery chandelier. And the political parties! Local big wigs denouncing McCarthy while leaning against his mahogany mantel, heedless of the booze he was pouring to lubricate their wallets for the benefit of the Democratic-Farmer-Labor Party.

Those days he had been so much more alive. The accident robbed him of both his wife and a life. Since the day Laura died, he had never opened his door for any kind of gathering, and Lija wouldn't either. Which was a shame, because that was what the house was built for.

Laura had loved telling the story. "It was built by the Voll family, after they amassed their wealth in the last decade of the nineteenth century. It was their first show place." She would tell the story in the school teacher voice he so loved. Then, affecting an expression of incredulity, "But they came to think the gambrel roof and white siding were too homespun." She would pause, waiting for her guests to shake their heads at the Voll's famous pretentions. "But with no market for such an unusual piece of architecture, they sold this treasure!" She cast her arms about the room. "For a song! To Lawrence's father!" No need for her to expound on what happened next. Everyone knew of the Voll's ever-so-much grander brick Colonial on the edge of Halcyon. Where nobody lived.

Lawrence shook himself out of the past. He could still take his opinions and bluster to the Halcyon Café. He lived. His girls lived. He was disappointed that this house was, in some ways, as empty as the other Voll mansion. It deserved a new lease on life. They could all use a new lease on life. A different life, because the past was gone. Still, it would be something for this house and this land to stay in his family.

5

HOT. HUMID. The farm offered no escape from the stodgy air that rubbed on Raki's nerves. Adding to her annoyance were gnats and mosquitoes buzzing outside the screened windows. How did the little devils even manage to slog through this slop? Go outside and they would sting and buzz her head. She could not wait until her and Lija's weekly evening in town. The city sprayed for bugs.

Lija lay across her bed, staring at the ceiling, picking tufts from the blue chenille bedspread, wearing nothing but a nylon slip and 'lift and separate' bra. Probably a D-Cup. Raki looked down at herself. Was there hope? Maybe tonight she would buy a training bra. They were on sale at J.C. Penney; she'd seen the ad in the *Halcyon Times*. No, Lija would say she didn't need one. Not yet.

"You still have curlers in your hair!" Raki screamed.

Did Lija not appreciate that the stores and cafes of Halcyon were open late only one night a week? Thursday. Tonight was Thursday! Did she not look forward to hanging out with friends from town? Eating food that wasn't homemade? Raki couldn't wait to get a burger, fries and a Bubble-Up at the Halcyon Café, followed by a piece of pie at Sis & Jim's Diner. Those places had air conditioning.

Wasn't there something Lija needed to buy? Never mind the training bra, Raki couldn't wait to get her hands on the latest editions of '*Teen, American Girl* and *Tigerbeat.* That's where she planned to meet up with her friends, Jody and Lynn, in front of the magazine rack at The Corner Drugstore. They would each buy one and swap them throughout the week until all three had read every word.

"What's the matter with you? Get up!" Raki yelled at her sister. "I'm supposed to meet Jody and Lynn. They'll be waiting for me! I can't be late!"

"I've got a lot on my mind." Lija looked like one of those sirens in old black and white movies. Sounded like one, too. Dreamy. All she was missing was the cigarette on the long holder, and the slim figure. She did look kind of skinnier though. Had Lija lost weight?

Raki stomped off. If she let loose with a swear word, she might not be allowed to go to town at all. So she took a deep breath and returned, crooning a poor imitation of Petula Clark's hit song. "Let's go *downtown,*" she sang, muffing the words. "No finer place, for sure, *Halcyon,* where everybody's waiting for you."

"Go away." Lija slid off the bedspread, pulling the curlers loose and settling in front of her vanity. Unlike Raki's own thick waves, Lija's corn silk hair needed an armor of Dippity-Do and hairspray to stay curled in place. Lija had a lot of work to do and barely enough time to do it. Raki went away as ordered.

By five o'clock Raki was in the passenger seat with Lija driving.

"So, what's bugging you?" Raki snooped when her sister offered none of her usual chit-chat.

"Riots in Watts," said Lija. Raki knew what she meant only because they'd watched Walter Cronkite on the news together the night before. Los Angeles was another world.

Raki rolled her eyes, leaning her head against the car window. Through the windshield, she watched the cornfields. Broad leaves glinted against the afternoon sun, like a crop of emeralds and diamonds. The air was visible, dense with vapor. Swooning over the fields, shimmering like a satin gown, swaying across a dance floor of immense proportions.

"Sorry. Seriously, I'm under a lot of stress."

"You didn't look stressed back home in your slip."

"You don't know what stress looks like."

"What's the problem?"

Lija paused before answering. "I'm not crazy about going back to college. Satisfied, Snoopy? Classes start in a couple weeks; I'm already registered and I'm not looking forward to it. But I'm nineteen and I've never had a serious boyfriend. I'm going to need a job someday." She sighed, "A career."

"That sounds exciting, Lija."

"What if I graduate and then can't find a job around here?"

"You can move to where you find a job," enthused Raki. "Minneapolis even."

"I need to be here. For you and Dad."

Raki considered this when all of a sudden, Lija's concerns burst forth like grain tumbling from the back of a truck after the gate lifts. "By the time I graduate from college you'll be in high school. You are going to be going to dances, and the prom. Dad is not going to be any help to you. He's no help to me, for sure. I used to think I knew what he wanted. I thought he wanted me to get a degree and be a teacher or something. Because he and Mom went to college. So off I went. But now he's sending out different signals. I don't know what I want. It's very confusing. And the most serious relationship I've ever had was a prom date." She sighed.

"James is kind of cute," said Raki.

Silence.

Raki started humming 'Downtown' to herself as they passed the sign: Halcyon, Minnesota, population 4,565.

"We're almost there. Where do you want me to drop you off?" asked Lija.

"Usual place, on the corner with the stoplight."

The summer sun was still high in the sky when Raki hopped out on the corner. If they stayed late enough, she would get to see the lights of the faded theater marquee twitch on, pulsing red, blue, green and white over the shoppers crowding the sidewalks. The row of giant neon diamonds in the jewelry store window would start blinking. Then the translucent plastic sign over the Halcyon Cafe would glow. And flood lamps would highlight the hand lettered 'Sis & Jim's.' Not what Petula Clark had in mind, probably, but pretty enough.

Raki recognized Jody's red-striped top and white slacks through the window of The Corner Drugstore. Familiar hand-me-downs from an older sister. Next to Jody at the magazine rack, skinny and blonde-haired Lynn wore a new sleeveless sheath. The pair was tee-heeing, skittishly pointing at a *Playboy*, which Raki was sure neither one dared touch.

"Sorry I'm late," said Raki, as she came through the door. "Nice top, Lynn."

"Trial run for my 4-H project. The blue matches my eyes." Lynn batted her lashes.

"It matches everybody's eyes," said Raki, rolling her own blue eyes. Even Jody had blue eyes and her hair was dark brown. Just about everybody in Halcyon had blue eyes.

Lynn already had the three magazines in her hand, doling out one to each. Of course she kept the *Tigerbeat* to herself. The Fab Four were on the cover. Raki angled for *Teen*. At least Ringo was on the cover. Jody got left with the *American Girl*.

"Where next?" asked Jody, stuffing the magazine under her arm.

"Let's go to Don's Records," said Raki. "I've got enough money for an album."

They each dug out a quarter to pay the clerk, then flounced out the door and down the street, past the lawyer's office and the bank with the fallout shelter sign, chattering earnestly and without interruption, until Sweet Tarts and nonpareils flirted at them through the window of the Five & Dime. Why resist? Raki bought a half dozen Hershey Kisses.

Toting their little candy bags, the trio bounced into Don's Records, the only store in Halcyon selling rock and roll. The tiny shop was crammed with kids. And Don didn't even have a neon sign. Jody and Lynn flipped through the latest 45 singles. What caught Raki's attention was the pure white cover and splat of red letters on the Beatles' new album, *Help!* Caressing the shiny slipcover, she calculated how many hours of bean walking it cost. She turned it over, reading the list of songs. A scratch of her fingernail left a skittered scar and spot of chocolate on the thin plastic. Well, now she had to buy it. But it was a good deal, with fourteen songs.

"Promise me you'll let us come over and listen to it!" begged Jody as she watched Raki hand over her three dollar bills.

"Me, too!" said Lynn.

"Of course!"

The door of Don's smacking behind them, they sauntered down the still simmering street, tossing their auburn, blonde and brunette hair, whispering catty remarks about the too-long hems worn by the older ladies. Not a single boy seemed to notice them. As usual. Disappointing. Sometimes they pretended to swoon, when the boy was really cute, but even that didn't earn any recognition, except sometimes winks from funny old men with bushy eyebrows.

They continued along the sidewalk, dodging toddlers not minding their mothers, keeping their eyes peeled for other kids from their class.

Seeing none, Jody suggested, "Let's see who's at Sis & Jim's. We can order some rhubarb pie."

Getting to Sis & Jim's involved walking past the Hoot & Hustle Pool Hall. The front door was propped open.

"Have you ever been inside?" whispered Jody.

"No way. I don't think *any* girl has *ever* been inside," said Lynn. "Not even any older lady, that I've ever heard of."

"My sister plays pool at the Bowling Alley sometimes," said Jody, "But even she never goes in . . . that place."

Making sure not to slow down or turn their heads, they cast six eyes sideways. Raki was hoping to catch the sight of tight jeans bent over a pool table. Lynn was probably more on the lookout for a guy in a leather jacket swigging beer and Jody could have been worried her dad was inside.

As they crossed the street to Sis & Jim's, Raki spied a young man escorting a young woman through the door to The Walnut Room. That took her mind off tight jeans and beer. The Walnut Room meant white shirts and ties, candlelight and wine. Or so she imagined, having never actually been inside there, either.

She skidded to a stop. Her friends, who didn't recognize Lija and had never met James, continued laughing and looking around for boys. How had she not noticed the new red empire-waist dress that Lija was wearing? The scene in Lija's bedroom came to mind with new clarity. Lija had not been lying there wasting time. She had been cooling down in her slip. Her make-up had been carefully applied and her nylons already clipped to her girdle. A new girdle! That's why she had looked so skinny. And the hair rollers. Lija had just been waiting to take them out so the curls wouldn't collapse too early in the evening. So intent on getting downtown to see her own friends, Raki had missed the obvious. Lija had been dressing for a date.

THE NEXT DAY, LIJA struggled with how much date talk was appropriate to share with a little sister.

"Why didn't you tell me you had a date? Did they have real candles? Or those little electric doo-hickies?" Raki badgered her. "What did you talk about? Did you use the fingerbowls? Did you drink wine?"

Lija picked at the threads of Raki's 4-H clothing entry, trying to ignore the onslaught of questions. *Save me from these annoying questions and insufferable knots.* Exasperated at her little sister's lack of focus on the job at hand, she still wanted Raki to learn this essential task. It was a skill she had learned from their mother, that she wanted to pass along. But she hated the tiny pins and the fussy thread as much as Raki did. God, she prayed, give me a hoe to whale away on some weeds.

"Pay attention to your project or you will never get it done in time."

"Aren't we going to trim the pattern?"

"Didn't your 4-H leader tell you that was a waste of time?"

"Are you and James going steady?"

"Questions like that won't get this project done. And I don't even know what that means," said Lija.

"Well, are you?"

"We've had one date. I don't think that qualifies."

How can one person be both sister and mother? Lija wanted to share her feelings, like a sister. But she also wanted to be a mom to Raki. Their mom had been confident and beautiful. Their mom never would have worried about being pretty enough, or nervous that she wasn't smart enough. Or too forward. Or not forward enough. Lija just kept pinning, in silence.

She wanted to tell Raki that yes, she drank wine, even though she wasn't old enough, and it made her a little too brave. When James got his pant leg stuck in his socks, she had teased it loose with the point of her shoe. Lija wanted to put into words how gooey she had felt when he smiled at her for doing that. It was a funny story, but she couldn't have Raki thinking she was a drunk, or that James was a hick. She pretended to prick her finger with a pin, peering closely at the nonexistent wound.

"I like James a lot," said Raki.

"I like him a lot, too," said Lija, and left it at that.

RAKI BROUGHT HER hand-sewn top to the 4-H Exhibit Hall a week later, confident it would earn a dazzling white. But never mind that. Her wheat bread and Lija's cucumbers were both good for purple, maybe even Grand Champion. How she wanted one of those enormous, ruffled, golden-inscribed ribbons. They reminded her of the Ferris Wheel.

Raki loved peering down from the Ferris Wheel, seeing the purple and yellow lights bejeweling the midway, that dirt patch carpeted in thick hay against the dust or mud, as the case may be. She loved the romance of it, circling high in the night, even higher than the grain elevator. Her friends complained when she asked them to go on it with her, so she quit asking. Kids her age, girls even, preferred the thrill of the Scrambler and the Tilt-A-Whirl, which slashed the prairie night like swordplay.

Raki and her friends ran from ride to ride, burning through their bean-walking funds and the cash their parents had tucked in their pockets. They stepped around wide-mouthed and petrified toddlers, scorned adults who were 'just people watching' and mocked the older girls who clung to their boyfriends and the boys who tried to win them prizes.

"Suckers," said Jody, pointing at the young men shooting pellet guns at the spinning wheel, their girlfriends cheering them on.

"You're just jealous," said Lynn, jostling Jody. "You would be proud to walk around with a boy on one arm and a big pink teddy in the other."

"It's cheaper to just buy a stuffed bear than to throw your money away twenty cents at a time," said Jody, shirking a little away from Lynn. "My dad tells my brother that straight shooters never win. You either need to be lucky, know a trick, or just keep trying until you spend so much money the carnie takes pity on you."

Raki intervened. "Come on, you guys. Lucky, smart, rich. Who cares how a boy gets the bear? If a boy wins me a bear, I'm taking it!"

"Speaking of rich, I'm not," Jody said to Raki and Lynn, scrumbling through the pockets of her pedal pushers. "I'm broke. Let's go to the Commercial Barn and pick up free stuff."

Besides going on every ride, they had already taken a dutiful tour through the animal barns and admired their own entries in the 4-H building, so they turned from the colored lights of the midway to the blazing fluorescent white of the giant Commercial Barn.

Jody was fishing through a bin of refrigerator magnets and Lynn was dishing herself free popcorn when Raki spotted Lija promenading between exhibits, James on one arm and a giant pink teddy bear in the other. Odd observations from that afternoon suddenly made sense: the girdle Raki had seen Lija slip on underneath her shorts; Lija's lacy new bra, the top button she had left undone.

"Hey," said Raki, "You guys have to meet my sister's boyfriend." Raki pointed at James and Lija, arm in arm yet gaping all around, seemingly mesmerized by the displays of Allis Chalmers balloons and John Deere calendars.

When they were close enough to hear her over the calliope music, Raki shouted at her sister, "Hey, Lija! Over here! Hi!"

"Well, hi, girls," said Lija in a tone of *savoir faire* that Raki had never, ever heard her use before. "Having fun?"

Jody and Lynn tipped their heads, pretending to be nonchalant. Their eyes betrayed them. They were both staring at James.

"Yeah," said Raki. She could hardly believe the giant pink teddy bear. She tried not to ogle it. What's an almost grown woman going to do with something like that? Not that Raki was jealous, but it would look better in a girl's room. She affected a careless tone. "Neat bear, Lija. Really neat."

Lija patted the bear's head. She looked over at James. He nodded.

"Raki, why don't you take the bear," offered Lija. "He's a big bundle for me to carry around all the time. Dad will be picking you up sooner than we—that is, James and I—will be going home. Plus, he matches your bedspread."

To carry around a bear won by a boyfriend. Not her boyfriend, but a boyfriend, nevertheless. Raki's heart couldn't resist. James gently unhooked the bear from Lija's elbow and handed it to Raki.

"All yours," he said. In her hands she noticed the fur was more scratchy than soft, but no matter.

"See you later," called Lija as she and James continued on, still arm in arm.

A week later the rides were loaded up on trucks and the barns swept clean. Raki couldn't stand to look at the deserted fairgrounds. The hot pink bear found a home on her pillows. Another year until the lights came back.

FALL OFFERED its own romance. Raki loved breathing crisp air instead of sticky heat and hearing the crunch of leaves instead of the buzz of insects. She even looked forward to going back to school and seeing her friends every day. And there was the fun of spying on Lija's 'courtship,' a word Raki got from her mom's old books, because nobody would call it that in 1965.

With Lija back at college during the week, and harvest from daybreak till past midnight even on weekends, James had precious little time for wooing, another word Raki got from her mother's books. No matter. Lija could pretend to be focused on canning vegetables all Saturday, but Raki knew she was really watching James through the window. Raki watched him, too, unloading the trucks and fiddling with machinery. She liked watching his arm muscles strain against his shirt sleeves. Sometimes she could hear him swear when he was trying to get something or another unstuck. Then Lija would cover Raki's ears or shoo her away. About the only time they saw James up close was when he came in for lunch, and Raki liked him well enough that she didn't even crinkle up her nose. Even on his sweatiest days. What she really liked, of course, was that Lija liked him. Because that might make him family.

FIFTH GRADE FRACTIONS were a mystery to solve, and not in a fun way, not like Nancy Drew stories.

Raki's teacher had flipped the numbers upside down and inside out and stirred them together with multiplication in a most confusing lesson. This had been the topic of discussion when Raki and Jody and Lynn headed to Jody's house after school. They were going to 'whip up a batch' of cookies, even though Raki knew there would be no 'whipping' involved, but a slavish adherence to every step set forth in Jody's mom's *Betty Crocker*. Which was why Raki found ridiculous Lynn's complaints about the real-world irrelevance of fractions.

"I'll never need to know this shit in real life," Lynn griped, Jody nodding her head in virtuous agreement.

Lynn and Raki had taken up swearing. Every 'damn' and 'shit' made them feel cool, like earning a badge on a Bad-Girl Scout sash. Jody objected, until they promised they would never use the 'f-word,' or combine 'damn' with 'God' or swear when it was not 'really necessary.'

Fractions distressed Raki just as much as Lynn, but she still pointed out, in as friendly a voice as she could, that they'd soon be measuring out quarter cups and half teaspoons.

"But Raki," reasoned Lynn, "the amounts are right in the recipe. The size of the cups and spoons are marked right on them. We don't have to figure out fractions. We just need to use the right size."

Later that evening, struggling through her arithmetic homework, Raki wished that Lynn was right. With her whole heart. But Raki knew first-hand that life followed no recipe. Baking didn't even follow a recipe. Sometimes you had to double it, or halve it. If you ran out of baking powder after the grocery store was closed, you could use soda instead, but just a fraction. Raki knew this from the notes her mother had left behind in her cookbook. Yellowed, crusted with smudges of old dough, that tear of notebook paper was Raki's security blanket. Her mother had written 'Emergency Substitutions' across the top in her neat schoolteacher penmanship. Raki reserved the use of these tips for true emergencies. She felt safe knowing her mother's wisdom was there to rescue her when she really needed it.

The real value of all this, mused Raki as she tapped her pencil against the pages of her workbook, is to teach you how to make do when things don't go perfectly. Like when your mother ups and dies on you, and you are left with just a three-quarter family.

6

BECAUSE HE HAD PROMISED Mr. Pederson, James registered for winter semester at Mankato State. He and Lija carpooled up and back and didn't always come home on the snowy weekends. He skipped registration for spring semester. It was warming up and he couldn't wait to get to planting. Somebody once told him summer vacation was supposed to allow students to work on the farm. Back then, when he lived in town, it made sense to him, but now he knew the busiest times were planting and harvest, when school was in session. So Lija had to start driving by herself again.

Winter semester had gone pretty well. Without animals, there was nothing much to do on the Pederson farm anyway. And while some of the other guys with agriculture majors resented their liberal arts requirements, he needed to take these classes just to keep up with his employer's ruminations. Whenever James didn't absolutely insist that Mr. Pederson show him how to fix something or figure something, their conversation veered in the direction of philosophy, politics, religion and science.

"Take a load off," said Mr. Pederson one spring day when rain and wind had chased them into the barn. The old man relaxed against the workbench, arms akimbo. James leaned against the wheel well of an old tractor, one he'd never known to run. Plenty of room to store antique implements when you don't have animals.

"Tell me what they taught you up there in Mankato last semester."

A small, dusty window let in little light. James peered at his employer. As long as they were wasting time, he'd get some useful information for himself. "Let me ask you something, Mr. Pederson." James kept his tone carefully casual. "You're always talking about religion, but in the abstract. What are your own beliefs?"

"Well, now that's an interesting question," Mr. Pederson said, straightening up. "Do you really want to know, or are you just humoring me? Angling for a bonus or something?"

"A little of both, I suppose, except maybe not the bonus. I hadn't thought about that."

"Oh, you have, too. And I'm not averse to a little brown-nosing, provided it's doled out in the proper proportion."

"Do I get a bonus?"

"Hell, no."

"So? Your belief, Mr. Pederson?"

"I was raised a Lutheran, as you may have guessed from my name, but my wife was Catholic." He harrumphed, "That was considered a mixed marriage back then."

"Still is. By some."

"I suppose. Anyway, I promised my wife and the priest to raise my daughters Catholic."

"Is that so? But Lija and Rakella aren't Catholic names."

"Well, sure they are. I told my wife no little girls of mine would be saddled with names like Clara or Theodora just because some woman five hundred years ago cured somebody of the flu or something. Wouldn't stand for that, but there are a lot more approved names on the list than you'd think. Lija and Rakella are Bible names, absolutely. You haven't read the Bible in Norwegian, have you?"

"Well, no."

"Neither have I, but their names are Norski-ized Old Testament. I swear it. Then we threw in top-notch saintly middle names—Lija Martha and Rakella Mary." He chuckled. "I thought I was bamboozling Father M., but converting a real Norwegian apostate was a coup for him. Those Norski names were his badges of honor. Good man, the father, forward-thinking, and a connoisseur of fine Scotch, too. More than once we raised a glass together."

"Let me know if I'm being too nosy, but you like the priest and yet I'm not sure if I've ever seen you get ready for Mass on Sunday."

"Well, I stopped believing in God, if that's what you want to know." Mr. Pederson turned his back on James, looking out the tiny window over the workbench. He picked up a wrench. James watched his shoulders tremble as he toyed with the tool.

"Why is that?"

"Because I'm mad as hell at God, that's why." Mr. Pederson slammed the wrench against the workbench with a thud and clatter, jerking his face toward James, his jaw thrust out. "I took Catechism classes and converted for chrissake. I kept my own personal beliefs to myself, but goddamnit I went to Mass every Sunday for over ten years. I gave money and flipped pancakes in that goddamned parish hall. I didn't sin any worse than any other bastard around here and what did God do for me? God took my wife away. I'm not interested in believing in that God."

Outside, rain fell like second-hand tears. It pounded on the roof like an organ dirge at a funeral, the barn like a cold and echo-y cathedral.

James stood up straight. He had heard Mr. Pederson raise his voice many times, but never like this. A wiser man would change the subject, but James was even more curious now than before. After a few seconds, Mr. Pederson's shoulders and jaw relaxed a little as he went back to leaning against the workbench. Safe to continue.

"How can you be mad at a God you don't believe exists?"

"Oh, he exists all right." Mr. Pederson wasn't shouting anymore. Now he sounded like one of James's professors. "So what? I mean, I believe Richard Nixon exists, but I don't have any interest in talking with him, or going to his political shindigs and I sure as hell wouldn't trust him with my retirement savings."

"What about Lija? And Raki? Are they mad, too?"

"Lija finds comfort in the rituals and the candles and the incense and all that rigmarole. She's very traditional; you must have noticed. It seems to me she embraces the faith even more strongly than her mother. Raki shows less interest. She likes the youth goings-on but sometimes she skips Mass. Lija really hates to go by herself, but she does sometimes."

And so when Lija returned Friday evening, James offered to accompany her to church on Sunday. Conversion would put his conscientious objector status at risk, but who cared where he sat for an hour on Sunday? There were no Mennonite churches in Halcyon, anyway. Staying put in his seat while the congregation trooped to the communion rail might make him feel like a stalk of volunteer corn sticking up in a bean field, but it was better than being shot at, so he wouldn't budge.

BY THE TIME James gave Lija a tiny diamond, just a few months later, he was at peace with the idea of promising the priest whatever promises he needed to make. His family was furious. They discussed shunning.

"It's not like I'm some long-haired hippie taking LSD or something," he argued.

That wasn't the issue.

"I'm not actually converting," he explained.

But the children, they responded.

The more they talked, the more he dug in his heels. How closed minded could they be? Screw 'em. What difference did it make, anyway? The priest read from the same Bible they did, mostly. If they were going to be like that, he'd be glad to throw in his lot with Lija and Mr. Pederson. That was how it had to be. And so on his wedding day the groom's side of the church was sparsely populated. A few high school friends, some rebellious cousins.

As her father had predicted, Lija's pent-up religiosity exploded. James could not embrace the dogmas, traditions and encyclicals with the same enthusiasm she did, but he had no grounds to argue with them, either. A very respectable eleven and one-half months separated the wedding from the baptism of baby Randall.

James was bursting with blessings as he carried tiny Randy to the baptismal font. The baby's little face poked through the neck ruffles of the heirloom baptismal gown. "I'll keep you safe, always," whispered James. Little Randy's face glowed from the sun streaming through stained glass windows, until a cloud passed over.

James's life plan was working out just so. He and Lija and the baby moved into the empty mother-in-law house across the road. It wouldn't take long to fill the other bedrooms. James was looking forward to taking on more and more responsibility for the farm. Indulging his father-in-law's view of himself as esteemed mentor and gentleman landowner was a job duty and means to an end.

PART THREE

Selfishness is one of the qualities apt to inspire love.

Nathaniel Hawthorne

Halcyon, Minnesota

1971 – 1972

7

RAKI SANG ALONG to the radio as she drove her cherry red Corvair toward home. The temperature was below zero, the heater cooking her feet while her ears still felt frostbit. Five months to summer vacation. Then senior year and she could bug out of Halcyon. Cool. Scary.

Chicago was blasting from the speakers, singing about what time it is, and if anybody cared. Raki belted out the familiar lyrics, off-key, but what did it matter? She didn't really care.

A stiff breeze swirled last night's snowfall across the highway, swishing and swaying in curlicues, like old-fashioned ballroom dancers. When the breeze lifted flakes into the sky, they twinkled against the blue horizon. The yellow sun, so alluring yet so weak, belied the arctic temperature.

She turned into the driveway, the snow squeaking and grunting beneath her tires. James always set his plow blade just high enough to leave a skim of hard pack over the gravel. With no animals to care for, planting still months off, and two toddlers and a baby packing his little house across the road, he seemed to spend as much time as possible outside, even in winter, behind the snow plow. The rhythm method had apparently failed them. Baby Randy had been followed a year later by Sandy, a little over a year after him came Lance. Lanny, James called him. Or maybe all these babies so close together were what they wanted. Hard to know.

Sometimes James hid out in the big house, studying. Raki always offered him cookies. He'd take a bite, sigh, and complain about the long drive to college, the crappy way the highway got plowed, how he felt like a serf to her dad, and that his grand plan for life was taking too long. How it was all turning into a drag.

Today, he was nowhere to be seen. Raki parked her Corvair, pulling together the pile of books sprawled over the passenger seat. Once inside, she piled them on the chair next to the back door, threw her coat on top, kicked off her boots, and set to work.

Every day was a good day to bake, but a cold one like this was best. With a test and research outline due tomorrow, she was doomed to stay home tonight, but all of that could be done while the dough was rising. She pulled canisters of flour and sugar off the counter, two envelopes of yeast out of the refrigerator, shortening and pans, two bowls and a set of measuring cups from the cupboard and set them on the scuffed oak table. She twisted the thermostat dial in the hallway, calling out, "Dad! I'm turning up the heat so the yeast will work."

Back in the kitchen, she tied her long auburn hair back into a pony tail, securing it with the wide cotton ribbon she had made from her mom's old red and yellow flowered shirt, after it had become too tattered to wear. She turned on the radio and washed her hands in the sink. Turning to her table of tools and ingredients, she scooped and leveled three cups of flour into a bowl, then added salt and sugar.

Outside the window, a truck rumbled past. She imagined that truck—no a fleet of trucks—with a picture of her bread on the side, a bigger-than-life loaf, maybe her face, too, smiling. Who wouldn't buy delectable bread from such a friendly baker? Her bakery company would be huge, with dozens of flour-covered bakers running around doing her bidding. How long before that might happen? Five years? It seemed an eternity.

Her dream was like yeast, and reality the salt that kept it from rising too fast. She had seen inside the local bakery. Enormous mixing bowls as scary as witch's kettles. Oven maws big enough to crawl into. Like a Grimm's fairy tale. Brick walls with no windows.

She shook off the image, refocusing on the flour billowing up out of the pink melamine bowl, sparkling in the winter sunlight, like snow. So white and pure. Yet, without adulteration, there would be no bread. Making a face, she used her fingers to dig out a big dollop of shortening from the can. What didn't go into the dough she smeared inside the pans and the second bowl. Then she turned to the sink, nudging the tap open with her elbow, letting it run. When the water was hot enough she slathered her hands with dish soap to cut the grease. Then she mixed some hot water judiciously with a little more cold, making it just the right temperature for her yeast.

She stirred vigorously, adding flour, mixing pure with profane. When the mass pulled free of the bowl, she dusted the table with flour and placed the dough in the middle, her hands massaging, folding and turning. Flour wafted up. More like talc than snow. Gradually the mass grew soft, rounded and smooth, like a baby's bottom.

Cold blasted through the door just as she placed the dough in the greased bowl to rise. In traipsed Lija with Randy and Sandy in tow.

"Close the door!" Raki scolded. The little boys dawdled on the threshold. Lija made no move to shoo them inside. Instead, she held the door open for James, who came in carrying Lanny. Couldn't Lija see there was dough rising here? Raki picked up her bowl and scurried it away from the draft. She scowled in their direction, but none of them even looked up. They were too busy with their boots.

"Wow, does it ever feel great to get out of that cramped little house," complained Lija, spreading her arms wide and revolving around the spacious kitchen like a very tired dervish dancer. Little Randy imitated her, throwing his arms wide and spinning until he whacked his hand on the table leg and began to cry.

Raki watched Lija kiss the boo boo on Randy's hand. "What's going on?"

"Dad called and asked us to come over. As glad as I am for a change of scenery, I gotta say that bundling up three boys for a walk across the road is a major chore."

"Come in here," called their father.

Two generations jostled down the hall.

"Make yourselves comfortable." Their father sounded like he was talking to accounting clients.

Lija took Lanny from James and settled down in the client's chair. James leaned against the door frame. Raki took the second client chair. "Scurry along," said Lija to her two older boys, "but don't break anything." Randy and Sandy decamped to the TV across the hall.

Their dad settled heavily into his huge leather chair. He leaned back. Wrapped his right arm across his chest. Gripped his chin between the thumb and forefinger of his left hand. What a show he was putting on. They were all family, for heaven's sake. There were times Raki would have found this amusing. Today she felt irked. Silence. Somebody needed to say something.

"Dad, I don't know what you have us in here for, but I planned on studying while my bread is rising."

"Sorry. It's just hard to know where to start." Another pause. Big throat clearing. "Well, I'll just start and fill in the blanks and backtrack as necessary.

"Lija, I've watched as you and James have filled up the little house across the road and get more and more crowded over there, while Raki and I rattle around this big place. But I couldn't pull myself away from the memories here. I have been selfish, holding on to what this house used to be, remembering the parties your mom used to throw. All that."

What was he going on about? Raki felt terrible that her memories of her mother had faded so much. Her recollections of those parties were mostly odd bits of laughter and lots of cigarette smoke coming up through the heater grate. She had always been tightly tucked in bed and sternly instructed to stay in her room.

"On the other hand, kids need room to grow. It's easy in the spring and summer and fall when you let them loose outside, but I see you going stir-crazy over there, Lija."

He looked over at James, spreading his arms wide. "Your husband here has proven himself capable of taking care of the land. Your family needs this house and I need to move on. Someplace a little warmer."

Raki looked at her dad's big hands, his wide arms, the ones that used to wrap around her and lift her in the air and make her feel warm all over. Warm and safe, even when he was flinging her into the air. Because he would always catch her.

"After Christmas I'm going to pack up and move to Arizona and do taxes for all those retired farmers living the life of leisure in their campers down south in the perpetual sunshine."

What? Sunshine? Raki looked out the window at the sun glinting off the snow. There was plenty of sunshine here. She once wrote a poem in grade school where she described her dad as smelling of earth, soap, sunshine and Scotch. She got an A, but after that her teacher sometimes asked her ridiculous questions. Did her father ever fall down? No! Did he fall asleep in odd places at odd times? Of course not!

"James has agreed to purchase what he can get a bank loan for and rent from me what he can't afford." The voice was the same, but this was a business man talking, not her father. "Whatever proceeds I don't need for lollygagging down in the desert I'll sock away and it will all get split fair and square when I die. Don't like to think about that, but . . .

"Anyway, once I hightail it out of here, you, Lija, just need to keep a room warm for Raki. Let her use her own room or get herself set up independent in your house across the road. Whatever works out. This house is yours, though, James and Lija, my thanks for all James's work, going on seven years. Plus, you really need it." He winked. "I'll be out of here before you really, really need it." Lija patted her hand on her belly.

Wait. What? Another one? Raki looked at Lija's waistline, incredulous. Three babies weren't enough?

Wait another minute. What had Dad said? 'Hightail' and 'out of here?' Did this mean her father, her only living parent, was leaving? She couldn't breathe.

Logic told her that, as a matter of accounting, little of his time was spent with her. If he wasn't in his office, he was out in the field or in town at the coffee shop or at the golf course bar. It had been many years since he had thrown her in the air and caught her. Still, he lived here, on this farm, always had.

He did not seem to expect any feedback. At the end of his speech he crossed his arms across his chest like armor. Any objections would certainly bounce right off.

"Thanks, Dad," said Lija. "We'll have parties here again, birthday cakes, candles and Kool-Aid."

Randy and Sandy ran in and jumped on their grandpa's lap. "Just don't let these little guys set the house on fire," he said. "It's all settled. Don't worry about anything, except maybe that I'll get bored and come back. I'll probably have to come back now and then and check up on James." He winked again. "Make sure he's not screwing up too much."

Raki was dumbstruck. She was still breathing, but each breath was so shallow she thought she'd faint. How was she supposed to react? What she was supposed to feel? She had been distancing herself, like a kite, flying ever higher and higher. But Dad was supposed to stay on the ground, holding the string. No string was long enough to reach to—where had he said—Arizona?

"I'm going to miss all of you, but I'm not going to miss this at all," he concluded, thrusting his thumb toward the window and the snow-clad prairie, the wind whipping froth into the late afternoon light.

Summer, senior year, graduation, college, that string of bakeries and the bread trucks with her picture on the side. Everybody moving along. No reason to be sad. Buck up. Be glad. It'll be all right. Better check on that bread.

Raki put on a fake smile, gave her dad a hug, and went back to the kitchen. James and Lija stayed in the office. The sounds of rustling papers and snippets of sentences, mostly legal words, occasionally wafted out of the office. Half an hour later James left with Lanny. Lija dragged the other two into the kitchen.

"Raki, your bread is risen enough," she said, reaching over to the bowl and punching down Raki's dough.

Raki erupted. "How dare you? That's mine!"

"Calm down. I just did what needed to be done."

"You have everything now, Lija! James, the kids, the farm, even the house! All I have is a promise! Someday I will get my share. Someday! And now you touch my bread, the only thing that's mine."

She slammed her book against the table and ran up the stairs.

FIRST MOM DIED, now this. Raki sunk her face in her bedspread's nubby chenille, stifling wails and soaking up tears. This was like being an orphan. Again. Only worse. At least Mom didn't leave on purpose. Lija got Mom for longer, and she had Dad here until she was grown up. And all the other stuff. What Raki got was a plate of leftovers, and even that was taken away before she was finished. She shook with the unfairness of it all.

But the dough needed to be divided, so she took a deep breath, steadied herself and went back down to the kitchen. Lija and James and the boys were long gone. Dad was still in his office.

Her tears dried as she shaped the dough and placed it in the pans. The salty film cracked when she moved her face. Honestly, what did it matter that Lija and James get the farm? Raki had other plans. If there was a farm she needed, it would be a wheat farm, not corn and beans. And Dad, well, why shouldn't he want to move on with his own life?

He was a good dad, even if he wasn't a mom, which was sometimes a good thing. She covered the loaves with a towel for the final rising. At least he didn't give ridiculous advice like Jody and Lynn said their moms gave them: you'll look stylish in these lacy bobby socks; be sure to button every last button on your blouse. But then Lija was as bad or worse. Don't use tampons because they ruin your virginity. Good grief.

Well, at least dad would be available by long distance. It was expensive, but there were cheap rates on Sundays.

8

LIJA SANK DEEP into the recliner, nursing tiny Jimmy, Jr., number four. Where had the months gone? Seemed such a short time since dad left, but it was cold then. God, she would sell her soul for some of that cold today.

She focused her mind on Jimmy Jr.'s weight against her body. He was a solid newborn, like his three brothers had been. The press of his weight was tranquilizing. Her sweat made him stick a little. She laid her head back and closed her eyes. Lanny crawled to her feet. What was he whining about now? Ah, the stench. She snapped her head forward and moved to get up. Finding insufficient energy, she flopped back into the chair. She lifted little Jimmy's eensy fingers to her nose, sniffing bits of stray talc to overcome the stink at her feet. It didn't work.

Across the hall, Sandy cranked the volume on the TV. A re-run of *Family Affair*, it sounded like. Lija pressed herself even deeper into the upholstery, anchored by the baby. She couldn't possibly get up to turn it down. She was too tired even to yell. The voices of Buffy and Jody and Uncle Bill and Mr. French leached into her consciousness. She imagined that idyllic scene behind her closed eyelids: the luxury city apartment, the 'gentleman's gentleman' round the clock to cook and clean, a perfect pair of adorable children, the lovable teenaged sibling, Cissy.

Lija's own teenaged sibling was—where? Not there to help, that was for sure.

Just for a day, no, an hour, no—just ten minutes. To live just ten minutes in a clean apartment—heaven. TV was not real life, but her life was real, too real. A big family in a spacious home on a prosperous farm. Should be wonderful. Not long ago this life she was now living had been her beautiful dream for the future. Now she had everything she ever wanted, and these boys were pooping all over it.

Where was Raki, anyway? At the beach flinging wet hair at the boys? In a bikini? Lija had never even tried on a bikini and there was no chance she ever would, now, not after four births. She struggled to forgive her sister for this selfishness. Or was it her own selfishness that needed forgiving? After all, Lija had been free to enjoy those things when she was seventeen—except of course in a skirted one-piece. But didn't Raki see how much help was needed? Didn't she feel grateful for all the things Lija had done for her, all the substitute mothering? Why didn't she come home and cover up and take care of Lanny's diaper?

She thought about that big family at church, filling up an entire pew with their twelve perfectly-behaved, well-scrubbed brats. Just four and she already had too many to handle. Too many to pay attention to, too many to clean up after, too many to—she was too exhausted to finish the thought. Another idea intruded of its own effort. It would be easy to stop at four. Lija prayed to shield her mind, but the temptation blew right past her religious defenses. She wouldn't be the first woman to take a pill in the evening and a communion wafer the next morning.

Lanny's whining turned into a wail, drowning out her thoughts. Jimmy quit sucking to join in the howl. Sandy turned up the volume even louder. Above all the wailing she could still discern the TV butler Mr. French teaching Buffy how to properly tear lettuce, at a volume so high it was like he was shouting at the top of his lungs.

Where was Randy? Ummm, too tired to look.

ॐ

DARK SWIRLS GATHERED themselves into a funnel over the corn fields. A little boy perched on his green John Deere tricycle in a yard. His tow head, grass-colored t-shirt and khaki shorts conformed to the agricultural palette surrounding him. Silver streamers fluttered out of his handlebars, mimicking the activity above him. A little chameleon boy, blending into the grass-lined gravel driveway. Only his barn-red, rubber-toed Keds stood out.

Chubby fingers gripped the handlebars. The black cloud danced over the house and the farmyard. The boy reached the road. He stopped on the shoulder. He looked up. Watching.

A Dodge pick-up driver craned his head toward the funnel cloud. An Oldsmobile sedan was speeding, swerving to pass the Dodge. All four of the Olds windows were wide open.

Suddenly, the Halcyon civil defense siren blared. The Oldsmobile driver pulled back into his lane too soon and hit the brakes. Dodge Pick-Up cranked right to avoid Oldsmobile.

The little boy scrambled his tricycle backwards just as fast as his little red Keds could push it. His balance failed him and he tumbled on his side. Dodge slammed on his brakes. Oldsmobile slammed to a stop. The drivers jumped out and ran to the child. Dodge crouched down. The little boy screamed "Mommy!" Oldsmobile ran for the house yelling, "Call an ambulance!"

And the funnel cloud rose back into the gray sky and disappeared.

RAKI REALLY WAS wearing a little yellow bikini, plus a lacey white cover-up. The drive home from the lake was sweltering. The wet beach towel beneath her thighs added to the humidity. She and Jody and Lynn had decided to leave the beach when the funnel cloud formed. Sated with sun and sand, they figured it was an omen and called it a day.

Raki's blue flip-flops, $1.00 at Ben Franklin's, rested a little too heavy on the gas pedal. She eased up. No sense wasting bean money on a speeding ticket. WDGY blared all the way from Minneapolis to her radio speakers. The Halcyon civil defense siren had settled down in time for her to hear Gladys Knight. An ad came on. Was that another siren? Fainter than the earlier one, but getting louder.

In the distance a mirage of red and blue and yellow lights seemed to be racing toward her, shimmering up off the hot, black asphalt, incongruous against the greens and tans of the fields. The siren was wailing now, deafening. The ambulance blurred past her, screaming toward Halcyon. James's truck followed a few seconds behind.

What the hell is going on? Raki's heart started pounding.

She pulled into her driveway, jumped out, ran into the house, yelling, waiting only five seconds before racing back out, already knowing there would be no answer. She ripped the car door open, threw herself back inside, pushed the blue flip-flops hard against the floor and aimed for the hospital. Screw the speeding tickets

THE HALCYON COMMUNITY Hospital was a flat-top affair, like a row of hay bales deliberately assembled on the crest of a small rise. The last blond brick was laid in the early 1960s, several years after Raki was born and just as the birth rate was tapering off. But a lot of her friends had gone there for tonsillectomies or broken bones, so the community still considered it an excellent investment.

She had seen photographs of the Catholic-run edifice it had replaced. The old red brick had made that one look kind of like a scab. The new fluorescent-lit facility was modern, clean, and staffed with secular nurses in crisp white uniforms. The habited nuns had scared the Lutherans and were now too scarce for the Catholics.

By the time Raki blew into the emergency room, Randy had been stretchered behind curtains. Lija was standing, Jimmy Jr. draped across her arm like a dish towel. Lanny was in his father's arms, his full diaper polluting the sterile environment. Sandy stood silent and squared-up, a two-foot tall obstacle in the midst of professional flurry. A nurse took hold of Sandy's hand, tugging him toward his father, where she silently removed Lanny from James's arms. "We'll find someone to take care of these children. They can't be in here."

The head nurse, an RN identifiable by her stiff white cap with its black band, handed the two off to an LPN with her lowly little unbanded cap. The head nurse lifted Jimmy, Jr. from across Lija's arm. "It's OK," she assured. "He'll be with us." Lija relinquished without protest. Raki stood with her hands shawling her shoulders, shivering beneath the lacy beach shawl.

"Who is this? And how old is she?" demanded the head nurse, looking Raki up and down, her lips pursed.

"This is Rakella, Raki we call her," said James. "My sister-in-law. She's seventeen."

"A sister-in-law is not immediate family and she's too young. Orderly!" The nurse barked toward a young man. "Escort this girl to the waiting room."

And so the orderly took Raki to the row of chairs across from the Admissions window.

"Is he going to be OK? What happened? Are any bones broken? Will he need an operation? He's such a good boy. Will he have scars? He's not going to die, is he?" Raki spewed question after question without waiting for the answers.

"Don't worry. The little guy is being well taken care of." What a soothing voice he had. "All I know is what I overheard. A car ran into him, but based on all the wailing, it sounds like he's strong. That's a really good sign."

His words salved her fears. The words 'good bedside manner' came to mind. He might make a good doctor. His current position seemed pretty menial, though.

"When will you know more?"

"I already know your—nephew?—is getting really good care. You should come back during visiting hours. Seven o'clock to eight-thirty. Plenty of time to go home and change. The air conditioning seems set too high in here." His lips turned up just a little. He looked to be trying to instill optimism, without trivializing the situation.

A little older than herself, but probably younger than James. Dark hair, longer and a lot less kempt than James's. Sun-bleached eyebrows beneath the dark hair gave him an interesting mis-matched look.

"I wouldn't worry too much. Worrying won't help anyway." He reached up and fingered his hair away from his forehead.

A secretary slid open the Admissions window, leaning her head past the glass. "Miss Pederson," she interrupted. "Do you want to take your other nephews home with you? That would be a big help. One of them needs a fresh diaper. Bad."

Raki stood up and nodded.

"See you around then," said the orderly, ambling down the short hall. "I'm Luke."

"Rakella Pederson. Raki for short. Pederson with a 'd' and an 'o.'"

IT'D BE NO trouble finding a babysitter in time to return to the hospital. Every woman and teenage girl within earshot of the ambulance trip would be willing to take on three boys for several hours just to be the first to hear what had happened. And because she wanted to help out. Because she cared, and maybe someday would need some help herself. Raki changed Lanny's diaper, then she called Jody. No charge for babysitting, offered Jody, provided Lynn came along, too.

As Raki waited for her friends, she traded out her beach wear. A gauze blouse came off the hanger. The long sleeves would protect her from the air conditioning, but the feathery fabric would be cool in the car on the way. She paced, and looked out the window, buttoning up. She had embroidered blades of grass on the cuffs and peace symbols down the front placket. *What is taking them so damn long?* The gauze caressed her skin. A thought of the handsome orderly sprang to mind. She bit a fingernail. Bell bottoms next. She sucked in her breath as she pulled up the zipper, straining to hear the sound of rubber on gravel outside. Nothing. She craned her head to look out the window. Only the screen kept her from leaning out. No car in sight. Her feet slid into a pair of embossed leather-strap sandals with chunky heels. *Come on, you guys! Hurry!*

She ran down the stairs, leaned against the screen door and peered down the driveway, kicking the toe of her sandal against the linoleum. Every minute or so she slammed out the door to look down the road. But it was actually more like every fifteen seconds. Sandy tossed Cheerios over his head and onto the kitchen floor. Lanny crawled through them, crunching half with his knees and palming the rest into his mouth. She knew she should clean it up, but her thoughts were at the hospital. At least Jimmy Jr. was out of trouble in his netted playpen.

Finally, the hum of a motor slowing. Raki was already at the driveway and tapping on the passenger side window by the time Jody came to a stop. Lynn cranked the window down and Jody leaned over to hear.

"Thanks a million, guys! I gotta run!" Raki's sandals spewed gravel on the way to her Corvair. "Wait up for me! Sorry about the mess!"

RAKI FOUND JAMES sitting by Randy's bed, holding the little boy's hand, croaking out most of the words to a nursery tune. "Hush, little Randy, don't say a word, Papa's gonna buy you a somethingbird . . ."

Lija sat crumpled in a vinyl chair in the corner, sniffling, smearing her cheeks and staring at the floor.

"He's going to be OK, Raki," said James, interrupting his lullaby. "Just a few bruises and broken bones. They gave him something to make him sleepy. He was lucky. We were lucky."

"I'm so glad." Raki leaned over to give her nephew a kiss.

James leaned over to stroke Randy's hair at the same time. Raki's hair brushed his arm. He flinched.

"You OK?" she asked.

"Better than her," he said, nodding across the room toward Lija.

"She must feel terrible."

"Make him leave," said Lija through her sobs. "Make him get out of here for a minute."

James stood up, heavily, and moved toward the door. "I'll get a candy bar or something."

The door swung shut. Lija collapsed even further. Raki scraped James's chair across the room to sit next to her.

"I can't do it. I can't do it. I'm not capable," sobbed Lija. "I'm in too deep and I can't get out and I can't do it and I can't."

"Can't what?"

Lija's hands were wrestling each other in her lap.

Raki worried Lija might break some bones from the contortions. She laid her own hands on top of Lija's to still them. "Can't what?"

"I can't be a mother. I don't know how to tell James, but I can't be a mother anymore. You tell him."

"I'm not telling James anything," said Raki, putting on a smile as real as a plastic flower from the Five & Dime. "You can be—no, you *are*—a good mother."

"No. It's hopeless. You know what I was doing? I wasn't doing anything. Nothing." She flung Raki's hands out of her lap. She spread her fingers like talons, seizing her head. "I wasn't watching Randy and I wasn't disciplining Sandy and I wasn't changing Lanny's diaper and I wasn't even feeding Jimmy because he was screaming. I was useless. I am nothing. Useless!" She was wailing.

"It's not your fault, Lija."

"Well, who the hell's fault is it then?" she sneered. "Maybe it's James's fault, because he was working." She quit sobbing, anger trading places with despair. "Maybe he should quit farming so he can watch these boys every single second of every single day. I sure as hell can't be trusted. Then we can all starve. No, no, wait. I know whose fault it is. It's dad's fault for gallivanting off to Arizona."

"What?"

"The almighty college-degreed accountant and farmer Lawrence Pederson doesn't give a rip for us or this land. He's sittin' in the sunshine having a high time, probably found himself some . . . woman . . . down there already. Miniskirt and bouffant hairdo I imagine. Never mind that James only has two hands and is working his ass off."

"Lija, I really don't know about a girlfriend, but it doesn't matter. Everything is going to be OK. No need to find somebody to blame."

Lija would not be soothed. "Maybe it's your fault, Raki," she seethed. "Maybe it's your fault because you have more important things to do. Get a good suntan today? That's an accomplishment. More than I did all goddamn day, I gotta admit that." Lija jerked her head away, staring at the wall, her shoulders shaking violently.

The onslaught left Raki speechless. Who knew Lija could swear?

"You know whose fault it really is?" Lija asked.

"It's nobody's fault, Lija." Raki sighed. "Like I said, accidents happen."

"Oh, it's somebody's fault, all right. It's God's fault." She paused. "They're always saying, 'God only gives you as much as you can handle.' Well, that's crap. Crap! God screwed up. Big time. He gave me way more than I can handle. Four more boys than I know what to do with."

"You're a good mother, Lija. Accidents happen."

"Bullshit. There are women who can handle six, ten, even twelve kids and I have four and one almost gets killed. Yeah, it's God's fault. He miscalculated when he was counting up how many kids I could handle. I can't do it. I can't do it." The 'it' stretched out into more sobs.

James walked in with his candy bar and stood beside Randy's bed. Lija turned her own chair, facing the corner like a child under punishment, her shoulders heaving.

"You can have your chair back," said Raki, getting up and moving toward the door, wanting to run but holding herself back. James picked the chair up and carried it back to Randy's bed.

"The priest is on his way down the hall."

The thought terrified Raki. If the priest started talking about God's will or the blessings of children, Lija might gouge his eyes out. The last thing Raki wanted was to be audience for that. "James, is there anything I can do? Bring something from home?"

"Raki?"

"Yeah?"

"Just give all the boys a big hug. Even if they're asleep. We're probably going to be here a long time. Tell them how much we love them. Whisper it in their ears. Please?"

"Of course." She slipped out of the room.

Leaving felt like walking out of a horror movie at noon. The fluorescent lighting blasted her back to reality. It wasn't really Lija inside there saying crazy things. She would calm down soon. Raki took a deep breath and turned down the hall. Luke ambled toward her.

"You were right," she said, faking bright humor. "Just bruises and broken bones. He'll be good as new." She spotted the priest's black shirt and crucifix coming toward them. Instinctively, she tugged the orderly's sleeve. "Umm, I'd like to talk to you, ask you some questions. Can we go somewhere?"

He looked quizzical, then motioned her to follow. "Taking five," he said, passing the nurse's station. Nobody even looked up.

The coffee shop was deserted. Luke put a nickel in the vending machine and a muddy brew sputtered into a paper cup. He held up an empty cup and wagged it at her. She shook her head no.

"They're only keeping him for observation, you know," said Luke. "Like you said, they checked him out really well and besides the broken leg, he's fine. They just want to make sure they didn't miss anything before he goes home."

"Oh, I understand that. I was just trying to get away from somebody. I needed to look occupied. You were just handy, that's all."

"Handy?" He squeezed his brows ever so slightly, tilting his head.

"At hand. Within reach. I didn't mean anything by it. It's not like I arranged for you to be walking down the hall just ahead of the priest I was trying to avoid."

"It's OK. Handy is a good thing. It's pretty much what they pay me for around here. What's so bad about the priest?"

"Oh, nothing against him personally. Aside from his boring homilies, he's OK. I'm not real devout, but my sister is. She even got my brother-in-law to convert—sort of anyway. By the way, will they let them stay overnight here?"

"No. They'll make them go home when visiting hours are over. The nurses will give a stern lecture about their need for sleep and their responsibilities at home. What are they going to do for him, anyway, when he's sound asleep?"

"OK. That's what I thought. Anyway, my sister is all freaked out about having too many kids. She thinks that's why this accident happened, because God gave her too many kids. I think she really needs The Pill, but I know for certain the priest is going to have a different opinion on that."

"Mmmmm." He sipped the coffee. "Want to try a little?" He held out the cup.

She took it without thinking, fighting hard to not wince at the bitter taste.

"Thanks. Plus, I didn't want him asking me when I was coming back to Mass or going to confession."

"I get it."

Through the steam coming off the coffee, Raki watched for Luke's eyes to start detouring toward the buttons on her blouse. This was the response she had been going for, back when she was choosing clothes from her closet. She felt a bit ashamed at herself. It wasn't as if she had thought about it specifically, in words, back when she was choosing her outfit, but while her injured nephew was drugged up against the pain and her sister was falling to pieces, Raki deliberately chose a pair of jeans a little snugger than the rest, and a blouse that hinted at being transparent, although it wasn't, not really. How shallow. A pair of looser slacks and a structured shirt had been hanging right there, too.

She had known, even as she held her breath zipping the jeans, there was no guarantee she would run into this handsome orderly again. She had also known, again without thinking in words, that if she didn't run into him accidentally, she might spend some time wandering the halls, perhaps pretending to be lost and in need of directing. It hadn't worked out that way, but she had been prepared. And yet, in spite of all that preparation, here he was, not noticing her clothes at all.

"Well, I promised to ask you a question, so here goes," she said, kicking back the shame and guilt to take advantage of the situation as best she could. Yeah, pretty shallow. "Where are you from? What are you doing here?"

"I'm a pre-med student at the 'U' working here as an orderly for the summer. To get some real-life experience."

A university student. All of a sudden the embroidered grass and peace symbols seemed completely silly. He would know real hippies. She was just a farm girl, faking it with her 4-H sewing skills. She tried rearranging her hands and arms to hide the colorful stitching, which just made it all the more obvious.

"Why here?" she said, pretending to relax. "I know you aren't from Halcyon."

"Because this is where I could get hired on. One of the doctors is my uncle."

"What do you do?"

"Whatever the nurses tell me to do. None of it is exciting or glamorous and a lot of it is gross." He bobbed his head back, draining his coffee.

"Is it making you want to be a doctor more? Or less?""

"Are you sure you don't want some? A cup all your own?" He got up and walked over to the machine. "Are you in high school or college?"

It was one thing to take a sip without grimacing, but a whole cup? That's what a university student would do. "Yes, I think I will have a cup, thanks."

Without waiting for her to answer his question, Luke continued. "When you go to college you will have to learn how to drink coffee. I know it tastes terrible, but we drink it. . ."

"Because you're sleepy?" *Oh, my god, what a stupid thing to say.*

He laughed as he handed her the cup. "Your first? Maybe some sugar? Sweeten it up, you know."

"That's a good idea." The coffee was hotter than she expected, the paper cup too thin. Her fingers got scalded.

"Anyway, in answer to your question. This summer hasn't helped much. I think I want to be a doctor, but I'm not sure. I could end up teaching biology, or work in a lab. I don't know. I'm still experimenting. Enjoy your coffee. I had better check in. I don't want to get fired. They don't pay much, but it's my rent money for next semester."

He tossed his paper cup in the garbage can on his way out.

RAKI COULDN'T WAIT to huddle with her friends, first assuring them Randy was going to be all right, then rhapsodizing about Luke. She wanted to watch their eyes get big as she described his cute behind and rumpled hair and that he was a university student. But her friends had not managed to get a single one of her nephews to sleep by the time she got home. Jimmy Jr. was crying; the TV was blaring; Lanny and Sandy were yowling along to the theme song to the *Beverly Hillbillies*. There was no space amidst the chaos for girl talk, at least not until the boys were settled down.

Jody and Lynn chattered in the living room as Raki shushed the boys and set to work upstairs, scrubbing their faces and pulling their pajamas up over their bottoms and down over their heads. The older two dragged their toothbrushes lazily across their baby teeth. She ordered Sandy to say his prayers as she changed Lanny and Jimmy Jr.'s diapers.

Then she remembered her promise to James. Sandy wriggled free before she had the first word out. Then she tried Lanny. He clung to her exuberantly, but could not possibly have heard her words of endearment. Sandy was howling at the moon.

"Shhh," she admonished. It was useless.

She picked up Jimmy, Jr. from his play pen. The infant had no choice but to be hugged and cooed at. She put each in his own bed, one, two, three, patted the empty pillow on Randy's bed, closed the doors and went downstairs. A few more howls, some rustling, then relative peace. Finally, she could go downstairs for girl talk.

"Thank you, guys," Raki whispered to her friends, exhausted.

"No problem," said Jody. A dramatic sigh implied a whole evening of problems. "Long night."

"How is Randy?" asked Lynn.

"He's going to be fine. Right now it's Lija who's in worse shape, I think. She blames herself. And everybody else."

"Is James holding up?" asked Jody.

"He's being strong. Not much comfort to Lija, though. Men can't handle emotional stuff." She twinged with guilt for badmouthing her brother-in-law. He had, after all, urged her to hug and reassure his children. She had, after all, been no more comfort to her sister than he had been.

"Talk more later," said Lynn. "Jody and I are going to meet the group at the drive-in. Sorry you can't come."

Raki opened her mouth to protest, but no words formed. They had managed to keep the boys alive, but little else, had been gabbing together while she worked, and now they were . . . leaving? Her eyes raked the room, willing the dust motes to turn into words, a smart sentence that would make them want to stay. A ball of resentment formed in her chest. If she and Jody were at Lynn's house, they wouldn't abandon Lynn to go to the drive-in. Or if she and Lynn were helping Jody, they wouldn't leave Jody to go hang with the group. Jody and Lynn didn't have squally baby nephews, but that shouldn't be an excuse. They should know that she needed to talk.

She clenched her teeth and watched without commenting as Lynn and Jody slipped on their sandals by the kitchen door. The crushed Cheerios, still all over the floor, spelled abandonment.

"See you," called Jody and Lynn as the screen slammed behind them. Raki stood at the window, arms akimbo, jaw trembling, tears streaking her mascara. Their car turned onto the highway.

"Screw you!" she screamed out the door when they were long gone. She turned on her heel, grinding cereal into the linoleum. Grabbing a broom from the closet, she swept angrily.

FLOORS SPOTLESS and tears dry, Raki was reading in her room by the time she heard James and Lija slam the car doors. She was glad the boys finally settled down. The earlier racket would have killed poor Lija. She felt a little irked, though, at their small effort to keep quiet. It wouldn't take much for the house to erupt again.

She got up and pulled the curtains back. The darkening sky muted the summer colors, but scraps of bright white paper stood out against the dark grass. Wrappers from medical supplies the ambulance driver must have discarded in his haste. Something else to clean up tomorrow.

She lifted her eyes across the road to the little house and the rows of corn and beans stretching east, dissolving into the horizon. It looked like her future. She could see where she was going, but not where she would end up. One thing she knew for sure. Her future would not be a houseful of babies. An image of Luke formed in her mind—the broad shoulders and firm bottom she had somehow detected beneath his uniform. She chastised herself. This was not the time to be thinking about that. Randy and Lija should be her only concerns now. But Randy would mend and Lija—well, she would have to mend, too. They had survived their mom's death and they would all survive a broken leg.

JAMES AND LIJA returned to the hospital before breakfast the next morning. They brought Randy home along with a bag of bandages, antiseptics and ointments. Lija also brought home two slips of paper—one a prescription for tranquilizers and another for birth control pills—which she tacked to the front of the refrigerator with magnets.

9

"IS RAKELLA HOME?" asked the voice on the telephone a week later.

"This is Raki," she said, suddenly shivering even though she was standing in the sunshine in the middle of a baking kitchen in July.

"Hi, this is Luke, you know, from the hospital. How are you? How is your nephew?"

"We're fine." Her legs were collapsing and her heart was working to beat its way out of her chest.

"I need to drive up to Minneapolis this afternoon to pick up some stuff. If you're not busy today, would you ride along? I'm tired from long hours, you know. I could really use a coffee-drinker to keep me awake."

While he talked, Raki tugged the long telephone cord, stretching it to reach the chair stepstool where she had stowed her purse. Her fingers rummaged through the jumble—cover-up stick, tampons, comb and brush, coin purse, a couple pacifiers she must have left in there after babysitting. Failing to detect the familiar cover of her pocket calendar, she answered anyway, "What time?"

He picked her up in a hail-pocked yellow VW bug. His hospital garb and soft-soled shoes had been traded out for a wrinkled blue madras shirt, frayed cut-off jean shorts and battered leather sandals. If not for his too-short hair and lack of a peace medallion, he might have passed for a hippie. And that he smelled of Ivory soap and Right Guard.

Anticipating an hour-plus drive under a hot sun with no air conditioning and wide-open windows, Raki had secured her long auburn waves with a rubber band and her signature floral hair ribbon. She had tied the tails of her sleeveless blouse into a bow beneath her breasts, exposing a cool midriff above a pair of yellow hip hugger short shorts. Beaded sandals completed the look.

It was ridiculous that this casual insouciance had taken a full hour to achieve. Luke's thrown-together vibe probably took him no more than a couple minutes. But guys didn't have to worry about looking too prim, or too slutty. Or the impossibility of looking fashionable and anti-materialistic at the same time. She had tried on everything in her closet except her Sunday dresses and still she looked like an ingénue who subscribed to *Seventeen* magazine. One with no legitimate reason for taking a drive to the Twin Cities with an actual university student.

Nervous and self-conscious, she climbed into the bug, struggling hard to look relaxed. Out of habit, she curled one leg under the other to keep her thighs from sticking to the hot vinyl. Luke had thrown towels over both bucket seats, maybe for the same reason. She lifted a corner. White threads poked through rips in the vinyl. She sniffed. Clean, for a guy's car. Of course the dash sported a custom-installed radio. Quality speakers boomed from the back seat. He turned down the volume.

"Thanks for coming along on such short notice."

She angled her shoulders toward him. Looking at him made her even more self-conscious, if that were even possible. Was the bare midriff too obvious, even in this heat? Her foot was tucked up beneath her bottom—was that suggestive? Or childish?

"It sounded like fun," she answered, tilting her head and shooing away the strand of hair that escaped the pony tail and stuck to her face. She prayed the humidity and sweat wouldn't melt her mascara. Luke looked remarkably cool. Cool in both senses. She noticed his thigh muscles. Dark hairs curled around the threads fraying from his cut-offs. He shifted into gear and focused on the road.

"Do we need to be back any particular time? I just have to pick up a few things from my house. It won't take long."

"Nobody is expecting me home. My dad lives in Arizona now, so I live with my sister and her family and they don't really keep tabs on me—unless I'm needed to babysit."

"With the little boy all banged up and all, maybe they need you? We can hurry back."

For a second she considered hurrying back into the house that very minute. Then she heard a voice from her own mouth say, "No, no, we have all the time in the world."

The little car scooted down the highway between the corn and the beans and the occasional alfalfa. Raki uncurled her cramped leg and twisted toward the window to cool herself with the rushing air. She and Luke made small talk for a few miles, shouting over the rush of wind through the windows. As they passed the twentieth or thirtieth barn, Luke motioned toward the new radio. Raki nodded and he turned up the volume. Singing along with the Top Forty could substitute for conversation. Not to mention take their minds off the hot distress of wet summer heat.

Humidity steamed Raki's skin. Anyone who considers Minnesota a cold climate never experienced a July sun scorching down from above, baked asphalt radiating up from below and air almost too heavy to breathe. She leaned back in the seat, spread her arms wide and laced her fingers behind her head—a futile effort to draw moving air across her skin. The Carpenters' 'Rainy Days and Mondays' seemed less like a sad song than a plea for relief.

Luke seemed unperturbed by the heat. An arm out the window was his only concession to the greenhouse effect. Slouching slightly, fingers of one hand casually caressing the steering wheel.

"Sorry I don't have A/C." He sounded more amused than contrite.

"I wasn't expecting it." Raki shrugged, remembering the air conditioning in her father's Oldsmobile. He had taken that to Arizona, which she had heard was even hotter than here, although that was hard to imagine.

Carole King replaced The Carpenters on the radio. Raki sang along softly but audibly. She could barely hold a tune, but thanks to high school and church choir, which took all comers, she was comfortable singing, and right now she felt just like Carole King did, her heart trembling whenever Luke was around.

He glanced her way. Was he checking her out? Did he think she was telegraphing an invitation? Was she? What if she was? Would he consider it a ridiculous presumption from a little girl? Was her heart trembling—or something else? Did it matter? Was this a date? Who knew? She stopped singing, took up humming and turned her face toward the cornfields.

Her thighs wilted, and not only from the summer temperature. They felt the way they did when the stars of a movie finally got around to kissing. Funny how she never got that feeling when a grabby high school boy kissed her. She didn't appreciate at all the way they tried to poke her face with their lips or fumble her breast, in cars that reeked of cigarette smoke, barnyard and Christmas-tree air freshener. Yuck. No boy had ever earned his way past her bra straps or panty elastic. The only redeeming aspect of those backseat overtures—a word far too grand for the reality—was that they proved a life of unrelenting chastity may not be her ultimate fate.

Not that she had any ambition to hold out for marriage, but she always managed to extricate herself because she damn sure wasn't going to waste her first time on some yahoo bungling around in a backseat of a stinky car. Her first time would include sufficient space and a modicum of finesse. And birth control. She and Lija felt differently about that.

Raki squirmed uncomfortably. The towel slid over the seat. She tugged at it, hoping the mundane feel of the terrycloth in her hand would snap the rest of her body back in control.

"We're almost there," said Luke. "It'll just take a few minutes at my house. We could get a burger in Dinkytown afterward. I'm sure to be hungry. And then, you know, it'll be later and not so hot when we drive back."

"Nobody keeps tabs on me. We can take all the time we want." Raki heard the unintentional double message coming out of her own mouth. She felt a little embarrassment and no regret.

It was four o'clock when the bug reached the Mississippi. The Hennepin Avenue bridge escorted them over the river, between the forty-foot-tall Gold Medal flour sign far off to the right and the giant red and blue Grain Belt bottle cap to the left. "Bread and beer are all you need," said Luke, pointing out the two iconic signs.

"Interesting, isn't it," said Raki, "that bread and beer are both made from grain and yeast. Yet so different. I never thought about that before." She was trying to sound intellectual. She was pretty sure it sounded sappy.

"The stuff of life can be pretty simple," he agreed, steering them onto Nicollet Island, leaving the sinuous Mississippi behind.

All Raki knew about the Twin Cities was that the state capital was in St. Paul, which she had visited on a school field trip; that the tallest building was the Foshay Tower, which stuck up into the skyline like a Midwestern-modest Empire State Building but would soon be eclipsed by a fifty-seven-story glass tower, a fact she knew from drawings in *The Minneapolis Tribune;* and that Southdale in Edina was the country's first indoor shopping mall. Once a year she and Lija got dressed up in their Sunday best to stroll the department stores, ride the escalators, and listen to the rich ladies with their string-handled shopping bags go click-clicking across polished floors of the chic atrium.

This limited exposure completely unprepared her for gone-to-seed Nicollet Island, where barefooted young women scuffled along pitted sidewalks hefting paper grocery sacks. Peeling gingerbread curlicues and other decrepit architectural frou-frou were a far cry from Southdale, or Halcyon for that matter. Tie-dyed t-shirts hung from clotheslines. Somebody had twisted twigs into a peace symbol. Most of the houses were peeling beyond recognition, but one was bright purple.

"Hippies or Vikings fan?" asked Raki, pointing.

"Both?"

Luke pulled the bug next to a chipped curb, parking underneath a towering elm, half its branches dead. A heaving sidewalk led to broad steps and a deep porch. Overgrown bridal wreath bushes slumped along the railing. Raki hesitated. She wondered if it was safe to get out. She told herself he wouldn't bring her if it wasn't. Then she wondered if she should wait until Luke opened the door for her, or pop out all womens-liberated, non-judgmental and delighted to be here. She decided to fake the latter. He walked to the front of the car and waved at her to follow.

"It's not glamorous, but it's cheap!" He zig-zagged to avoid crumbled sections of concrete. Raki stayed several steps behind, watching her feet. She noticed a little patchwork in the concrete. Although the walk was desperate for work, this was not repair. Imbedded in it were three tarnished spoons, a glass coaster with lavender sprigs sealed inside, a trio of keys and a smattering of charms, the kind young girls hang on bracelets.

"One of my roommates, Carol, is an artist," explained Luke, standing on the ramshackle porch.

Raki had read about women living with guys they weren't married to, but had never known anybody who actually did it. She wondered if this Carol was Luke's girlfriend. That would be really embarrassing.

"Watch out. Those steps will swallow your ankle if you aren't careful," said Luke.

The double doors swung open to a grayed interior decorated with Rolling Stones posters, peace symbols and gigantic orange cushions.

"Who's there?" A woman's voice echoed as the door clunked shut behind them.

"It's me, Luke, and a friend. I just dropped by to pick up some clothes."

The woman who emerged could have been nineteen or twenty-nine, Raki couldn't tell. Her unlined complexion and hippie clothes looked young, but something about her seemed disconcertingly mature. She was carrying a toddler who was naked except for a diaper. Both of them were covered in flour. The boy was licking it off his finger, the woman blowing it off his hair.

"Can't be much stuff if you brought a friend. That car of yours is no moving van." The woman extended her free hand toward Raki. "I'm Carol," she said. "Pleased to meet you." The strings on her peasant blouse swung to and fro across breasts that also swung to and fro, a little more than Raki was used to seeing. No bra.

This was all too weird. Raki wiped the sweat from her palms on her yellow shorts before shaking Carol's hand. She had no idea what to say. She felt scared, but didn't know what she was scared of.

"Just a suit and good shoes," explained Luke, as he pivoted toward the stairs. "Dr. Uncle informed me that I cannot continue my employment if I don't show up at some fancy party he's throwing. Dressed like a dandy, of course."

"Whatever, for the man," laughed Carol. She set the boy on his feet.

Raki stood at the bottom of the stairs, shifting her feet back and forth. She wanted to follow him, but that could seem forward. If Carol was his girlfriend, then it would be really forward, not to mention embarrassing. She wished she had more clarity about this situation. But if Carol was not Luke's girlfriend, and Raki stayed downstairs, then she'd look like a prude. What to do?

"You don't want to see my mess," Luke said. "Hang out down here. Listen to Carol complain about what a lousy roommate I am." She watched him propel himself up the stairs, alone. A good girl would feel relieved. Raki felt disappointed and a little confused. *Why am I here?*

"I would not sully your reputation with your girlfriend," Carol called after him. That was a relief.

"I'm not really his girlfriend," said Raki, instinctively, although now she knew she wanted to be, and that Carol wasn't.

"OK, then what are you?"

Carol pulled up a pair of cushions and sat. Raki kept an eye on the little boy, out of habit from watching her nephews, but she didn't see anything in the house that he could break, unless he fell through some broken floor boards or something.

"Just a friend, keeping him company for the ride." Raki sat down.

"Uhmm, hmmm," said Carol. "Nice friend. It's hotter than hell and you spend two hours in an overheated German jalopy just to keep Luke company. I'm not that good a friend to anybody."

Intimidated speechless, Raki looked down at her hands.

"Oh, dear." Carol's tone softened. "I think I've scared you. Let's get you a glass of water. That will help." She rose, extending her hand to help Raki off the cushion. "How do you like our humble abode?"

"Who all lives here?" asked Raki.

"Has Luke told you nothing? Such a man. Well, my baby and Luke and Brian and Janie and me. They are all real students, enrolled and all. Me, I just take classes. Art, cooking, meditation. Mostly I'm earth goddess, caretaker and bread baker. We all have our roles. Luke bandages our boo-boos."

"Is this like a . . . commune?"

"Oh, girl, what have you been reading? *Time* magazine? The frippery section of *The Minneapolis Tribune*?"

Raki looked down at the tatty grey rug, embarrassed by she knew not what.

"Oh, I'm sorry again, you were just being curious. Well, we prefer to call ourselves 'a bunch of roommates who can't afford anything better than a broken-down old house.' I have never met anyone who admitted to living in a commune, even in my meditation classes. The word is so pretentious, like your home is some kind of political statement or act of rebellion. I mean, I'm political and damn rebellious, but this," she said, sweeping and twirling again. "This is shelter. And friendship."

Raki followed her into an open dining room past a gigantic table blotched with water rings and worn to splinters. "Modern art!" exclaimed Carol, stroking the wood. "I found this treasure in the alley. So much better than the Formica table we used to have." Raki noted the mismatched chairs – an aluminum and vinyl job that probably used to match the Formica-topped table, a three-legged stool and a cane-seat antique that looked unsafe.

"Don't worry," said Carol. "We hardly ever all sit down at the same time." She pushed open a swinging door to the kitchen.

A muddle of potted herbs, cereal boxes, dough-smattered cookbooks, assorted cooking utensils and baby food jars packed the counter on one side. Opposite that, four pans of bread rested, rising vigorously in the summer heat.

"This place is going to get hotter than hell when I put these things in the oven," said Carol. "Baby and I may have to sleep in the back yard again tonight." The little boy, who had followed his mother, got hoisted to her hip. She gave him a squeeze and he buried his pudgy cheeks into her neck.

"Water! I promised you water. Or maybe, maybe even a soda. Pop, as you say here." Carol opened the little refrigerator opposite the sink. "Bubble-Up? RC? You're too young for the beer."

"RC is fine." She remembered her manners, "Thank you." The cold and heavy can felt so familiar inside her palm, refreshingly real. She pressed the aluminum against her forehead.

"Let's take your drink into the yard." Going out the back door, Raki recognized the sweetly herbal, slightly-skunky fragrance. Just like what wafted out of cars in the Halcyon High School parking lot. Pot. Clear plastic sheeting was stapled to raw lumber, then twined to the deck railing for a makeshift greenhouse. Five leafed plants sat on dilapidated old chairs. "Brian's farm," said Carol. "You're not gonna call the police, are you?"

"No, of course not," said Raki.

"Oh, who am I kidding? This place is a commune!"

Luke appeared, a dry-cleaning bag on a hanger slung over his shoulder, black leather shoes hanging from two fingers. "Sorry it took so long. Carol, was it really necessary to show her Brian's, um, medicinal agronomy experiment?"

"She's cool," said Carol.

"Raki, don't worry, not my thing." Luke turned to go back into the house, his dry-cleaning bag thwacking Raki on the shoulder. She followed, grateful for an excuse to leave the 'farm.'

"Before you go," said Carol, detouring to a cupboard as they traipsed back to the kitchen. She handed Raki a loaf of bread wrapped in a dishtowel. "A gift for you. Yesterday's, but still fresher than from a store."

Luke laughed again. "She doesn't need your bread, Carol."

"It's a gift you idiot."

"Thank you," said Raki. *A kindred soul.*

"WANT A TOUR of the island?"

Raki took a deep breath of fresh air. "Sure."

Luke led her down a secluded path, greenery arching overhead, then crossed a street toward the tree-lined riverbank. He slid his heels on a bed of last year's leaves as they descended, releasing the sweet aroma of decay.

"The Mighty Mississippi!" He skidded to a stop.

Raki tripped over a lady's high heeled sandal. Abandoned next to an empty bottle. "Obviously, we aren't the first ones to come here."

"No, obviously not." He gazed at the river. She gazed at the river. She waited for a kiss. This would be the perfect place.

"Come on," he said, grabbing her hand and pulling her back up the bank. "Let's go visit the priest." What the hell? A priest?

Past more weeds and crumbled concrete, a solid brick edifice rose up amidst actual green grass and a statue of a cloaked man holding a book.

"Meet Father De La Salle," said Luke, pointing toward the statue. "And this is his High School."

"I think I've heard of it."

"Did I scare you?" The corners of his eyes crinkled.

He knew how she felt about priests. She should be annoyed. But that would ruin everything, and they still had a really long ride home. Better laugh it off. "Did he just have lunch?"

"What?"

"The way he's holding that book open with his hand over it. Like he's brushing off crumbs."

"Yes, well, that reminds me I promised you food."

RAKI WAS RELIEVED to leave the island to go somewhere normal. Luke parked the bug in Dinkytown, across a bridge from the university. On the sidewalk sat a man, cross-legged against a brick wall, his feet tucked beneath the frayed hems of crusty jeans. Unwashed hair and a hank of love beads told her he was younger than he looked.

They walked past a movie theater next to an old tailor shop next to a head shop down the street from Gray's Drug Store above which, Luke told her, Bob Dylan once lived. The stale reek of burnt toast and runny eggs oozed out the door of Al's Breakfast. She prayed a quick prayer to her new saint of lunch, De La Salle, that Luke wouldn't want to eat there.

"Annie's is good," he said, pointing to a new but old-fashioned sign. Lightbulbs studded a kind of blue metal cloud that tufted around the name. Prayer answered. Should do that more often. They climbed steep metal stairs to the second story. Being summer semester, the place was mostly empty. They slid into a wooden booth by a window. Sunshine glared off the table top varnish. A bored-looking waitress took their orders.

Raki asked about his classes. That gave him a lot to talk about, a relief. The more he talked, the less chance there was she'd accidentally say something stupid.

The waitress interrupted, bearing two plates of burgers and fries, bits of grease dripping off the sides, winking in the sun. That's when the conversation lapsed.

"Do you, um, participate in demonstrations and sit-ins and stuff like that?" she asked. No matter what she said, it always came out sounding hokey.

"Not really. Carol and Brian and Janie do sometimes." Luke nabbed a limp French fry before continuing. "Once, though, a bunch of people were parading around and I saw a guy from anatomy class. I fell in with the group and he caught me up on a lecture I missed. We marched in a circle and I carried his anti-war sign when he had to stop to tie his shoe. But it's more my thing to save the world by stitching people up than by picketing in the streets."

"My brother-in-law is going to save the world by growing corn and soybeans." She bit into the burger. Salty grease glossed her lips. She licked it off.

"We each have our calling."

"What's Carol's 'calling?'" Raki was dying to know more about the odd roommate.

Luke tented his hands in front of his lips. "Revenge."

That she hadn't expected. Carol seemed so sweet. Crusty, but sweet.

"Revenge and art, to be fair," said Luke, breaking the long silence.

"She seems like a nice person."

"Oh, she is. Have you heard the phrase, 'living well is the best revenge?' She survived terrible things and lives making art and bread and meditating and taking care of her little boy."

"Who, as far as I can tell, does not have a name."

"Baby's name is Owen."

"So what's the revenge for?" Raki licked a bit of ketchup off her lips.

"I shouldn't have said that."

"But you did." Raki was consumed with curiosity. As her tummy filled with familiar food, she was starting to feel more like herself, comfortable, bold even.

"Later. Maybe."

With that, Luke offered to give her a tour of the campus.

Back on the street, the same hippie sat fingering his beads exactly as before.

"Let's go back to the car, so I can get the bread out, before we go on tour," she suggested. Luke looked puzzled, but agreed to the detour. She leaned into the bug as lady-like as she could manage. Jody and Lynn said her butt looked good in these shorts. She hoped he noticed.

She brought out the towel-wrapped gift, trotted back to the hippie and handed it over.

"Bread, man," said the hippie, chortling softly as he peeled back the cloth. "I mean, lady." She didn't stay to chat.

"What was that for?" asked Luke as they crossed the bridge over the railroad tracks.

"What do you mean?"

"Why did you give an addict your loaf of bread?"

"Well, I'm pretty sure he can't shoot it up, now can he?" She looked for his reaction; couldn't tell. "Carol's gesture was generous, but I bake my own. That guy . . . it seemed like he might enjoy it. Besides, it makes a good story."

"What kind of story?"

"I can tell people in Halcyon I gave a loaf of bread to a hippie. They'll ask me what he looked like and everyone will marvel at what it's like at 'the U.'"

"You could have given your bread to a poor person in Halcyon."

"You're kidding, right?" They crossed through stone pillars onto campus. "People in Halcyon may wear love beads and fringes and kids smoke weed and all that, but a guy who sits on the sidewalk all stoned out? Never."

"Not hippies, but a poor person."

"In Halcyon? We're all middle class. Except for the one family that lives in the ramshackle house. The kids don't comb their hair, but it's impolite to mention it."

"So if you paint your house and comb your hair you're in the middle class?"

"You make it sound silly, but yeah."

"Everyone the same?"

"Well, no. My father considered himself above average, because he has a degree and good taste in booze. Not because we are rich, which we aren't. Halcyon does have one rich family. The Volls. They own a big mansion, but nobody knows them. Too scary."

"Scary?"

"My dad can act all sophisticated but if he flubs it like a hick, who's to know? The Volls would know. They're scary."

The topic lapsed as they walked amidst the campus shade. They took a break on The Knoll, which is what Luke called the grassy expanse in the midst of the academic buildings. She told him of her plans to major in business and own a chain of bakeries. They crossed a pedestrian bridge. She looked down at the water running beneath and imagined walking here with a U of M sweatshirt on her back, books in one arm and Luke on the other.

She knew what she wanted. She had it all figured out.

THE HIGHWAY HOME followed the contour of the river. Steep banks of oak and wild sumac alternated with well-kempt farmsteads. An enormous Jolly Green Giant stood guard over the highway. Scenes from the day mixed and swirled through Raki's head, like colors in a pop art painting. She couldn't get the non-girlfriend roommate off her mind.

"So, tell me all about Carol."

She could see he was thinking by the way he scrunched his brow and twisted his lips.

"Carol's story, what she tells of it, is not secret. The part she keeps secret, I don't know anyway."

"So, what do you know?"

"Hmmm." He took a breath. "Carol comes from a very powerful family somewhere, we're not sure where. Probably not the south, because she doesn't have the accent."

"Somewhere where they don't call Bubble-Up 'pop.'"

"Right. She doesn't speak Minnesotan." He laughed. "And she likes to remind us of it. Anyway, we don't know her real last name. Her father deposits a large sum of money in her bank account every month. All she has to do is not tell anybody her real last name—or go home."

"Why? Because she got pregnant and wasn't married?"

"Carol had two abortions while she still lived with her family, so pregnancy wasn't exactly the issue."

Raki knew a lot of women had abortions. People whispered about it. She had never known anyone who admitted to it. She considered her response carefully, wanting to sound empathetic, not accusatory. "She's lucky to be alive. I hear back alley abortions can kill you."

"Illegal, maybe, maybe not, but definitely not back alley. Her father paid top dollar for the very best medical care."

"So why did she decide to have Owen?"

"Different father. Not her father."

"I'm confused."

"The first two—they were his."

"Whose?"

"Her father's."

"Oh, my God." Raki's stomach clenched. Bile rose up her throat. She swallowed hard.

"But not Owen. When Carol's father found out she was sleeping with a boyfriend, he refused to pay. Said it was the boyfriend's responsibility. Carol thought about getting married, but her boyfriend didn't have two pennies to his name so she got a better idea."

"What was that?"

"Blackmail. As long as her father sends money, she keeps his secret. But if he ever misses a payment, she will tell her story to the *New York Times*, or whatever is the biggest paper in the state she's from. She's saving a lot of the money. That's why she lives in our dump. She wants to have a pile of dough saved up before her father dies."

"What happened to her boyfriend?"

"Who knows? She won't say. Maybe Daddy had him killed."

"You're kidding, aren't you?"

"I don't know if I'm kidding or not. He sounds like one mean dude. One mean rich dude."

AS THE LIGHT disappeared, the heat enveloped Raki like a thick quilt. She drowsed.

The crunch of familiar gravel roused her as Luke pulled into the farmyard. She shook her head to clear the cobwebs. "I'm afraid I wasn't much help keeping you awake. Apparently not enough coffee."

"It's all right."

She opened the door.

"Uh, Raki, by the way, will you go with me to my uncle's party?"

"Sure." A thought popped into her head, fully-formed. "I enjoyed today. Can I repay you with a visit to a place I really like?"

"I get off at three on Wednesday. I can be here by four."

"Bring your swim trunks. There's water involved."

10

RAKI FLUNG A TOWEL onto the backseat of Luke's sweltering car.

"Four o'clock, right on the dot!"

"The water part sounded tempting."

Wavy red strands of hair eddied around her face and flew out the open window as they scuttled down the backroads. Water towers ballooned across the horizon. Train tracks zippered through the grid of fields. She saw it all with fresh eyes, as if for the first time. It was beautiful. Even the dust, spurting behind the tires. Like psychedelic pop art, just without the colors.

A pair of spruce jutted from the farmland, apparently planted a lot of generations past.

"Turn right here, between the trees," she directed.

He parked just past the weathered sign. 'Prairie Dels' it read. A mowed meadow surrounded a small parking lot.

Raki climbed out of the hot car, peeling her t-shirt away from her sweaty belly, fanning herself with the fabric. A pair of yellow bikini strings were tied at the nape of her neck. Her bikini bottoms were bunched under her cut-offs. Luke grabbed the towel and his swim trunks.

"I wonder why nobody has plowed up this meadow," he commented. "This is valuable cropland."

"Oh, no. It's a lot more than that."

She led him through the meadow. Tall grass fringed the edges. It tickled her thighs. She heard the blades scrape against Luke's jeans.

Hot sun and open fields gave way to a dappled shade. Thickets laced the seldom-used pathway. With both hands, she pushed through. *God, please, don't let there be poison ivy.* Faint music of falling water grew louder, the insects adding grace notes. Amidst a jumble of moss-tufted gray boulders, a waterfall fed a tiny pool. The secret glade smelled like fresh rain.

Raki sat on a red rock shelf. Luke crouched beside her. A dragonfly flashed shimmery wings beside his cheek. He swept it away.

"If I recall my high school geology," said Luke, "this is the same rock the Indians made their pipes from. It's soft and easy to carve."

Oh, good grief. Geology? "Look," she said, tracing the rough heart carved into the rock next to him. "George and Mary were here in 1932." She scooted her bottom a few feet. "This is the oldest one I've found. Johann und Marta 1867."

A grasshopper chirped, landing beside her foot.

"I love the sound of a waterfall," said Luke. "Like tiny bells."

Tiny bells. Big improvement over carving pipes. She leaned back on the mossed rock shelf, scouting out a soft spot for her elbows. Luke sat next to her, upright, his arms embracing his knees.

"Tell me more about your dream, Miss Rakella."

No boy had ever asked her that before. Luke was turning out to be even more perfect than she had hoped. "What do you mean?"

"You told me you wanted to own a bakery."

"Well, flour and sugar, they're beautiful," she answered. "You dump ingredients into a bowl in front of a window and the flour whooshes up in a fluffy white cloud. The sugar sparkles in the sunlight."

"Mmmm," he said. "Sugar."

"Sugar is a crystal, you know. Like diamonds or sapphires." *Uh, oh.*

I meant like jewelry, not rocks. Don't let him start in with the geology again.

"Better, because you can eat it," he said.

She didn't really want to talk food any more than she wanted to talk rocks, but at least she knew something about it. "Alone, sugar is too sweet and flour out of the bag is awful. The magic comes when you mix them together."

"Adulterated with butter and yeast," he said.

Does he know we're not talking about bread anymore?

Luke turned away, pointing toward the deep pool. "Is it safe to jump?"

"I've done it dozens of times and I'm still here to show you."

"Where can I, you know, change?" Luke swung his head, looking around.

"Behind those bushes." She gestured to the left. "I promise not to look."

Raki's bikini was on underneath, so she just pulled her t-shirt off, wriggled her cut-offs down and jumped first, cannonball style. Luke plunged in right behind. It took him a frighteningly long time to emerge. He flung his hair, droplets spraying in the sun. She splashed him. He splashed back. She paddled a few feet, but while the pool was deep, it was no size for real swimming. When she was almost ready to give up on him, he put his hands on her shoulders and kissed her.

This was not like her first kiss, the one in the back of the band bus in seventh grade, or like any other kiss ever before. The water heated up between them. She feared she might lose control and drown, but no matter. Then Luke broke off and swam to the edge, scrambling up the rocks, turning his back to her.

The drive home was quiet. She didn't know what to say. Luke broke the silence as her farm came into view.

"Will you still be my date to my uncle's party?"

He called it a date! "Of course. I would love to."

"Saturday, then, around seven."

RAKI'S CLOSET CONTAINED just one piece suitable for an adult cocktail party. A mini-length dress, taupe, sleeveless, a cascade of roses falling down one side. Red sandals matched the flowers. She burnished her hair with a hundred strokes and barretted it at the back. Just enough foundation to mask a few blemishes, mascara and a couple flashes of blusher. She considered the blue eye shadow Jody and Lynn had pressured her to buy. No, not really her style.

Luke showed up a few minutes before seven o'clock, wearing the suit they had picked up at his house. His polished shoes reflected the porch light. She handed him a small plate of peanut butter blossom cookies, the kind with the chocolate kiss in the center, covered in plastic wrap.

"You do know there will be food at this party."

"Dessert. For later."

He took the plate and held out his arm like an old-fashioned gentleman, escorting her to the car and slipping the cookies into the back seat.

His uncle's house oozed sophistication. A sprawling, single-story, multi-winged, highly air-conditioned ensemble of carpeted rooms, large paned windows, dark paneling and abstract art. After brief introductions, Luke headed straight to the hors d'oerves buffet. He piled a complicated tower of tiny foodstuffs atop a cracker. Raki plucked a cheese-stuffed slice of celery and a couple green olives off a tray. She nibbled them off a tiny plate, hoping the pimento wouldn't get stuck in her teeth.

Henry Mancini crooned from the console hi-fi. Luke pulled open a sweaty bottle of beer, even though he probably wasn't twenty-one yet. Raki poured herself a pop. She sipped, peering through the bubbles, marveling at the architectural hairstyles of the older women. She calculated how much they spent on hairspray.

"How is your old dad making out in Arizona?" Luke's uncle asked, having mingled his way around the room and back.

"Just fine," guessed Raki. She didn't really know, which bothered her. Dad called late every Sunday evening, when long-distance rates were lowest, but she didn't learn much. He asked about school. Fine. She asked about the cactus. Fine. After those subjects petered out, he spent a half hour with James, discussing fertilizer, grain futures or whatever. His moving away created more of a void than she would admit to a stranger.

"We certainly miss him here. Life of a good party, you know. Must be pretty damned hot there right now, but I guess that's his business, am I right?"

A few of the older guests approached Luke and inquired how he liked his summer job and about his plans for a specialty. Braver souls asked his opinion on the war, and what his draft number was. All expressed pleasure at meeting Raki, even though almost all of them knew who she was.

When Frank Sinatra replaced Henry Mancini, Raki whispered in Luke's ear. "I think we've done our duty."

Expressing dismay at having to leave so early, she waited until Dr. Uncle and Mrs. Aunt's backs were both turned, then nipped a bottle of champagne from a cart.

The evening humidity walloped them as soon as the door swung shut. And the doctor thought Arizona was hot.

"Let's take my cookies out to the Dels," she suggested.

"Good idea," he said.

He drove without directions this time, even in the dark, parking in the same spot. Raki handed him the bottle. She carried the cookies.

Fireflies spirited around the meadow, flickering like fairy candles.

"When I was a little girl I loved to run around the yard and catch these and put them in a jar. My sister would turn them loose before putting me to bed. She's good at taking care of things."

Out of sight of the road and the parking lot, Luke sat on the grass.

"Do you have anything in your trunk that we can sit on? So I don't stain my dress?"

He returned to the car, came back and dropped a blanket. Raki stooped down and spread it flat.

"Found these, too," he said, holding up paper cups. He popped the cork and poured the yellow bubbles.

He held his high, motioning her to do the same. "I heard that the inventor of champagne exclaimed, 'I'm drinking the stars!'"

The bubbles tickled Raki's nose. She gazed up at the real stars spread horizon to horizon.

After a few minutes, she peeled back the plastic wrap over the plate. The chocolate was still soft from the warm car. She dipped her finger into the melted candy kiss and smeared it over his lips like lipstick.

The tip of his tongue poked out to lick it off. Then he pulled it back in. She looked into his eyes, unblinking, breathing deep.

"Do you want to kiss it off?"

"Yes," she breathed. He leaned toward her. She licked his lips. Sweet, so sweet. Gingerly at first, savoring it like that first taste of a chocolate-covered caramel pop. This was what she had been planning for.

He moaned. Very softly. "Are you . . ." he started.

She leaned down into the blanket, pulling him with her, fingers entwined in his hair.

"Do you . . ." he started again.

She kissed clean the corners of his mouth with two flicks of her tongue. No, no words. She could feel his hot breath. He loosened his tie. She snaked it from around his neck, sensually.

If only boys read the kind of books they needed to learn how to conduct a proper seduction. *If you want something done right, you need to do it yourself.*

He pressed his body heavy upon her. Sharp pebbles and spears of dried grass poked through the thin blanket. No matter. This was so much better than dirty car smells and roustings about in some backseat. His tongue slid between her lips and hers met his, like in a dance, an old-fashioned dance, a waltz.

His hands slid down her back, cupping her buttocks. The heat of his hand coursed through the fabric of her dress. She felt her legs melting, but his hand went no further. He pulled back from the kiss, his eyes staring straight into hers. She did not blink. He kissed her ears, first one, then the other. His lips moved down to her neck, nibbling, then sucking.

She pushed him away. He looked at her, startled, until her fingers found the top button of his shirt. Pushing it through the buttonhole with one hand took more dexterity than she anticipated. He reached up to help. The tip of her finger found the little depression below his

Adam's apple. She tickled him there. Six more buttons came undone and she buried her face in his chest, the hairs tickling her nose, scraping her cheeks. His fingers raked through her hair, down toward her neck, searching. He fumbled at the tiny metal zipper pull. She leaned into him, making space for him to grasp it.

She could never recall, later on, how the rest of their clothes came off, only that somehow every inch of her skin was freed to the night air, every inch not covered by his.

He entered and her toes curled, so tightly she worried the bones would break. His rhythm drove an intensity of focus. As if every cell of her body had a life on its own, all marching toward one irresistible goal. She cried out. Her fingers splayed, then her nails dug into his back. His skin, already damp from humidity, erupted in sweat. She cried out again. He shuddered. How long did it take? Ten minutes? An hour? She had no idea.

He rolled off, panting. Her mind felt erased. Her breasts jutted up toward the stars, caressed by the night breeze. Her own sweat, like dew, gathered itself and slid off in rivulets. He said nothing, gazing up toward the sky, his breathing slowing. She followed his gaze. Stars. Like a billion candles. Romantic. Constellations. What was it she learned in astronomy class? There it was. Virgo. How perfect.

"Let's go swimming," she whispered, when the silence became overwhelming. She leaned over to pull him up by the hand. She had never been totally naked in front of anyone, that she could remember. She thought she'd feel funny about it, but it felt natural. They followed the melody of falling water, grateful for what little moonlight they had.

She tried to jump first, but he tugged her back.

"Together," he said.

They leapt into the water ramrod straight, feet first, whooping as their torsos hit the cold. The splash sounded like a cymbal clash to the waterfall melody. Underwater for just a second, she shot out from the surface. A half second later his head burst through. He flung the water from his hair, droplets shimmering like the fireflies. She floated atop the ripples, her nipples interrupting the surface. She could tell he never took his eyes off her.

She had no idea what time it was when they finally took to

gathering up their clothes. The dress stuck to her wet skin. She wadded her pantyhose in a ball. Luke poured the last of the champagne into the paper cups and handed one to her.

"I didn't expect that," said Luke, "Not any of that."

"I know." She raised her glass.

In the car on the way home, leaning deep into the upholstery, humming softly to 'Color My World' on the radio, she felt proud for saving herself for something like this, unsullied and uninhibited. Passionate, not desperate. It was even better than she had expected.

"Are you OK?" Luke asked.

"Better than OK."

"I tried not to think that way about you because . . ."

"Because nothing," she interrupted. She made a show of looking away from him, out the window, humming a little more loudly.

Better than the firsthand stories she heard from friends. Better even than the 'good parts' in the books the girls passed around, the ones they discovered, unassisted, on the racks in the drugstore and the shelves of the public library. She smiled in the dark, glad to have fought off all those other grimy boys with their dirty minds, saving herself for mature love.

The yard light from her family's farm drove her back to reality.

"I want to see you again," said Luke as the engine sputtered off. "I worry, though, because I'm so much . . ."

"So much perfect," she said, kissing him quickly on the lips. "Keep the cookies." She leapt out before he could say anything she didn't want to hear.

BEFORE THE WEEK was out, they had found the hay loft in his uncle's barn; Luke's bed, when his aunt and uncle were out; a cot in the back of the medical clinic, after hours; the cushions in her friend's boat, with permission. Lija said nothing the night she spotted Raki coming into the house, even though her blouse was inside out.

ON THEIR TWO-WEEK anniversary, Luke and Raki escaped again to the Twin Cities. Raki ignored the scowl from Lija's eyes when she said she couldn't babysit. Randy was healing, but he needed a lot of extra attention. He and his boisterous brothers were exhausting her sister, but as much as she wanted to help, Luke was a magnet whose pull she could not resist. Nicollet Island the second time felt different. Normal. She smiled at the little spoons embedded in the sidewalk, skipped up the rickety steps, hugged Carol and patted Owen's head. As soon as Luke hauled in their bags, they raced together up the stairs.

Descending an hour later, in search of chips and beer, they found Carol tying flowers with ribbons. Carol looked the pair up and down, her lips curling up in a friendly smirk.

"Do you know anything about arranging flowers?" she asked, looking at Luke.

"Me?"

"Why not you? Equality of the sexes and all that. Right, Raki?"

"What are you making?"

"A wreath, for my hair. I've got a gig at the Renaissance Festival."

"Which is what?" asked Luke.

"It's the first one, so I don't really know. I hear it's like a county fair, but with jousting instead of a demolition derby."

"That reminds me," said Raki, turning back toward Luke. "Our county fair is next week. You'll come with me, won't you?"

"Cotton candy and cows?" He laughed. "I wouldn't miss it for the world."

But he would.

"HEY, LYNN," said Raki over the phone the next day. Are you free tomorrow to drive to Mankato with me?"

"Long time, no hear from you."

"Only a week. And I've been busy."

"More than two. And so I've heard."

"Really, I need you. And Jody, too. Can you come?"

"We're helping clean out the commercial barn and set up the tables. So, no."

The fair. She had no plans for a 4-H entry. No baked goods. No sewing project. For the first time in memory, and she didn't care.

"Can't you do the tables another day?"

"It starts tomorrow. Can't you go to Mankato another day?"

"I already made an . . . oh, well, it doesn't matter."

It sure as hell does matter. You're my best friends. You're supposed to be there for me when I need you.

Raki had already been to the Halcyon Public Library, found the right section, 613 in the Dewey Decimal System, pulled *Our Bodies Ourselves* off the shelf and sat cross-legged on the floor between the stacks. Something less trouble than condoms, more reliable. She read up on and contemplated all the various options. Diaphragm – icky; spermicide – messy; IUD – scary. *The Pill. Of course.*

Then she had gone to the out-of-town phone books in the reference section, looked up Planned Parenthood, scribbled the number on a slip of paper, and driven home. She had waited, biting her nails until Lija and James were both out of the house long enough for her to make the call. It had taken every bit of nerve she had to dial the number and talk to the receptionist.

She sure wasn't going to call back and reschedule now.

"What did you want to do up there, anyway?" asked Lynn.

"Oh, just shopping." It wasn't exactly a lie. Shopping for birth control was still shopping. Still, it would be a good idea to pick up a new blouse or something, too, a cover story.

"Well, don't spend all your money. You need it for the fair."

So Raki drove alone the next morning, passing the fairgrounds where the carnies were bolting together the rides and pulling up the gambling booths. She focused on the road ahead, occasionally cursing her friends for not being there when she needed them. She wondered if she should have told Luke what she was doing. No, this was a girl thing.

On the outskirts of Mankato, she pulled out her map and spread it over the steering wheel. Left here. Two blocks. Somewhere on the right. There's a parking spot. Oh, God, where were the coins for the meter? Her heart was pounding. She got out, looking for the address on the paper clutched in her hand. There, on that old brick office building, a tiny logo stenciled on the window of the scuffed old door. She took a deep breath and reached for the knob. Her hands were so wet they slipped. Out of the corner of her eye she spotted a familiar form. A young man coming out of another office. The cut of the dark hair, the saunter. What was Luke doing here?

The sign on the building he exited was much more obvious than hers. Army Recruitment. He saw her, waved and ran over.

"What a surprise!" he said, panting.

"What are you doing here? Why were you over there?" She pointed at the Army sign.

"Let me buy you lunch and I'll explain."

Dumbstruck, she followed him. Around the corner was a Woolworth's. The fluorescent lights and shiny chrome of the lunch counter made her dizzy. He slid onto a swivel seat, spinning the one beside in invitation. She thought she might throw up.

"I enlisted," he announced. "Signed the papers. I'm going to be a medic." He reached for the greasy menu.

She grabbed his wrist. "You have a deferment!"

"No better training for a future surgeon than to patch up soldiers in the jungle. I've been thinking about it a long time."

"You never told me!"

A waitress approached. Raki glared and the woman backed away.

"I've been thinking about it longer than I've known you. We haven't known each other very long."

It felt like a gut punch. She looked at her watch. Already late for her appointment. But what was the point of The Pill, now?

"You told me you weren't a protester, but you enlisted?" She said it in the volume of a whisper with the inflection of a scream. "Nobody enlists! People go to Canada. They don't *enlist*."

"Sure they do." Luke spoke in a normal tone, scanning the menu. "I leave day after tomorrow. We'll have one last really nice date, before I leave."

Her teeth clenched and her cheeks burned. The smell of grease made her stomach turn. She stared at the side of his head, hard, but he did not turn to face her.

"I'll bring the flowers, you bring the goodbye kisses," he said.

"Go to hell."

"Some people would say that's exactly where I am going." He looked unfazed as he finally turned toward her. "But hey, don't be mad. This will be a great experience. People like me are really needed, you know."

"But it's an evil war!"

"Since when did the baker get an opinion on the war?"

"That's what everybody knows." The waitress was eyeing them from the far end of the counter.

"Not everybody. And the guys fighting, they're just regular guys. Some are from Halcyon, right? And they don't ask to get shot. All they ask is to get stitched up after they get shot."

"What about . . . us?"

"It's been wonderful, Raki. I'll never forget it."

He didn't say her. He didn't say he would never forget her. He said he would never forget *it*. He was stomping on her heart, grinding it into the dirt with a muddy boot. A combat boot.

"Go. To. Hell."

11

LIJA STARED OUT the window, or rather at the window, her eyes fixed on the children's dirty finger prints smearing the glass. A towel to polish them off was close at hand. Why bother? The bang of a car door shook her out of her stupor. She looked out beyond the smear.

Raki leaned against her car, forehead pressing on the window frame, shoulders shaking, fist pounding the roof, feet kicking a tire. Lija considered going out and asking what was going on. But why? She knew what had happened. The boyfriend. A fight or something. What did it matter? Lija had no advice to give. Raki wouldn't listen anyway. She didn't care. Nobody did.

"Mommy!" screamed Randy from the davenport in the living room.

Lija turned from the window, shoulders slumped.

"Mommy!" echoed Sandy, running in from the yard.

She wanted to lock herself in the closet.

Jimmy, Jr. began to wail in her ear. She winced. Where was Lanny? She'd find him later, when she wasn't so tired, so weary, so very weary.

The screen door slapped on its hinges. Raki steamed into the kitchen like a hot prairie wind. "Do you need help?" Raki demanded, her hands on her hips. "I might as well get the boys ready for the fair. I have no date. Anymore."

She lifted Jimmy Jr. from Lija's arms and grabbed Sandy by the hand, hauling them both upstairs, yelling down, "I'll get you in a couple, Randy!" Lanny crawled to the bottom of the stairs and plopped his bottom on the floor. Where had he come from? Two more trips and Raki had wrangled all four upstairs.

Lija looked at her hands. Empty. She smoothed her palms down her skirt. No child clinging there. When was the last time she stood awake without a child on her hip? She could not remember. A chance to run away, if only she had the energy. At least now she would have a little help.

Sounds poured down the stairs. "Yellow! I wan' yellow! No red!" Randy wailed. Sandy screamed that he was clean enough. Lanny and Jimmy Jr. cried in concert. Lija sat on a hard kitchen chair, hands over her ears. She knew she should be getting ready herself. *Oh, God help me. The fair.* In her mind's eye she saw the boys sticky with cotton candy, slobbered with ketchup and mustard and dust. James having to carry broken-legged Randy like a baby. Depressing.

Stop it, she scolded herself. Count your blessings, like the priest advised. Husband, home, hundreds of acres of fertile soil, good enough crop prices; food on the table three times a day. Four sons. Randy somehow managing to avoid getting himself killed. Let it be enough, she prayed.

The problem was that it was too much. Too much passion, for one thing. Another baby would kill her, she was sure of it. Yowling annihilated her thoughts. Exhaustion fixed her to her chair. Let Raki deal with all this, just for once.

All of a sudden, Jimmy, Jr. was in her arms. Raki must have carried him down the stairs. He smelled of talcum. She couldn't resist. She placed her nose on his head, tears matting his fluff.

Lija carried the baby outside to escape his brothers' racket. In the near distance, tidy rows of corn and soybeans, selvedged neatly at the edges, soothed her soul, a little. She gazed at the barn, gleaming white in the late afternoon sun. She raised her face to the blue sky. She jounced Jimmy, Jr. on her hip. He smushed his chubby cheek against her shoulder. Just like a picture book, except this was real.

Real kids would sooner rip the pages of a book than look at the pictures. They don't quietly pull a wagon like Dick, Jane and Sally. Real boys push the wagon down the hill, laughing to see the teddy bear fly out into the ditch. *The Jolly Barnyard* Golden Book doesn't reek of anhydrous ammonia.

James walked up behind her. He put one arm around her waist. "Is Raki all right?"

"Not our concern."

"Are the boys getting ready for the fair?" he asked.

"She's taking care of it."

"I can help her," James said. He gave Lija a side hug, kissed her ear and strode into the house, closing the screen door behind him.

She could not recall the last time he helped her with the kids. Then she thought on the hug and the kiss and resolved to smooth down the bitterness. She would fix her hair and find her brightest blouse and prettiest skirt. She would enjoy the colored lights and the tinny music. She would even gag down a corn dog. Picture book for a night.

An hour later James stowed a stroller in the trunk of the sedan. Both generations crammed together in the seats, three adults up front and four kids in the back, sitting neatly in a row, Randy holding his baby brother in his lap. After a half mile, Sandy crawled onto the back ledge, wedging himself under the rear window.

James pulled into the fairgrounds parking lot, a field of dirt and smashed grass. Lija faked a smile. *Nothing ever changes, including the old guys selling tickets at the gate. Except the grandstand acts have longer hair and better amplifiers.*

Attendants flagged the cars into wobbly sorts of rows. Once parked and unpacked, Jimmy Jr. and Lanny alternated in the stroller and Lija or Raki carried whichever one wasn't being pushed. James carried Randy, who insisted he was too big to ride in a stroller, no matter his broken leg. Sandy walked, gripping his dad's hand, struggling to keep up as best his short legs could go, his head swinging back and forth. *What a bewilderment this must be to him.*

At first, Lija enjoyed the boys' wide-eyed wonderment. Then they turned to whining, and she fatigued. James offered the two older boys a ride on the merry-go-round. His strong arms steadied their sons as they bobbed up and down on their fanciful steeds, circling round and round. High-pitched chortles underscored the notes of the calliope. Then Lanny screamed at not being included. Jimmy Jr. began to wail, too. The ride ended. Lija crumpled.

"I'm so tired. This is too much stimulation for the boys. And Jimmy's diaper is disgusting. We need to go home."

"Noooooo!" squalled Randy at the top of his lungs.

Raki shushed him. "Poor Randy is bored to death sitting home all day," she said.

That was true enough. Lija wished she had the strength to care.

"He needs some fun," Raki continued. "I'll watch him while you two take the little ones home. James can come back to pick us up later."

"You can't carry Randy around by yourself," James noted.

"Why not?" said Lija, "I've been hauling him around the house by myself for weeks."

"Randy, do you want to get a corn on the cob at the Legion booth?" Raki pointed toward the bright white lights of the temporary clapboard diner.

"Yeah!!"

"When he's done eating I can carry him around just a little bit," Raki said. "Then we'll come back here and wait for you."

"Give me an hour," James relented, offloading his broken son. He motioned for Lija to follow. She felt sick, torn between guilt for ruining the fun and relief at having it over.

JAMES DROVE, silent in thought as the middle boys squabbled in the back. Lija, slumped exhausted against the car door, the baby in her lap, looked withered as a cornstalk drooping from drought. Just a few hours ago he had felt cheered watching her dress up for the evening. Like the joy of watching rain clouds gather, smelling the relief they promised.

She had even left open an extra button on her blouse, so it billowed when she moved, touching her breasts here and there. Her skirt swung loosely, caressing her buttocks like he himself had so often done. Of course, he didn't mind watching the behinds of other girls strutting the midway in their tight shorts, but the swooshing of his wife's full skirts served up a deeper sensuality. His body loved hers. His hands, cleaned up with pumice soap, had grasped her around the waist just a few hours ago. She had leaned against him in the yard.

But now, only a few hours later, everything about Lija was sagging—her eyes, her shoulders, her breasts. The blouse slumped like a tarp shielding a load of grain. He wondered if they were in love, if she loved him, if she ever had. He prayed for a magic wand if it made his wife yearn for him again. Tonight, if at all possible. James pulled up to the house.

He helped Sandy and Lanny out of the car and up the stairs into their bedrooms. Then there were pajamas to pull over heads. He heard Lija changing the baby's diaper, then dropping into bed. With one eye on his watch, he let the middle boys skip tooth brushing. Raki was doing them a favor, watching over the bored, cast-legged Randy. James needed to get back to the fair.

JAMES SPOTTED THEM at the Legion booth, as promised. Randy faced away from the aging Legionnaires who were flipping burgers and hauling French fries out of the boiling oil. Swinging his good leg back and forth on the whitewashed bench, Randy's eyes followed the flashes from the whirling rides, the carnies yelling from the gambling booths, the slow twirl from the lights of the Ferris Wheel. Raki lounged against the hard bench, her suntanned arms loose at her sides, bare legs jutting forward, ankles crossed.

James breathed deeply as he approached. Earthy scent from the barns wafted amidst the enticements of buttered corn and wieners-on-a-stick. He maneuvered through the throngs of laughing neighbors, the strings of lights and spinning gambling wheels. The whoosh of the Scrambler. The smell of diesel. He looked around for Jody and Lynn, or other of Raki's friends, worried that her babysitting duties had spoiled her fun, but she was alone, except for Randy. She waved at him.

"Sorry it took so long," he apologized.

"No problem. Randy and I are having a marvelous time!" Raki poked Randy on the shoulder. "The Ferris Wheel!" she exclaimed, pointing with exaggerated motion. He had always loved her enthusiasm. But tonight, it all seemed kind of off. Too much. Overworked. Was something the matter?

"He already did the merry-go-round, again," said Raki, responding to James's look. "He's too heavy to carry around the barns and his leg can't be jostled in the big rides, but gee, the Ferris Wheel is just the ride for him!"

James hoisted his son onto his hip and followed Raki to the Ferris Wheel, dodging slow grandparents and darting kids. He bought three tickets at twenty cents each and they climbed in an empty car, Randy in the middle. The carnie brought down the safety bar and the car swung forward as it rose slowly up in the air. Randy wrapped his hands around the bar, as tight as dough around a corn dog.

"I always like to take a ride on the Ferris Wheel at least once while the fair is going on," said Raki. "My friends think it's boring, but I think it's, what's the word, nostalgic."

Ever so slowly they revolved, rising high above the raucous midway on every turn. Rounding the top, spread out below, starry dots from farmyard lights sprinkled across the prairie farmlands.

"Oooh," said Randy.

Nobody ever said it better, thought James.

"If boys were smart, they'd take their girlfriends on the Ferris Wheel," Raki continued. "It's very romantic, the lights and all, but boys just want to go on scary rides so girls will scream and cling to them."

"Do you wish you were up here with your boyfriend?"

"What boyfriend? There's no boyfriend."

The car swung to a stop. Mechanical problem, sick rider? James put his arm around his son and squeezed his shoulders. "It's all right. Having fun?"

"Pretty," Randy said.

Very pretty. James glanced at Raki. He lifted his hand from his little boy's shoulder, fingers grazing Raki's arm. "Are *you* all right?"

She hesitated.

"We're stuck here anyway. Might as well tell me what's going on," he urged.

"Sometimes it feels like everyone abandons me. Mom, then dad, then my friends, now my boyfriend. I guess Lija hasn't abandoned me, yet. Or you."

"I'm rooted. Not going anywhere. You can depend on that." The Ferris Wheel started up again. He continued, carefully. "I know how it feels. To be abandoned."

She looked over Randy's head, straight into his eyes. "By whom?"

"My parents. Plus, there's more than one kind of abandonment." It would have been better if Lija hadn't built up his hopes earlier—no build up, no let down. He didn't expect Raki to put her sister down, and she didn't.

"You know what was nice?" said Raki, her tone brighter. "That bouquet of ditch roses you gave me. Remember that?"

A picture of a girl in a flowery shirt sprang to his mind. "I just remember you holding that gas nozzle, offering to fill my tank. So much cuter than the boys in their greasy uniforms at the Shell Station."

She laughed. He always loved that laugh.

It felt good to put aside worries about rain and yield and crop prices, forget the demands the banker was going to make. He relaxed against the vinyl cushion. Randy was healing. Lija was home safe. He was just having a good time.

After they disembarked, James headed straight to the cotton candy stand. "A man does not live by fried chicken and creamed peas alone," he said, taking three fluffy-topped cones from the attendant and handing them around. He pulled off a hefty pink strand and stuffed it into his own mouth, grinning. Raki giggled.

James wished the evening could go on forever, but even fueled by spun sugar, Randy exhausted early. Weeks of lying in bed and watching TV from the davenport had sapped his stamina. As much fun as they were having, Raki insisted they needed to take the little boy home to bed. Randy fell fast asleep on the way home, sprawled across the backseat, grinning even in slumber. Raki and James talked softly, stopping to laugh together at the child's little snores.

"You don't have to go away to go to college you know," said James.

"Of course I do." Confusion colored her voice.

"But your dream is to own a bakery, right? You could get a job at the Halcyon Bakery. On the job training. Take business classes at night or on your days off. Stay here."

"Why would I do that?"

"Me. And Lija. And the boys. What's the opposite of abandon?"

"I don't know. Protect?"

"We can protect each other. Protect each other, from abandonment."

WHEN JAMES FINALLY crawled into his own bed, he had forgotten his earlier disappointment. How easy it was to get all wrapped up in day to day chores and miss the beauty right there in front of your eyes. Who spurns a gift? He drowsed with a smile on his lips. He really could have it all.

WITH THE FAIR barns hosed clean, the carnie booths disassembled and the Ferris Wheel and Scrambler loaded onto trucks, Halcyon turned toward autumn. Temperatures cooled, humidity dried up, corn fields turned brown like a sea of brooms, their handles buried deep in the soil, tassels gently sweeping the gray sky, housecleaning for the winter ahead.

Raki and the other seniors settled into a familiar routine of lectures, bells and long walks down the halls between classes. The farmers settled into tractor seats for long days and nights weaving up and down their rows of corn and soybeans.

Raki helped Lija feed James and his hired hands. She kept an eye on her nephews. She helped Lija gather in the harvest of green beans and sweet corn from the garden. She didn't rebut Lija's complaints about how the weeds had taken over everything, although, as far as Raki could tell, the vegetable harvest didn't seem at all diminished.

The summer weeks with Luke had estranged her from Jody and

Lynn. Her old Beatles' album *Help!* caught her attention. Funny, wasn't it, how Jody and Lynn never had come over to listen to it. The girls still went to keggers together, sat on logs, watched the fire and drank beer. Jody and Lynn ogled and flirted with boys in tight jeans and long hair, sometimes leaving with them. Raki always drove home in her own red Corvair. Alone.

Whenever she got home late, Lija and the kids were always tucked in and fast asleep. Sometimes Raki watched James's tractor lights tracking up and down the rows as he worked late in the fields. Other times a light from the barn told her he was tinkering with an engine.

When the harvest was trucked to the elevator and tucked in the silos, James came inside for the winter. Every morning she found him at the breakfast table, a newspaper or a farming magazine spread before him. In the afternoons she heard pencil scratching from her father's den, as she still considered it, where he worked on his accounts, or sometimes she heard squeals from the boys, when he roughhoused with them. Lija continued trudging through the days and staring out the window.

Corralled by horizon, thought Raki, looking out of the same window as her sister. Unless you focus on the roads, all leading away. Should she take a road out? Or stay here? She looked at the calendar for the eleventh time that day, afraid to count the days.

Leaving had always been the plan, but James wanted her to stay. Times are changing, like Luke's commune on Nicollet Island. Family is not like *The Waltons* or *Leave It to Beaver* anymore. Maybe it never was. It's love that matters. Not the old conventions.

THE DAY BEFORE Thanksgiving Raki woke to see dawn whipped in a white froth. She flicked on her nightstand radio. Finally, she heard it: ". . .Halcyon Elementary and Junior and Senior High Schools, closed; Halcyon parochial schools, closed; Killon . . ."

No quizzes today! She snuggled deeper under the covers as the radio's looping litany lulled her back to sleep.

Like a surprise gift, a snow day is best unwrapped slowly. Ten thirty was early enough to make toast and begin enjoying a free day. Instead she descended into Lija's chaos. The boys were bored and whining. The kitchen was in shambles. Raki couldn't stand it.

"Put on your coats and boots and bundle up, because we're all going out to build a snowman!" Her exclamation was insincere but exuberant.

James began gathering up snowsuits and boots and mittens for his sons.

"They're too little. And it's too cold," said Lija, looking out the window like she was considering it anyway.

"It'll be fun," James countered.

Lija opened the refrigerator. "I bet there's a carrot for the nose in here," she said, pulling out the crisper drawer.

Raki was surprised by her surprise. Such a little thing, looking for a carrot, yet more effort than she had expected from Lija.

"Randy, come here!" yelled James.

The little boy ran on his fully-healed leg, straight into his dad's arms. "Are you old enough to build a snowman?"

"Yes, Daddy!"

"Will you get too cold?"

"No, Daddy!"

"What about your little brothers?"

"No, they're too little, Daddy."

"Nonsense. They can supervise."

"What's supervise, Daddy?"

"Never mind. Help us find eyes and mouth."

"Here's the carrot," said Lija. "But who has coal anymore?"

For the mouth, Raki and Randy emptied an old Herman's Hermits eight-track tape that nobody listened to anymore.

Lija disappeared into the bathroom, returning with caps from two spray deodorant cans. "These will work for the eyes."

For the snowman's outfit, Raki found a tattered stocking cap of her dad's and a handful of buttons from Mom's old sewing box.

Thirty minutes later, James and Randy were rolling sticky snow into a ball. Sandy was running around in circles, sticking out his tongue and falling down. Over and over again. Lanny toddled here and there, patting extra flakes onto James and Randy's ball, or rubbing them onto his own snowsuited tummy. Jimmy Jr. supervised from a high chair, covered in a mound of blankets. A county plow truck rolled by, the snow quit falling from the sky, a few patches of blue punctured the gray overhead.

Raki turned her face up toward a bit of weak sun poking through. She detected a trace of weak sound, too, unfamiliar and familiar at the same time. James and Randy stopped rolling the ball. Was Lija laughing? Sandy came to a standstill. Unbelievable, but yeah, that sound was coming from Lija. Lanny toddled over to hug her legs. The sound grew. Jimmy Jr. banged on the tray of his high chair. Had he ever heard his mother laugh?

A car pulled slowly into the driveway and a young man stepped out, a camera slung around his neck.

"Excuse me," he called as he plodded toward Lija. "I'm from the *Halcyon Times*. Taking 'happy kids playing in the snow' pictures. Miss Richter would love one of your family on her front page. Do you mind?"

"Not a bit," said Lija. She turned and beamed at the photographer. "But you'd better hurry up before they're all done. I'm going inside to make cocoa! With marshmallows! You can have some, too! You look rather frosty!" She tromped enthusiastically through the deep snow, throwing her head back to the sky. Laughing.

Raki and James stared at her, open-mouthed. Then they gathered the boys and smiled for the photographer. He snapped a half dozen photos of them, the snowman and four kids making faces.

"This is like a Norman Rockwell," the photographer enthused. "Miss Richter will just love it."

THE THERMOMETER DIPPED even lower as Lija's spirits rose higher. Whenever she started to feel overwhelmed, the snowman revived her smile. She nicknamed him 'Jolly Joey.' When the *Times* came out on Wednesday, she clipped the photo and taped it to the refrigerator.

Christmas preparations she embraced with merry enthusiasm,

frolicking through the Ben Franklin store, picking up brown stuffed bears and green toy tractors for her boys. She strung colored lights along the railing of the wraparound porch. She popped corn and showed Randy and Sandy how to string it with cranberries to make garland.

James suddenly came back into her focus, too. In the grocery store, she remembered to pick up steak as well as Frosted Flakes. When she saw him headed to town, or just to the barn, she found a way to extract herself from the boys long enough to kiss him goodbye.

She started talking with Raki again, too. She asked advice on how to add pizazz to her wardrobe. "Scarves! And big pendants!" came Raki's answer. They discussed the current fashion in hem length. Lija looked down at the faded skirt that skimmed her knees.

"Let's drive up to The Cities," she suggested. "James can watch the boys. We'll get Christmas gifts you can't find here." Then, whispering, "Maybe a few tidbits for us, too."

Lija called the high school.

"I told them you were sick, which wasn't exactly fibbing," Lija told Raki, "if senioritis is an actual disease."

LIJA RELISHED the piped-in carols swirling through the mall atrium and the toy stores. Do I splurge on a talking Mattel-O-Phone, she wondered. The rakish chords of 'Jingle Bells' signaled, 'Do it. They're only young once!'

Laden with almost more toys than she could handle, Lija waltzed through a department store into the lingerie department. Her undie drawer was sadly lacking in frou frous. The stacks of lace caught her breath a little, but she soldiered on, capturing a bag full of pastel niceties.

Raki tip-toed around, fingered a couple nighties, then excused herself. She returned a few minutes later with a bulky sweater in school bus yellow with a red stop sign. The boys would get a kick out of it, she claimed. It was far too large, and alarmingly childish, but Lija was not qualified to advise Raki on fashion.

On the long drive home, Lija asked Raki if she had heard anything from her boyfriend. Raki shrugged. "It was just a summer thing," she said, closing her eyes and reclining against the car door. Lija recognized the signal. She dropped the subject.

࿊

RAKI'S MIND was roiling and the lull of the car trip did nothing to quiet it. *Thank God Lija stopped with the interrogation. What the hell am I going to do? And what was that lingerie deal about?* Weird. When had Lija started caring about stuff like that?

The snow cover glowed blue under the moon. It reminded her of a different chilly night, many years before. How long ago had it been? Lija had yelled up the stairs for Raki to throw down her slippers. The floors in the old house were frigid. Not ungrateful for the interruption to her homework, Raki had leapt up. What had she been working on? Fractions, maybe. Raki remembered bending over to reach the slippers, and what she had seen.

She had carried the slippers down the stairs, finding Lija on the davenport, legs curled beneath her, flipping through the pages of a seed catalog. What was the song that had been playing on the radio? Somehow she recalled it had been Dusty Springfield.

"Cat got your tongue?" Lija had asked after too many minutes passed.

"No."

More minutes. Dusty Springfield gave way to the Beatles, who sounded odd singing at such a low volume. Even as a teenager, Lija had behaved so much older than her years, listening to rock 'n' roll at level two on the volume knob.

"No jokes about my stupid garden?"

"No."

"Are you wondering why a young woman such as myself is comparing squash varieties in a seed catalog instead of eye shadow colors in a *Seventeen* magazine?"

"No," said Raki.

"Don't think I don't care or that I have given up."

"Given up on what?"

"On boys."

"I thought you meant on life."

Lija had crossed her arms over her chest and leaned back. "Oh, my, aren't you the melodramatic one. What's eating you?"

Raki recalled how scared she had been. "I can't stand any more dying," she had answered. So earnest for such a little girl. "I can't live here with just Dad. He died a little when Mom died and he will die some more if you die and then it will be just me and a fraction of a dad." Yes, now she recalled, she had been working on math.

It was the blood that had scared her. She had seen it when reaching for Lija's slippers. Everybody talked about the blood when their mom got killed in the car crash. She knew about stopping a little blood with a bandage, or getting stitches. But sometimes there was too much blood.

It had taken Lija a little while to figure it out.

"It's OK, Raki," she finally said. "Let me give you something Mom gave me." From her bedroom Lija brought out a thin pamphlet.

Raki had stroked the glossy paper and turned it over gingerly. On the back was a picture of a blue box with a white rose on it.

"You got this from Mom?"

"And now it's yours. Read it and then you can ask me questions."

"I saw blood in your wastebasket. Sopped up blood. I saw it." Now, years later, she was astonished at how ignorant she had been. And grateful to Lija for explaining.

"Every month?" Unbelievable.

"Well, it depends." Lija explained that she was as regular as could be, every 28 days on the dot, but other girls were what was called 'irregular,' she said, and so always had to be prepared, because those girls just never knew.

Later, snuggled in bed, young Raki had reached under her pillow and pulled out the fuzzy robe she kept there. She rubbed the fabric across her cheek, breathed deeply and opened the little booklet to page one. The illustrations were dated, but the message was timeless and she imagined her mother's voice reading to her as she fell asleep.

Now, all these years later, Raki was scared again. She considered how her insides were as unlike her sister's as their personalities. If only. She stared out at the blue snow. *If only I were less erratic, more regular. Then I would have realized sooner.* Soon enough to do something. Or at least in time to consider other choices, all the options.

Damn it. What now?

12

LIJA'S FINGERS were cramping from addressing Christmas cards. She stretched, then checked on the boys in the living room. Early morning cartoons had given way to soap operas. The boys were tossing blocks out of the toy box. On the TV, two actresses sat on a white sofa, grasping each other's hands. *Must be a serious talk, like the one I'm going to have to have with Raki.*

That damn boyfriend, she swore under her breath as she switched off the program. He had been too old for Raki, too experienced. Would a stern lecture have done any good? Motherly advice? Lija wouldn't have known what advice to give. It wasn't like teaching Raki how to pull weeds. Lija knew nothing about fending off boys. James hadn't been like that.

Lija wriggled her fingers over the cards, picked up her pen, then set it down again. She had let her little sister down. Had been too deep in her own depression to look out for her. What would Mom have done? Even girls with moms get in trouble. At least three girls in Lija's high school class 'had to' get married. Would they even be able to find this boy, this 'summer thing,' as Raki called him? Luke? Would he agree to do the right thing? What was Dad going to say?

Lija licked the back of an envelope, smoothing it sealed. None of that mattered. Everything would work out all right. She would make sure of it.

The clock ticked throughout the day. At three-thirty Raki walked through the door.

"Hey, sit down here, Sis, for a minute." Lija's jolly holiday tone belied the thumping of her heart.

Raki dumped her textbooks on the table. Lija poured two cups of coffee and motioned for Raki to take a chair. Lija looked through the steam. All that thinking, and she still didn't know how to start. "Well . . ." she finally sputtered.

"Well, what?"

"Well, when are you going to tell me?" Lija blurted it out.

Raki put her palms up and tilted her head.

"You know what I'm asking, Raki."

"No, I don't."

"I've had four children. The big sweaters, trips to the bathroom every five minutes. You're not freshening your mascara in there."

She waited. Raki said nothing.

"OK, well, when are you due?"

"May, I think."

"You think? Have you seen a doctor?"

"Yeah, in Mankato." Raki's eyes, flitting ever so slightly, betrayed the lie.

"And he said May?"

"Yeah," Raki lied again. It was easy to tell.

"OK. Maybe you should get a second opinion. Maybe not from a doctor right in Halcyon, but one who's closer than Mankato."

"What good would that do?"

"You need good medical care."

"I suppose. There's a doctor in Winton. That's closer."

"Good. And Dad's coming home for Christmas. Are you going to tell him?"

"I suppose."

"What are your plans?" Lija didn't want to distress her sister, but as long as they were finally talking, she may as well put it all out there. "Have you notified the father? Luke? Are you going to get married? Or give it up for adoption?"

Raki looked away, touching her belly through the thick yellow sweater, tears leaking through her lashes. "I can't do either of those things."

What other options were there?

"I was hoping I could just stay here, with the baby," said Raki. "Once I've graduated I can be around more to help you. My baby will be cousins to the boys. They can play together."

Lija tried to stay sensible. "I'm sure, if we contacted the Army, they could find the father."

Raki ignored her. "I wouldn't be the first girl to keep her baby when she isn't married. Really. Please, just for a while. Until I figure it all out?"

Not the first? Keep a baby without being married? Lija had never heard of such a thing. But then she didn't know what people did in other places. Times were changing, everybody could see that. Maybe it could work. Raki really had been a big help lately. The two of them taking care of five babies would be easier than Lija taking care of four.

"I'll get a job, too. I can be a typist or something. Help out with the utilities and all." Raki was pleading.

Lija knew she would miss Raki, and if she didn't want to marry this Luke, nobody could force her. Even Dad couldn't do that. Lija considered it. She stood up and paced. This wasn't a decision to be made in haste.

The words popped out of her mouth unbidden, like a weed between the garden rows. "All right. We're family. You can stay here with the baby." She got up and gave her sister a huge hug. "Now, let's go tell James."

࿓

DAD WOULD BE HARDER to tell. Raki didn't want to ruin his holiday, but surrounded by boisterous boys and drowning in Christmas wrapping paper, the news seemed barely to register with Grandpa Lawrence.

"Another grandchild!" he boomed, with the unaffected bonhomie available to a man who would soon drive two thousand miles away from the small-town gossips. "A girl, this time, I hope!"

It was all going to be OK. Better than OK. Maybe even perfect.

Part Four

Is there no pity sitting in the clouds, that sees into the bottom of my grief?

William Shakespeare, *Romeo & Juliet*

Halcyon, Minnesota
1972

13

MARGARET DENING, CO-ED, soon to be bachelor of arts, summa cum laude, could not make up her mind. She stood, hands on hips, vacillating like Hamlet. Which was braver—telling her secret or keeping it buried? She wanted to talk with somebody. Or did she? A minister would listen. There'd be one inside this stone church. Go inside or go home?

Her legs wobbled. She sat on the church grass, 'Indian-style' as her teachers use to call it way back in grade school, 'cross-legged' her cultural anthropology prof would have corrected. Either way, the rear of her new pants was getting stained green. No matter.

Long, straight brunette hair billowed lightly in the breeze, the part down the left side as straight as the margin of notebook paper. Her purple bell bottoms poured over her twenty-two-year-old frame, hems spraying out over yellow shoes. A red t-shirt with matching purple sleeves snugged her trim curves. A braided belt tied it all together.

The goal of this insouciant ensemble had been to impress her future mother-in-law, in a fashionable, confident, semi-womens-libber kind of way. She had been so worried that the mansion and the rich Mrs. Voll would make her feel inadequate, inept, unqualified, ineffective . . . her English-major brain, when procrastinating, turned into a thesaurus.

The who-knows-how-many-bedroom monstrosity, the thing her fiancé's parents were giving them as a wedding present, had been quite overwhelming, in fact. Doric columns, a butler pantry and, good grief, servants' quarters? But Mrs. Voll had been so kind, funny even. Not much of a snob at all. Margaret felt guilty for assuming she would be. More guilt.

Margaret counted off her blessings. A university education, handsome fiancé, well-off. Everything a girl could want. The guilt came from knowing she had done nothing to earn it. Nothing. Everything had come easy. Even after she failed the one big test, it all turned out A-OK. Why? She wasn't special. Jeannette had been special. Not Margaret.

Guilt was the secret she buried deeper than a footnote in a literary analysis on the bottom shelf of a library stack. But if she was going to go forward in life, she needed to dust it off and open it up. The only thing for it was to just walk into that church and confess.

৯০

MONDAY WAS the brand-new Reverend Samuel Bergstrom's day off, but he came into church anyway because he had nothing better to do. The other ministers in Halcyon spent Mondays tossing baseballs around with their sons, or sitting with their knees up to their chins sipping tea with their tiny daughters, or so he imagined. He didn't really know. The associate minister at St. Peter Lutheran Church, commonly known as the Swedish Lutheran, knew he was likely to remain an 'associate' for the same reason that he had nothing better to do. No wife and kids.

So unfair, he griped to himself. An image of his dad popped into his head: "Life's not fair," Dad lectured at him. Twenty-five years old and he still couldn't get his dad out of his head. *Sheesh.*

Still he couldn't shake his frustration. Priests were forbidden to marry, but for protestant pastors it was practically required. At least to make it up to Senior Pastor. Otherwise, people might 'wonder.' Sigh. And he couldn't just marry anybody. She had to be virtuous, and play the organ. How often had he and his fellow seminarians snickered at that inside joke? It wasn't funny anymore.

So he had spent the morning cleaning the toilet and scrubbing the bathtub in the little apartment the church council had chosen for him. At least the priests got a housekeeper. Then he made himself a Velveeta sandwich, heated up a can of tomato soup ('mmm mmm good') and came in to the office because, what the heck?

He checked in with the church secretary so she would know he was there, although it was unlikely anyone would care. Services had just been yesterday, so his congregation certainly still felt adequately inspired today, ready to finish up Spring Planting with pure hearts, strong arms and hearty appetites. This time of year they were really too busy to sin, so they wouldn't need confession anyway, not that anybody had ever come to the Reverend Bergstrom for confession. That little task got tidied up nicely in unison on Sunday morning. Even in the dead of winter, with nothing to do but feed the cattle, his congregants would be hard-pressed to think up any individual sins worth coming all the way into town to confess.

Of course they were sinning right and left. He knew that. Taking the Lord's name in vain dozens of times a day. Not loving their wives as God intended. Being cruel to their kids, some of them. Not caring about their neighbor, at least not the ones next door. The ladies trooped to the church every Tuesday to sew up mesh bags filled with soap scraps to send to poor people in Africa, but not the ones on the corner of Tenth and Main, no matter how often the ladies complained that those kids smelled. But the Reverend Bergstrom confessed in his heart that he was no better. That family was a problem for another pastor. They came from Missouri, so they must be Baptist, or maybe Methodist.

The Reverend Bergstrom considered all these things with his feet up on his desk, looking out the window at the grass littered with dandelions in full bloom. Apparently the lawn care committee hadn't gotten around to pulling the spring weeds. He went out the back door and pulled up a handful of the yellow blossoms. Out of the corner of his eye he spotted an unfamiliar young woman in a red t-shirt and purple pants. Feeling sheepish, he turned his back so she wouldn't see his clerical collar, and pretended to be just a helpful soul tending the lawn. When he got a small bundle, he brought them inside, walked up the steps to the fellowship hall and rummaged through the church kitchen cabinets. He found elaborate cut glass vases, but kept searching until he located an empty jelly jar. Church ladies could always be counted upon to never throw anything away.

He really didn't know why he was doing this, except that ministers with little kids would probably get jelly jar dandelion bouquets to put on their desks, so why shouldn't he? He carried it back to his office and placed it front and center. His little jar sported a picture of Pebbles Flintstone landing a fish. Perhaps he could get some inspiration for a sermon from that.

"Reverend? Are you free?" The church secretary tapped at his door jamb.

"Really, 'Pastor' is better, or even just Sam," he responded, in as patient a voice as he knew how to make. He and she had had a long discussion at the golf course bar about how the term 'Reverend' was theologically suspect. Plus nobody revered him, they had agreed over too many beers, which is probably why she forgot the conversation.

"There's a young woman who says she wants to talk to a minister. I didn't ask about what."

"Show her in, please."

A few seconds later she appeared, the red t-shirted, purple pants'd one he'd seen on the lawn. Her outfit was snug enough to make the church ladies cluck, but he didn't mind. His secretary/golf course confidant gave him a look that told him to inquire into this young woman's musical resume, but she also left the door wide open when she left. *Am I not to be trusted?* He wondered.

AN ENORMOUS DIAMOND on her left hand sparkled as she extended her right. How had a good secretary missed that?

"Margaret Dening. Pleased to meet you."

"Likewise. So we haven't met. What a relief. I was ready to be embarrassed that I didn't recognize one of my own congregation members."

Sam guessed she was a year or two younger than himself. She was trying to smile, but the sides of her mouth twitched. Her legs looked a little wobbly, so he scooted a chair to her as quickly as he could. He was a bit embarrassed by the worn upholstery, but she didn't seem to notice. He sat down, too, and looked across the desk at her. She gulped a dose of air.

"I don't know where to begin so I'm just going to start talking. Do you have lots of time?"

He wished she assumed he was super busy, just offering up his time from the magnanimity of his Christian soul. But truth is truth. It was a Monday.

"Take all the time you need."

She nodded toward the door. "Do you mind?"

"Of course," he said, jumping up to close it.

"OK. OK. Here goes." She dosed in another big breath as he returned to his desk. "I'm engaged to Mike Voll. Michael. Do you know the name? We're going to be married next month. Then we're moving here. My hometown is just up the road. He's going to manage his family's land. I'm going to teach. English. I graduate next week. When we move here we'll join his church, one of the other ones, a bigger one. No offense. Norwegian Lutheran or something. Not German Lutheran, even though I get them mixed up. At any rate, not this one."

"OK." Pastor Bergstrom noted the nervous prattling. He considered joking about the outdated ethnic designations, but got the feeling that levity would not be appreciated.

"I'm here because I have a huge secret. Really huge." She paused, sighed and took another deep breath. "I can't bear to tell Mike, plus my parents would never forgive me. I have to tell a stranger. Somebody who's sworn to secrecy. Like you."

He suddenly felt under-qualified. "Are you confessing something?"

"Well, I don't know. I guess not. No. It's just that." She paused, fixing her eyes on the dandelions in the jelly jar. His attempt to cheer himself up now seemed rather foolish, but this woman was neither available nor a member of his congregation, so he let it go.

"I feel guilty because I don't deserve anything I've got," she continued. "I did something really bad, or at least, didn't stop something really bad from happening, when I had the chance."

"A sin of omission rather than commission?" he prodded, gently, he hoped.

"I don't know if what I did . . . didn't do . . . is a sin, but my sister died, and she didn't have to. Since then, everything has gone right for me. It doesn't seem fair."

Survivor guilt? He thought back to the new psychology theory his counseling professor had mentioned at seminary. *'Bout time that class came in handy.*

"God offers grace, not judgment," he said, wondering if that came off as wise or ridiculous.

"I don't need grace or judgment. I guess I do need to confess."

"Really?" he said, probably too enthusiastically. "Most people don't know that Lutherans do individual confession. I'm honored."

She looked at him oddly, then said "All right," a little too loudly. He detected a struggle to steady the quivering of her voice.

"This all happened ten years ago, when I was twelve," she began. "My sister, Jeannette, was fifteen . . ."

"I WILL NEVER forget the day it all started. My sister came home from school carrying all these textbooks: chemistry, world history, geometry. She also had a load of spiral bound notebooks in colors to match her textbooks, all doodled with hearts. Teenage rococo art, as it were. Jeannette was a really good student. She even sang in the church choir. I guess we all did. I remember she was wearing a white starched shirt, pleated wool skirt and matching cardigan. Navy blue. We dressed so differently back then. So conservatively.

"I couldn't believe those heavy textbooks. And the notebook pages crammed with handwriting. All I had was a worksheet and a pencil. And how did Jeannette get any studying done when she spent so much time carving hearts into the cardboard covers?

"I didn't say anything, because a lot of my friends doodled hearts, too, and also because when I brought it up to my mom, she put me in my place. 'The only marks that matter are the ones on her and your report cards.' That's how my mother lectured me. Since

Jeannette got all A's that was the end of that.

"I'm rambling. But you need to know what Jeannette was like. She was pretty and well-dressed and polite and smart. School smart, anyway.

"But one day, when she was showing me how to darn socks, she learned that in home ec, she whispered, 'I got married.'

"Can you imagine? I was shocked. She was fifteen, a freshman in high school. It was crazy. She whispered the whole story to me and never stopped sewing. How after her boyfriend got his driver's license they drove all over trying to find somebody to marry them. Of course they couldn't get a marriage license, not without their parents' approval, and that was never going to happen. They were too young, and my dad and his dad hated each other. Jeannette had been sneaking around with this boy for months and I had known it all along. But I didn't see what the dads had to do with it, so I kept her secret. But even at twelve I knew that getting married at fifteen was nuts.

"Jeannette and her boyfriend drove around to little towns where nobody would recognize them, asking around for a minister that might break the rules. For a good cause. I'm sure the people they asked thought Jeannette was expecting, you know 'in trouble,' but she wasn't.

"Jeannette told me she thought it was good enough to get married in the eyes of God. She wore her confirmation dress, because it was white. As soon as they found somebody who would agree to do it.

"There was an old minister that the kids in some little town called 'Friar Drunk.' Jeannette's boyfriend had twenty-five dollars and a fifth of whiskey he stole from his dad's liquor cabinet. Apparently, Friar Drunk took that as sufficient payment to break the law and the rules of his church, assuming he even had a church. She swore that he wore a collar, like yours, but do they check your credentials when you buy one? Maybe he wasn't really entitled. Who knows?

"Anyway, she got married in a white dress and then they went home and didn't tell a soul. 'Til me. They knew they couldn't support themselves. So they went on just like normal.

"After she told me, her boyfriend's—um, husband's—dad found the fifth of whiskey missing and all hell broke loose. The neighbors heard the yelling, and blabbed about it afterward. Her boyfriend tore out of the driveway like a maniac. He rammed another car a mile from our house. He died, and so did the lady in the other car. That night Jeannette killed herself, too.

"Like Juliet, when she found Romeo dead. But it wasn't a dagger. It was as a coat hanger. She did it in the bathtub. There was blood everywhere. And it wasn't her heart she stabbed. I can't say what she did. But you know what desperate girls do with hangers."

THE REVEREND BERGSTROM realized, too late, that he should have been sitting in the chair next to her rather than across a desk. In hindsight, this business office arrangement was not set up for taking confessions, or even having a conversation.

The tormented young lady on the far side of his desk looked down at her hands, her long hair swinging past her cheeks, veiling the water leaking through her mascara. She pulled her face tight and pursed her lips to dam it up. A moment passed. She looked up, her complexion reddened. "I knew she had locked herself in the bathroom. I should have known what she was doing. Maybe not exactly, but that it was something bad. I could have stopped her. Told mom. Dad could have broken down the door. But I didn't do anything."

He took a box of tissues down from a shelf and handed the box to her. He sat down on the chair next to her, belatedly, but said nothing. Struck dumb like Zechariah, but not from any good news, for sure.

Her mascara had run, painting jagged black scars down her face. She used the tissue to swab her cheeks clean. He considered his words. He thought about saying, "I don't really see that you have anything to repent. You were only twelve."

Obviously she knew that. He ransacked his brain for some nugget of wisdom from that seminary counseling class. His training felt locked up, as in one of those little girl's diaries with a side strap and little gold lock. He searched his brain for a key, but couldn't find one.

The huge silence walloped him, so he blurted. "I have no idea what to say. I'm so sorry about your sister." He paused to consider a trope about grace, a loving God, heaven. He believed it all, but words wouldn't cut it.

She sat up straight, looking thoughtful. Reading his mind, she said, "No, I don't need any words from you. I just couldn't carry this secret, this guilt, all by myself anymore. The coroner ruled it a suicide. It wasn't really an abortion, you see, because there wasn't any baby there. Ironic, right? We'll never know why she thought there was."

He didn't dare ask how she would know that. He wondered how long he should let the silence go on.

Finally, when the quiet was making him sweat, he muttered, "Well, is there anything you want me to do?"

"Just keep me in your thoughts, your prayers even," she said. Then she stood. "No, actually, I don't care that much about your prayers. No offense. I want to do something. What's the word you guys use? Atone. And I don't care if you believe in it or not. I want you to find somebody who needs help. I wasn't able to help my sister, but maybe there's somebody I can help, somehow, some day."

She stood up and he followed her lead, extending his hand, "Good luck with your wedding plans."

"Thank you," she said, dropping her hand toward his desk. fingering the tiny yellow petals poking out of the jelly jar. "One question, though, before I leave. What's with these dandelions on your desk?"

"They're symbolic."

"Symbolic of what?"

"I don't know. Gotta figure that out."

14

LIKE MOST LITTLE girls, Margaret and her friends had playacted weddings. One girl would drape a dishtowel over her head, parading in her most dignified gait. Another would play pastor, the sleeves of her dad's old suit coat dragging on the floor. The 'guests' would hum the processional. And no girl ever wanted to be the groom.

Jeannette's death had wrecked the illusion. Then women's liberation made it seem silly. By college Margaret had decided she had no interest in marriage. Then she saw the cutest guy in her cultural anthropology class. When he showed up again in Brit Lit, she changed her mind.

Mike's old money, older even than the state of Minnesota, bought him a *savoir faire* she had never seen before. He wore his hair trimmed and his pants pressed, yet hung out with shaggy-haired boys in dirty jeans and didn't for a second pass judgment. He studied for fun, never worrying about grades. So different from Margaret, whose union-label dad taught her to work hard, get A's, and land a job with a pension.

Pension was not a concern that ever entered Mike's head. His family owned land, 'ancestral acreage,' he called it, and lots of it. After graduation he would manage it, so amongst his classes in literature and anthropology, he squeezed in some business and agriculture.

Mike confessed his Midwestern landed-gentry roots back when he had proposed to her. The Volls, he made clear, had never been the 'tired and poor' of Emma Lazarus fame. His forefathers were among the first Norwegians to immigrate, their pockets jingling with sufficient coin to buy an early foothold.

The first immigrant Volls amassed as much fertile soil as they could, paying only $1.25 an acre, always legally and sometimes ethically. When the Homestead Act passed, they were the ones holding open the 'golden door' for the 'wretched refuse' of the teeming fjord. Unfortunately, or fortunately as it played out, Norwegian city dwellers and fishermen did not always turn out to be enthusiastic farmers. When the need arose, the Volls were ready with cash to rescue their compatriots from their plows. Ready-made sod-busted fields were purchased at a 'fair price' and rented out to more suitable types. Swedes and Germans.

Nowadays, Mike assured her, everything was completely above board and no Voll ever got his hands dirty, actually or ethically. No Voll had even lived near their land since his dad was a boy.

The empty mansion they were getting as a wedding present was the second home the Volls had built in Halcyon. The first, a white clapboard home with a Gambrel roof and wrap-around porch, was still occupied. In 1925 Grandfather Voll sold that old house to one of his renters, for as much as farmer Pederson could afford to pay, and built the much grander neo-classical brick manor on the other side of town. Never mind the expense of shipping bricks across the prairie by train.

Mike's Grandfather and Grandmother Voll lived in the mansion only four years. Their lifestyle took a detour thanks to the Great Depression. With more than a few tenants in arrears, their liquid assets were suddenly insufficient to pay boarding school tuition for their children, not to mention that they were ostracized. Once the Voll's dunning letters hit the rural mail routes, tenants and everybody else imagined them feasting on caviar paid for with the sweat of farmers who could barely afford seed for their own gardens. So the Volls covered the furniture with cloths, boarded the windows, and turned it all over to a groundskeeper for safekeeping. They moved to swanky Edina. Mike's father attended the very best public school in the state. The family collected rents at an address in the Foshay Tower. A few times a year an emissary drove down to make sure the caretaker was earning his keep.

And now, over four decades later, Mike told her it was time to move back 'where I can see what I'm managing.' Which was how it came to be that he and she and his mother had all driven a hundred miles to check things out. His mother got there first.

"Mike, Margaret," Mrs. Voll had proclaimed when she flung open the grand doors for the two of them earlier that day. Margaret had met her future mother-in-law only a few times before, always as briefly as politely possible. She had been intimidated by the older woman's etiquette book demeanor, not to mention the precise hair, elegant skirts, Italian-leather pumps and cashmere sweaters, always draped over her shoulder, just so. But there was no avoiding Mrs. Voll any longer. There was business to attend to.

"Welcome to our ancestral home," Mrs. Voll announced, swinging wide the immense double doors. "Lovely outfit, Margaret. Very colorful."

Margaret hadn't been able to tell if the becashmered woman was sincere or sarcastic. Better assume the first, to be on the safe side. "Hello, Mrs. Voll. It's so nice of you to do all this work for us."

"Work? Me? Never. But a whole team of other people is getting this place in shape for you. Really, why you want to live down here in the sticks is beyond me, but we're happy to get rid of it. Lord knows there's no joy in keeping up an empty house."

Margaret couldn't stop gawking. *The Great Gatsby* came to mind. She ogled the chandelier hanging two stories above a marble-floored foyer. "We could throw quite the impressive party here," whispered Mike.

"That might be fun," she had whispered back, thinking, "If we can manage to make some friends."

As if reading her mind, Mrs. Voll piped, "I do hope you have better luck fitting in down here than my in-laws did."

Leaving the fresh air of the foyer for the formal parlor, Margaret had managed not to crinkle her nose at the musty smell. Mrs. Voll read her mind again, visibly sniffing, "Don't worry. We'll air it out.

Fresh paint, floor wax, the works."

Next stop had been the dining hall. As long as a bowling alley, Margaret thought. *Gawd. Bowling. How working class.* Margaret was glad she hadn't said it aloud.

Late morning sun glittered through mullioned windows. Another chandelier sparkled light in her eyes. Then the butler's pantry, opening to a startlingly small kitchen. A miniscule powder room huddled in a corner, like a chambermaid hoping not to be noticed.

Next the three paraded up the curving stairway, like the one in *Gone with the Wind.* Margaret felt underdressed for the trip. When they reached the second floor she gasped, grabbing Mike by the elbow. The master bedroom alone was bigger than the house she grew up in. More spacious bedrooms, and on top of all that the third floor. A tiny window at the very top of the stairs looked over a park with trees and flowers. No, not a park. There were headstones. A cemetery.

Ahead, a claustrophobic warren of tiny rooms opened off a narrow hallway lined with broom closets and linen closets. Servant quarters?

"I hope Margaret's teacher friends won't think you two are pretentious for living so high on the hog, as they say down here. But, this is a pretty nifty wedding gift if I may say so myself. Which I just did." Mrs. Voll had laughed at herself as they descended the narrow back stairs to the kitchen.

"Let's have lunch!" Mrs. Voll pulled a pitcher of lemonade and a plate of sandwiches from the glossy new harvest gold refrigerator, so modern next to the Roaring Twenties-era cabinetry. She poured ceremoniously, placing filled glasses on a handled tray before proceeding to the back patio. She handed the tray to Margaret and carried the sandwiches herself.

"Relax," Mrs. Voll had said, settling into a lawn chair. "It's just a house. Just lots more of it than most."

Margaret nibbled a bit on her sandwich and sipped daintily.

"Lemons from Byerly's," Mrs. Voll had said, pointing toward her glass. "The trees are watered with champagne, the rinds caressed daily. With feathers from royal peacocks. That's why they cost so much."

Margaret burst out laughing. She couldn't help it.

Her future mother-in-law guffawed. A couple professionally-permed hairs escaped free. "Now we're having some fun!"

So Margaret did relax, a little, although now she felt bad for all those times she had scoffed at Mrs. Voll's 'materialism.' Where was the harm in a little high class lemonade?

"Whatever happened to Mike?" asked Mrs. Voll, eyeing the lone full glass left on the tray.

He reappeared carrying a Hamm's beer, pulling the tab off the top, pushing it through the hole and swigging a long quaff. Mrs. Voll feigned disapproval, her mouth turned down in an extravagant frown.

"Ahh," he sighed, licking the foam off his lip. "Mom? Lemonade? Seriously? No wonder the locals chased us out of town with pitchforks. Time for a new era. Beer and booze will tame the natives."

"Provided you don't insult them with Hamm's," answered his mother.

"Budweiser then?" Mike was smirking. His mother resurrected her fake frown.

"OK, OK. Miller High Life," said Mike, as if surrendering.

"Really, we Volls must keep up standards," she said, wriggling her pinky finger and lifting her chin.

Focused on graduating with honors and putting the final touches on the wedding plans, Margaret needed to get back to her books and notebooks. First she helped her future mother-in-law tidy up before excusing herself for the drive back to the university. Mike stayed behind to help his mother deal with the air conditioning installer, take a drive around the fields, and generally avoid studying for finals.

It was then, exiting the long Voll drive, alone, that she had decided to detour a few blocks to the unfamiliar church.

I don't deserve all this, she had fretted. All this luxury. All this perfection. A handsome fiancé, beautiful house, funny mother-in-law. What she needed was somebody to talk to. A stranger. Somebody sworn to secrecy.

NOW, AN HOUR LATER, she felt unburdened. Such a nice young reverend, he was, taking so much time to listen to a stranger. She pointed her car up the highway toward the university, slipping easily between the deep black fields, the baby green shoots just now poking up through the soil.

MARGARET EXITED down the aisle on Mike's arm, her tulle veil fluttering behind. The wedding had all gone so well. Not as posh as they might do in Edina, but her union-label parents had put on quite the impressive to-do. Flowers. Candles. Beautiful bridesmaids with long flowing hair. Handsome groomsmen whose long flowing hair got barbered off for the occasion. Solo sung. Vows and rings exchanged.

Now to the church reception. Cake. Coffee. Nuts and mints skittering across luncheon plates. Guests in heels and slippery soles on waxed linoleum, navigating between banquet tables and folding chairs.

Margaret swished her white train around the room, her groom a half step behind, chatting up relatives and their parents' friends. When a respectable hour passed, and a sufficient number of guests had departed, they were grateful to decamp with the rest of the bridal party. Wild spring sunshine burst through the open doors as the twenty-somethings swept out of the hall.

"I need a drink," said the best man. No one protested.

Her own parents would be going home to rest, but Margaret was not surprised to find her new in-laws already at the hotel bar. Mr. Voll ('I couldn't possibly call him Dad.') was chatting with a group of men, his tie loosened. On the other side of the room Mrs. Voll ('That's my name, too, now.') motioned to them.

"I want you to meet my friends," Mike's mother said, tilting her champagne glass as if in toast. "Never mind their names. You won't remember them anyway. These are my oldest and dearest. We have played cards, drunk gin, told tales on our husbands and our kids, and now, 'Cheers!' we're done."

Mrs. Voll took a drink. "No, no, not done with the cards and the tales and the gin. Done raising kids. Well done. And I guess we're into champagne now." She took another swig.

"Mom, are you drunk?"

"Well, not yet, son. But I do plan to get quite tipsy. Eventually.

Right now I'm just a little tipsy."

Mike rolled his eyes.

"Nice to meet you," said the ladies one by one, the bouffant, the bee hive and the French twist.

"Beautiful ceremony," said Bouffant.

"Lovely soloist," Bee Hive added.

"Nice sermon," French Twist opined.

"Really, my dear?" said Mrs. Voll. "You paid attention? What did he say?"

"Never mind."

"My son, here, plans to take his bride to the middle of nowhere and play Lord of the Manor down in the soybean fields. Margaret plans to teach English."

"How lovely. We wish you the best."

"He thinks if he offers the locals a Bud they will become his friends," Mrs. Voll laughed, "but I fear these two are going to be very lonely." She affected a dramatically rueful expression.

"Mother, we agreed on Miller High Life," said Mike, joining in her ribbing.

"No, no, I think bud would be more tempting," she said. "As long as it's not beer, you know."

Bud? Not beer?

The coifed matrons burst into chortles, spraying spittles of champagne on the bride. Mrs. Voll took an ever so dainty sip this time, peering at them over the rim of her crystal.

The bridal couple's mouths dropped open.

"Oh, get over yourselves. You think because we get our hair permed we're ignorant!"

Bouffant poured a refill into Mrs. Voll's glass. "Your mother's just having fun," she said, hoisting the bottle over her head.

"Mother? Bud? Since when do you speak stoner?"

"I read *Time* magazine, son," she answered, swinging one leg, her pump dangling from the tip of her stockinged toe.

"We all read *Time*," said Bee Hive, nodding around at the table.

Mrs. Voll leaned close to Margaret and Mike, stage whispering. "Plus, we . . .experimented . . . just a little bit . . . one time."

"Mother, no . . . Where did you get it?"

"We stole it from her son." Mrs. Voll said, pointing her thumb toward French Twist.

"He rather owed me, don't you think?" slurred French Twist, smoothing a stray hair back into her do. "Childbirth and so forth. And what was he going to do? Go to the police? Complain that his mother took his stash?"

"How did he find out it was you who took it?" asked Bee Hive.

"Maybe he didn't," said French Twist. "He grumped around the house for a week. Taught him an important lesson. Be more careful about taking care of your things."

"How was it?" Margaret couldn't contain her curiosity. These middle-aged matrons had managed more of a counter-cultural experience than she ever had. Birkenstocks were radical as she got, not that she actually owned a pair.

"Mostly it didn't live up to its reputation," said French Twist. "We did it on my patio. Sank back into our chaise lounge chairs and gazed into the swimming pool. Staring at chlorine water isn't as fun as it sounds."

"Yes, it is," said Bouffant.

"Then it didn't occur to us to get back up again," added Bee Hive. "We got terribly sunburned. Finally we got up and ate a whole bag of potato chips and a box of graham crackers."

"Stuffed and crispy. Like chicken Kiev!" Mrs. Voll hoisted her crystal glass again.

"I don't suppose they do such things down where you're moving," said French Twist, "What was the town again?"

"Oh, please, if we're doing it around the pool, they're doing it at the pig roast," said Bee Hive.

"People are all the same, doing all the same things," agreed Mrs. Voll. "Son—and daughter—Just don't pass judgment, and you will get along fine."

ॐ

TWO WEEKS AFTER the wedding, a week after the honeymoon, Mike swiveled onto a seat at the counter of the Halcyon Café, getting a start at fitting into small-town life. A big man's voice boomed over the noonday hum.

"Hey! Little landlord! Come over here and introduce yourself!"

Mike followed the bellowing to a corner booth, where a group of men were seated.

"Gentlemen, I believe this is the famed young Mr. Voll of the big mansion," the man continued, in a quieter volume as Mike got closer. "These two gentlemen on my right," he gestured with the panache of an orchestral conductor, "are among those who will be paying you rent and plowing up your vast acreage, yet they claim to never have met you."

"I've been meaning to introduce myself," said Mike.

The men maneuvered to their feet, shook hands and muttered their names.

"And I'm sorry, you are?" Mike turned to the interlocutor.

"Lawrence Pederson. I live—used to live—in the house your great-grandpa built, maybe great-great, who knows?" Mr. Pederson continued the introductions. "This fellow on my left will be fitting you and your children with glasses someday. And down at the end, our finest local attorney, whose services we all hope you never need."

Mike straightened up. "Pleased to meet you," he said with as much gusto as he could manage. "Don't worry. No evictions planned. Good news, except for those in the legal profession."

"Aww . . ." said Mr. Pederson. "How is our attorney going to afford new glasses from the fine doctor here if you don't cough up some fees?"

Mr. Pederson motioned for Mike to sit. "Hope you aren't offended by the 'little landlord' thing. Just hazing. Like a fraternity."

"How did you know who I was?" asked Mike.

"Oh, I didn't. These geezers saw you walk in and somehow they knew and huddled together cackling about you like a gaggle of fussy old hens." Mr. Pederson shook his head. "I couldn't stand it, so I made you come over here."

Mike surveyed the group. The two farmers' foreheads were branded from the bands of their seed corn caps, the green Pioneer and red Northrup King hanging from hooks on the wall. The professionals must have arrived hatless, but they probably owned wool fedoras, gathering dust somewhere. Mr. Pederson was hatless, too, and extraordinarily tanned for so early in the season.

"We were just discussing babies," said Mr. Pederson. "And feckless young men, yourself excluded of course."

Ancient ceiling fans twirled slowly overhead, gently stirring the smoke-stained spring air. Mike arranged himself on the new vinyl cushions, which megaphoned his discomfort.

"My fifth grandchild will be born out of wedlock. Any day now," announced Lawrence. "The father volunteered for the Army and took off for Vietnam. We were discussing that for all of our medical advances, girls still get themselves in trouble."

"More than ever, it seems," said one of the farmers. Mike knew on account of the line across the man's forehead. "Older generations knew how to behave."

"Pshaw," countered the lawyer, or maybe it was the optometrist. "What about the girls who disappear suddenly and go tend to their invalid aunts for five or six months? Or get sent to a home for unwed mothers, like that awful place that shut down a few years ago?"

Mike lost track of who was saying what.

"It wasn't so awful. Muckraking newspaper woman. Didn't need to shut it down. A little poison to kill the rats, tape up the exposed wires and unlock the fire escape—that would have been good enough. Better women have lived in worse."

Mike noted the other men's eyes trying not to roll. A couple times one opened his mouth, then closed it again.

"The point is, that place was operating for many years. If girls in the olden days didn't get in trouble, who was living there then? Hmmmm?"

"Shotgun marriages." The speaker blew on his finger, like it was the end of a gun barrel. "It's a well-known fact that a remarkably large percentage of first-borns arrive less than nine months after their parents' wedding."

"I'm not much of a shotgun kind of guy," said Mr. Pederson. "I'm an accountant, for chrissake. But what could I have done anyway? I don't even live here." He looked at Mike. "Just back here on a visit." He addressed the group again, "And the boy, he's over the ocean in a jungle. With more guns than I have. I haven't shot a thing since the war."

"The Supreme Court of the United States is, right now, as we speak, debating if we should legalize abortion. Their decision will have a major impact."

Mike figured that must be the lawyer talking.

"Not in Halcyon," said one of the other men. "That's not something a Halcyon girl would do, legal or not."

"Oh, grow up," said another man. "Halcyon girls are no different, never have been. My mother's best friend went up to Minneapolis twice for a D&C. Second time left her ruined."

"Your mother told you that?"

Mike detected a measure of incredulity.

"Of course not. But a kid has ears and I knew how to use 'em."

"I'm sure you misheard," came a pious retort. "Our mother's generation wouldn't even know what that was. I knew your mother. She didn't have any friends who would consider such a thing, assuming they had cause to consider it, which I highly doubt."

One of the farmers rolled his eyes. Mike was glad they hadn't asked his opinion. And then.

"Young Mr. Voll," said one. "What's your take on the Sexual Revolution?"

Mike hesitated. "Apparently, it passed right by me."

Pederson guffawed. The others chuckled sadly.

"So," said one of the farmers, turning to Mr. Pederson. "What are Raki's plans now?"

"She and the baby are going to stay on the farm with James and Lija. Raki will help out with all of Lija's kids and the chores and so on. Raki can take classes, part-time, at the college. She still wants to get a degree and go into business. James has a few more classes to take, too, although he's pretty close to done. Come winter, those two can carpool. Save on gas. Can you believe how prices are going up? Gonna hit fifty cents a gallon, mark my words. Anyway, they have it all worked out."

IT DIDN'T WORK out, though. The next time Mike heard that peculiar name, Raki, it was from Margaret.

"Her dad is back in Arizona and her sister threw her out, her and the baby," she told him.

PART FIVE

I loved him, or thought I loved him, which is the same thing.

Coco Chanel

More Letters
Halcyon, Minnesota
1949 – 1951
Read in 2016

15

June 15, 1949

Dear Katherine,

Your last letter about your French "beau" – how dashing he sounds – would have made me unspeakably jealous, except that I have my own romantic news. But, first, I am so very happy for you! You said he flew in the Service Aeronautique and that he is handsome, but that's not what I want to know. When you greet him at the door, does he whip out a bouquet of fresh flowers from behind his back? Do you picnic on a blanket in the park with an umbrella, one of those long loaves of bread, and a hunk of cheese? Does he pour you wine in the middle of the day? I would swoon to imagine such French romance, but as I hinted above, I am in the throes of middle-America style passion right now.

Yes! I met a man. He served in the Army Air Corps. Now we call it the Air Force, but either way it still does not sound as romantic as Service Aeronautique. It is quite the coincidence, isn't it, both of us dating fly boys? His name is Claude and of course he is very, very handsome. We met when I stopped in to the Halcyon Café late one afternoon. He was sitting alone when I walked in and there were few empty tables.

"I come here often at this time of day and it is always busy. It seems selfish to

take a table all to myself when I could share with a lovely young woman and make a place for other hungry folks, don't you think?" he said, pulling the chair out for me. It's not flourishing a bouquet of flowers or a wine and cheese picnic, but I fell for it!

He lives in Winton, and—you won't believe it! He is also an only child who cares for his parents. He's been coming to Halcyon about once a week or so, he said, to get away and relax. Winton, of course, is even smaller than Halcyon. He said he can't have any fun there. He takes dinner at the Halcyon Café and then gets himself a drink at the VFW and talks to the other vets.

Well, I hadn't told the Judge and mother that I'd be gone for dinner. I just went to the café for a pop. So eventually I had to excuse myself and go home and heat up soup for them (and me), but (I confess!) for the next two weeks I made it a point to walk into the café—ever so nonchalantly of course—every day at about 5:00 and eventually it paid off. There he was again!

More confession. I told him it was my twenty-first birthday, which was a lie because my birthday was the week before. Naturally he felt the need to treat me to a drink, so we walked down to the Walnut Room. He ordered us both Sidecars and then told me this cute little story about how he and two English Royal Air Force officers invented it after an air raid in Paris. Having fibbed about the exact date of my birthday I felt only a little bit bad about pointing out that I had heard the Judge order a Sidecar even before the war. Claude was unfazed. He laughed and said the whole story was actually true, but that it was World War I and the American officer wasn't, of course, him.

This is when I knew, for certain, that he was courting me. He personalized that story—to impress me!

I have never spoken as honestly to anyone else, even you, as I can speak with him. I pour my heart out, and he to me. By our third Sidecar I had even told him about my plans for law school. As soon as it fell out of my mouth I was sure he would respond with a lecture about leaving careers to the men, especially the men who served so valiantly, etc. etc. Instead, he looked delighted! I need to work out exactly what that means, but it felt good. Stay tuned!

Your friend,

Dolores

P.S. You need to tell me what your French beau looks like. There are many varieties of handsome.

July 22, 1949

Dear Katherine,

Thank you for your description of your dashing French beau. Looks like Clark Gable, you say? I certainly cannot top that!

My Claude is a cross between Cary Grant and Mickey Rooney. I hear you laughing over the ocean, but it's true. He is, alas, not as suave as Cary Grant, because he has this impish quality, hence Mickey Rooney.

He picked me up for our date to go dancing, and you'll be floored to hear this. Mother and the Judge approve! I imagined them tsk-tsking because no man would ever be good enough. When Claude told them we were going dancing at the Bloody Bucket, I thought for certain Daddy would bar the door. (Even I think the name of the place makes it sound dicey, but The Bloody Bucket is really quite respectable. Don't judge a book by its cover or a dance hall by its name.)

Instead they merely questioned him about his family and his job (he sells pharmaceuticals, I don't think I mentioned that). Then they talked about how much fun they had going dancing during the Roaring Twenties, before I was born. Daddy talked about going to Speakeasies. The Judge! Breaking the law and admitting to it! Imagine!

Over breakfast the Judge offered to fund a new dress.

I feel a little bad writing about drinks, dancing and a new dress while you and your Clark Gable still live with rationing over there, and doing heroic deeds and working so hard. I know you will forgive me this newfound shallowness because you know how starved for romantic affection I have been. Just the idea of Judge Richter threw ice water on all the boys at Halcyon High. As for college, well, the men there all seem to have sweethearts pining for them 'back home,' wherever that is.

Anyway, I'm so happy that we both are enjoying new love for our lives.

Carry on, friend.

Dolores

August 1, 1949

Dear Katherine,

Thank you, dear friend, for your concerns about my love life. Never fear. I am quite the sensible young woman. In just one month I will be starting my final year in college and then moving to Minneapolis for Law School.

Speaking of Minneapolis, Daddy made good on his promise of a new dress. We found the loveliest gown in green watered silk. It has a sweetheart neckline, fitted bodice, shirred straps and sweeping skirt, ideal for spinning over the dance floor. It hints at being risqué but isn't, really.

Enough silly girl talk. I hear that the recovery in France and England is going quite well. The Minneapolis Tribune *reports that the roads are getting rebuilt and food and medicine are becoming easier to obtain. I expect soon you will be running out of work and have to bid 'adieu.' Or will you find a romantic reason to stay and raise little French children? Would they wear berets?*

Now for the hometown news. Halcyon is booming and you will not recognize it when you get home. Where we used to have one grocery store and one hardware store, we now have two of each! The Veterans of Foreign Wars have broken ground on a new meeting hall. The Norwegian Lutheran Church is talking about pulling down the old white wooden building and replacing it with a much grander brick structure. So much for Protestant understatement. Lots of young men discovered God among the hedgerows of Europe and in the jungles of Asia and the ones who came home are willing and eager to help build. More power to them!

The County Fair is coming up. You know I'm not one for canning pickles, but Claude and I have plans for going round and round on the Ferris Wheel. I still see him no more than once a week, since he needs to stay close to home in case his parents need him. I am grateful my own parents are at least capable of taking care of themselves during the week while I am at school in the fall, winter and spring. Thank goodness for that.

Take care of yourself over there.

Your Friend,

Dolores

July 1, 1950

Dear Katherine,

Congratulate me! I am graduated with a lustrous Bachelor of Arts and received in today's mail a letter of acceptance on embossed stationery from the University of Minnesota School of Law. Best of all, I also received a delivery of roses from Claude, who is taking me out for a celebratory dinner at the Walnut Room.

As you know from my letters, which have been terribly boring of late, Claude and I saw little of each other while I was in my last semester. His mother apparently requires constant tending and his father is of little use. Alas, my studies left me rather no time for dating anyway. Now that I am home, the two of us have much catching up to do!

Even as I write these lines, I am dressed in my best green dress and all made-up, waiting for Claude to ring the bell. As soon as he does so, I will have to break off and finish up later. It is such a relief to be done with finals. I almost wish . . .

Well, Katherine, I no longer recall what I 'almost wished' last night because I heard the jingle of our front doorbell and had to break off from writing this letter.

Daddy answered the bell even before I could get to it, and invited Claude into the house. Mom and Daddy do enjoy Claude's company. Imagine this—Daddy does not even mind when he loses to Claude at cards!

Before we left the house, Daddy told Claude that if it got too late, he was welcome to sleep in our guesthouse out back rather than risk falling asleep on his drive home to Winton. Maybe he sneaked out there for a late-night whiskey and a Cribbage rematch.

I know that other girls like their romance with a little more dare and danger. Perhaps you? I'm content spending my time with an upstanding man whom my parents admire. Still, if you have some Service Aeronautique romance you could share with me, I am eager to rip open your letters and devour your tales of daring and danger.

Your friend,

Dolores

P.S. So relieved that Claude served his tour already and came back in one piece as it appears we are mobilizing for war again. There are already Halcyon boys going over to Korea. We haven't yet mopped up our mess from the last war, as you well know.

ॐ

CLAUDE. Raki paused in her reading. She ran her fingers over the handwriting, Miss Richter's impeccable handwriting in black ink on the light blue paper. The name Claude reminded her of something. Something that happened in the Seventies. She couldn't remember. Too many decades had intervened. Claude. An image came to mind. Miss Richter, a camera, red wine and something about a pearl handled pistol. That didn't make any sense. But that name. She shook her head a little, clearing the thought.

"Mom, are you all right?"

"Yes, of course," she said, and continued reading.

ক

December 20, 1950

Dear Katherine,

I was so touched by your story of locating the grandparents of the orphan begging for francs in front of the Louvre.

By comparison, my problems seem trivial, but they are consuming me. Where do I start? I've been crying so hard I can hardly see the paper to write. I locked myself in my room. Mommy and Daddy think I'm up here studying or wrapping some big Christmas surprise.

My Christmas surprise is already unwrapped and I don't know what to do. You know how Claude was such a gentleman. Roses, telephone calls, weekly dinners and dancing. I truly believe, believed, that we were head over heels in love.

We bonded over the joys and frustrations of caring for invalid parents. It seemed his parents were in even worse shape than mine, so I did not think of burdening them with a visit. I don't know what made me think it would be a burden, considering how the churches are always reminding us to visit the shut-ins, but that is what I thought. I had no other reason to go to Winton. Why would I? Winton is even smaller than Halcyon, and not on the way to anywhere.

Then, bored from my winter break, it occurred to me to do it. Visit the shut-ins. I borrowed Daddy's car and drove down to Winton. When I got there, I realized I didn't know where he lived. It's a small town, but not that small. I couldn't knock on every door. I found a phone booth and looked him up. I didn't even know his telephone number. I had never called him. Why would I? A lady waits for the gentleman to call her. But it would be rude to show up completely unannounced, particularly when visiting invalids. I put a nickel in the slot and dialed the number. Then everything fell apart.

A high, little voice answered the phone. A visiting nephew, I assumed. I asked to speak to Claude. I'm such an idiot!

'Daddy is over helping Gramma and Grandpa right now,' said the little voice. 'Would you like to speak with Mommy?'

Please, Katherine, please don't judge me. I have fallen apart completely.

Your friend,

Dolores

January 1, 1951

Dear Katherine,

Your letter arrived yesterday and I'm so relieved. You are very understanding. A few weeks ago survival seemed impossible, but since then I have come up with a plan.

I have not told anyone what I found out or how I found it out. The next time Claude showed up at our doorstep I told him to leave and never come back. I told my parents that I had broken things off. They can see I am heartbroken.

I intended to return to university, make the Judge proud. However, I realized it would be impossible to concentrate. I would certainly flunk the semester. I decided to get away. I absolutely must. <u>Get away.</u>

Please help, Best Friend. I'm laying upon you a huge responsibility without your permission, but I beg you to cover my gigantic lie. It's almost as big a lie as Claude told me. Bigger, really. His lie was in what he did not tell me. I committed straight-up perjury. I told Mommy and Daddy that in my heartbroken state I would be taking a year off to join you in Europe.

You know I'm not nearly brave enough to do that. I'm going to escape somewhere, but it will not involve crossing an ocean or learning a new language. I can't have them thinking I'm abandoning them to accomplish nothing more than finding a place to cry. You wonder how I can leave them. It seems my devotion was more for my own benefit than theirs. Being a good daughter was an easy life, at least until another option presented itself. At any rate, they have the financial resources to take care of themselves and seem willing to do so.

Tomorrow I take the train someplace. I'll let you know where. My parents will be corresponding with me through you. Please, please play along. Forward their correspondence to me at the address I give you and I will respond through you. I will reimburse the cost of airmail so it won't take so long.

Your trusting friend,

Dolores

෨

DECEPTION AND SUBTERFUGE. Miss Richter did have a secret, and they might be getting closer to it. How many more letters before they figured it out? Raki peeked in the box. Too many.

"Mom, be patient, said Joey.

PART SIX

"Tish-ah!" said the grass. "Tish-ah, tish-ah!" Never had it said anything else—never would it say anything else. It bent resiliently under the trampling feet; it did not break, but it complained aloud every time—for nothing like this had ever happened to it before.

O.E. Rolvaag, *Giants in the Earth*

Halcyon, Minnesota
1972 – 1974

16

RAKI STOOD in the principal's office between the other pregnant girl and the boy whose guard sat outside waiting to take him back to jail. Her eyes misted when the principal handed over the black leather folder. Her diploma was inside, but she wore no cap and gown. No band played 'Pomp and Circumstance.' No speech. No applause. The principal hadn't even bothered to clean the clutter off his desk.

For thirteen years her class had done everything together. Slid down the same slide, swung on the same swings, scrawled math on the same chalkboards. All one hundred forty-nine of them filled in the same little bubbles on the same standardized tests, fell asleep to the same slide shows, cheered from the same bleachers, danced to the same bands. Not today. Today the others would get their diplomas handed to them on stage. Wearing flowing robes. Robes big enough to hide a swollen belly. But that didn't matter.

The other pregnant girl had no family there, so Lija and Dad sat outside chatting with the guard. They had come to witness this 'graduation' of sorts, but the principal had pushed them out. "Too cramped in here already," he insisted. Lawrence blustered his objection, but the principal held firm. Raki was grateful for how kind Lija had been through the past months, and that Dad, in all his tanned glory, was back from Arizona for this visit.

"To supervise James, make sure he doesn't screw up my farm," he claimed when people asked, adding "and of course I want to see my fifth grandchild!" He puffed out his barrel chest when he said it, daring anyone to question his sincerity.

When she left the office, Lija and Dad congratulated Raki as the guard cuffed the boy and the other girl shuffled past, looking over her tummy at her feet.

"I love you, Dad. I love you, Lija," Raki said.

"We love you, too," her father said, "no matter what." The last three words stung, like peroxide on a skinned knee.

WHEN THE LABOR pains finally started, Raki sought out Lija. Lija walked beside her to the car, one arm around Raki's bulging waist, the other steadying her at the elbow. Lija drove. It was the first time they had been to the hospital since Randy's accident. Since the day Raki met Luke. Nobody mentioned it.

Lija helped Raki up the steps and answered the receptionist's questions. The nurses loaded Raki into a wheelchair. She begged for Lija to be allowed in the delivery room.

"Just to hold my hand," she argued with the nurses. "I'm scared."

Not allowed. A doctor, a nurse and the mother, nobody else. Those were the rules.

During the most intimate and intense hours of her whole life, she would be surrounded by strangers. Worse than strangers. People who knew her name and her family, but not who she really was. A doctor who put his stethoscope on her chest once a year. A nurse who had given her vaccination shots. Raki's thoughts dwindled as increasing pain medication blurred her brain. Voices swooned in and out of her consciousness. What were they talking about? Her moral reputation or some kid's oral report? Who was the father or how was the weather? She awoke with no memory of the delivery, no surprise. "They knock you out cold for that," Lija had warned her.

It took hours for her brain to unfog. Lights, blurry forms, an unfamiliar blanket against her skin. It all gradually coalesced back into reality. Visiting hours began. Lija and Dad crept into her room, as if not to wake a baby, but the baby was down the hall in the nursery. Raki sat up, smoothing her auburn waves, even wilder than usual because they had not been combed.

Her father beamed. "It's about time we got a girl!"

"She's beautiful, Sis." Lija took Raki's hand.

"She's tucked in and lined up in front of the window with all the others, like so many bars of soap in the grocery store." He was convincing as the proud grandpa.

Raki looked toward the door. "Is anybody else coming in?"

"They won't allow the kids, of course. James is at home, making sure the boys don't burn down the house," explained Lija.

When Raki couldn't sit up anymore, after her eyelids started drooping, her visitors crept out the way they had crept in. Lija returned the next morning, as soon as visiting hours allowed. Raki was drifting in and out of sleep.

"Are you doing OK?" Lija leaned over and stroked Raki's hand. "I bet you're still exhausted."

"I'm fine. Is anybody else here?" Raki yawned.

"Dad is watching the boys. James is at the nursery, checking out the baby."

"Josephine," said Raki.

"Josephine?"

"I'll call her Joey. Like the snowman, because that was such a happy day."

"That's a good name and a good memory."

"I got to feed her," said Raki. "She screamed bloody murder."

"Yeah, well, babies don't know what's good for them. She'll soon like it." Lija used the tone of a woman who knew what she was talking about.

"Mmmm. Can you go ask the nurses if you can bring her back in here? If they'll let you. I want to hold her. They don't let me do that enough."

"Sure. I'll come back with James and the baby—Josephine."

Lija pushed open the door. Fluorescent light from the hallway spilled into the room. A whoosh of antiseptic aroma swept in as the door swung shut. A few moments passed. Raki waited. She waited some more. What could be taking so long? She strained to hear. From far away came a muffled cry. The scuff of soft-soled nurse shoes. The click click of trolley wheels. Hushed voices.

It seemed like an hour before Lija returned. Maybe longer. James wasn't with her. Lija had the baby in her hands, not cradling it. Carrying her like a sack of garbage. She handed over the bundle to Raki.

The tip of Joey's nose and one finger poked out over the top of blanket. Two tiny feet dangled out the open bottom. Raki tucked the baby's feet into the cloth and pulled the covering away from the baby's mouth. "Hush, little baby, don't say a word," Raki sang softly.

"I sent James home." Lija's teeth gritted and her lips barely moved.

"I see."

"I'm sure you do."

Lija's soft features had been replaced with something hard and artificial, like melamine.

"I'm sure you must realize you can't come back to the farm."

So formal. Raki had never heard Lija speak like that. What the hell happened out there? She had heard nothing, but then she wouldn't. A hospital was like a church. Lija wouldn't raise her voice in a hospital, no matter what.

"We're a family, Lija," Raki said. Baby smelled of talcum powder. Raki buried her nose and eyes in the baby's blanket so Lija wouldn't see the tears welling up. "Families don't abandon each other."

"Sisters don't betray each other." Lija's voice was cold.

What about James's promise on the Ferris Wheel?

"You," continued Lija, her teeth still clenched, "cannot live with us any longer." Her voice was on fire, destructive, yet only as loud as a sizzle. Lija would never alarm the nurses or make a baby cry. How could so few decibels scream so loudly?

"You would put me on the street? With a newborn? I don't believe it."

"You should have made plans already," said Lija.

But she had made plans. Work at the bakery. Learn the ropes. Take classes. Tend the babies. Live on the farm. Everybody one big happy family. Like Luke's commune. Like James's promise.

Truth was the ingredient Raki had left out of the fantasy. Hope, like yeast, had fed and fattened her plan, but without the salt of truth, it had been guaranteed to collapse. Raki knew that, knew she'd been foolish, but couldn't admit it. Not yet.

"Take *our* house and *our* farm and *your* fine husband and *your* squalling kids. I don't need any of it! Fuck. You." Raki was not sure she had ever said that word when anyone could hear it, but if there was ever an occasion, this was it.

"When you find a place, I'll have your things brought over."

"I wouldn't dream of bothering you, Lija." The blanket had blotted her tears. She looked up. "Where's Dad?"

"He's, what shall I say, disappointed. He's on his way back to Arizona."

There would be no good-bye, no big, muscly hug. What had she expected? His accountant side avoided drama. His farmer side stood with the land. In the lowest audible tone Raki spat, "Send the nurse in. I hope Dad has a safe trip."

Lija's flat soles thudded across the tile to the door. She tried to slam it, but the swinging door just flapped in her wake.

The tears welled up again. One splatted Josephine's forehead. Raki wiped it away. Then she sniffed, set her chin and determined she would make no more.

What the hell am I going to do now?

A nurse came in. Her starched uniform, white stockings and smart little cap made her look like just the kind of capable professional qualified to figure things out. Raki talked. The nurse listened, nodding now and again.

"Of course. Of course. I know who to call," White Cap said.

A half hour later a blue-blazered woman walked in, carrying a clipboard. "County Social Services," she introduced herself, extending her hand.

"Nice to meet you." Raki shifted the baby in her arms to extend her hand. Another nurse hustled in, extracted Joey and hurried away.

"In a bit of a pickle, are you?"

Raki didn't know how to respond.

Blue Blazer barreled ahead. "I brought the forms so you can give it up for adoption."

It? What? Where had she gotten that idea? "No, ma'am. I do not want to give up my daughter. I just need a place for us to live."

"How old are you? What about your parents? Legal guardian?"

If Raki knew how to answer that, this lady wouldn't have needed to come in the first place. She said nothing.

"Cat got your tongue? Well, there's AFDC, welfare," the woman said, flipping the forms in triplicate on her clipboard. Raki caught a whiff of the rancid oil smell of carbon paper. It made her sick.

"If you qualify," continued Blue Blazer. "It'll take a few weeks to process." The metal clip snapped like a door hinge clapping shut.

"What about tonight? Tomorrow night?"

Blue Blazer looked at her doe-eyed, like a bad actress in an afternoon soap opera. "If you're not terminating your parental rights, there's nothing I can do that quickly. You should have planned ahead."

I did plan ahead! Raki wanted to scream and rip the official county pin right off the woman's prissy jacket. But then the lady might call her 'unfit,' and they'd take Joey away.

Raki faked calm. "I'll figure something out."

"I'll be back," the woman said, laying a stack of forms at the foot of the bed.

"That's not necessary."

"It's my job to decide what's necessary," she said, emphasizing the 'my' and patting her pile of papers. Then she exited, as officially as she had entered.

Raki kicked hard. Papers scattered across the floor. Now she faced hard truth. Her plan had been stupid. Why did that woman insist on coming back? To bring diapers and formula? Probably not. To take Josephine away? Maybe. Could she do that? Raki's twenty-first birthday was a lot of years away. Everybody was talking about the legal age going down to eighteen, but when? Not that it mattered, even that birthday was a few weeks away. Raki looked out the window, terrified. She had no idea where to go from here. Blood from her heart flooded her brain.

White Cap returned. Raki didn't hide her despair. "Perhaps your priest can help," the nurse suggested, glancing at the chart at the end of the bed.

"Oh, please, no." White Cap wasn't so smart at all. Raki hadn't been to Mass or Youth Group since she started showing. It had been over a year since her last confession.

"How about our chaplain on call? He's Lutheran."

Raki thought fast. "Only if he's already here. Don't call him in special." She couldn't risk waiting long enough for that social worker to come back.

The minister who walked in the door a minute later was a lot younger than Raki expected. Half the age of Father M. And very, very medium. Medium height, medium weight, medium brown hair cut to a medium length. Not boisterous like her father. Not determined like James. Not romantic and rumpled like Luke. Pressed trousers, plain black shirt and a round, white collar. Plus a cross.

White Cap introduced him. The Rev. Bergstrom.

He sat on the metal chair with the thick, green vinyl cushion. She told her story, as much as she was willing to tell. When she finished, he leaned back in the chair. The vinyl squawked. He looked thoughtful. Or maybe reverential.

"I wish I could help," he said. "Shall we pray on it?"

She folded her hands and lowered her head on cue. Her mind had other priorities. Will prayer keep Blue Blazer from stealing Josephine? She couldn't risk waiting to find out.

SAM COULD NOT believe the lame words he had heard coming out of his own mouth. *I wish I could help? Shall we pray on it?* He left the hospital haloed in failure.

AS SOON AS Josephine was back in her arms, Raki swaddled her up, slapped on her own clothes and slung her purse over one shoulder. She peeked into the hallway. Yes! There it was. A backdoor at the end of the corridor. No nurse's station between here and there. Coast clear.

SAM DROVE back to church, his brain thrumming. Who could he ask for advice? Senior Reverend Solquist? And megaphone his incompetence? Mom? Oh, for heaven's sake, an ordained minister can't go to mommy for help. Was there a book? As soon as he got to his office he would look on his shelf, even though he knew that was futile.

NO ALARMS WENT off when Raki carried Josephine into the sunshine. She hadn't heard any footsteps behind her, but there was no time to waste. Running was out of the question. She walked fast, aiming only to get out of sight.

The baby cried. She had no bottle and no formula. Raki's breasts ached. That would be the cheaper way to go. She found a bush to hide behind.

SAM PUT HIS ELBOWS on his desk, his head in his hands. What were the options? His apartment had a second bedroom, but that would look improper. Maybe the church basement. Who would have to give permission? He considered calling an emergency Church Council meeting. For an unwed mother? Who's not even a member?

JOEY FELL ASLEEP in Raki's arms. She pulled open her purse and counted the cash. Exactly $5.80, plus a checkbook showing a balance of $65, all that was left of last summer's bean walking money. A week in the Halcyon motel and they would be stone broke.

Camping seemed an option, but where? Underneath that tree? The most 'roughing it' Raki had ever done was a pop-up trailer.

SAM WRACKED his brain. *The woman at the well, Bathsheba, he who is without sin throw the first stone, think, think, think.* There had to be someplace, somebody. *Think, think.*

IN HER WHOLE LIFE, Raki had never heard of a person who didn't have a place to live, not counting Mary and Joseph in the Christmas story or the hoboes in the Depression. Joey woke up and started screaming. Raki wanted to scream, too.

Maybe the barn. They could hide there. Lija almost never went into the barn. James could sneak in a pillow and blanket. No, no. That was a terrible idea.

SAM'S EYES CAUGHT on the wilted dandelion in the Pebbles Flintstones jelly jar.

Holy Shit, that's it.

FRIENDS. Raki had friends. And what are friends for, anyway? She started walking to Jody's house.

SAM'S FINGERS FLIPPED through the thin phone book. *V, V, V, V.* He found the number, 782-8960. He dialed the seven. An eternity elapsed as the dial spun back to the beginning. Eight. More waiting. This was taking forever. Five more numbers to go. His heart pounded. Finally, zero, the longest spin of all.

RAKI KNOCKED on Jody's front door.

Her mom answered.

"I'm so sorry, Raki." Jody's mom had the same soap opera doe-eyes as the social worker. "Jody's sister and brother are both home for the summer and we have no extra room." She patted Joey's head. "I really wish we could help. I do." She waved her fingers in front of her nose. "Better change that diaper." She turned her back. The door clicked shut.

SAM WAITED for an answer. Ring, ring, ring. He tapped his fingers on his desk. A voice in his head reminded him to wait twelve rings before giving up. Twelve rings. Another eternity.

RAKI KNOCKED on Lynn's door. No answer.

"They're on vacation," a neighbor shouted from across the street. "Won't be back for two weeks."

SAM HEARD a click through the receiver. Finally.

"This is the Voll residence. How may I help you?"

RAKI WALKED AWAY from Lynn's front door. She needed a quiet, dark place to calm the baby, and to think. Think. She tried the door to Lynn's garage. Locked. Who the hell locks their garage door? She sat on the gravel in the alley.

SAM JUMPED IN his black Cutlass and raced back to the hospital. The young mother's room was empty. The bed clothes were rumpled. He checked the nursery. Baby Pederson's bassinette was empty. He inquired at the nurse's station. No, the Pederson girl had not checked out. Something told him not to say anything more.

RAKI ROCKED JOEY desperately. Nobody came down the alley, except for a woman emptying her trash into a metal bin, who didn't look their way. Joey's diaper really did stink. Even if she bought another diaper, how could she wash it?

SAM HAD NO particular plan for tracking them down. Finding a scared young mother with a newborn baby in a town a mile square could not be all that hard.

RAKI HAD NEVER seen a baby's face get so red. Like a maraschino cherry. But finally, finally, Joey fell sleep. Thank God.

SAM HAD BEEN up and down every street in Halcyon at least twice. For God's sake, they had to be somewhere!

RAKI GOT UP from the alley and began walking toward downtown.

SAM STOPPED at the Five & Dime, because they sold baby stuff.

"No girl with a baby in here today, Pastor."

RAKI'S BODY ACHED. Who knew seven pounds could be so heavy?

SAM CHECKED LEFT as he pulled away from the curb. Could it be? He squinted, then ripped around the corner.

RAKI'S KNEES BUCKLED. It was too soon for so much walking. She grasped Joey tighter. Brakes squealed behind her.

SAM LEANED OVER the passenger's seat and hollered out the window. "Get in! I found you a place!"

17

MARGARET WATCHED HERSELF hang the receiver back on its chrome hook. What had she just agreed to? Had she taken leave of her senses? Mike would surely think so. The suitcases from their honeymoon were still waiting to be unpacked.

She had not really considered the possibility that the pastor would take her up on her offer. Not to mention so soon. In hindsight, going to his church, telling her story in his office, had been a really dumb idea. Impetuous. Imprudent. Naïve. And she had been so earnest. Practically begging him to let her help somebody. No wonder he thought she was serious.

The story of this Raki girl (what an odd name) made her tear up. Bringing a total stranger and a newborn baby into the house? Crazy. She couldn't back out now. Good thing about that third floor. The girl and the baby could stay up there.

Her final words to the pastor echoed in her mind. "Well, OK then. Bring them over."

By the time Mike came home, the girl and the baby were already settling in.

"Her dad is back in Arizona and her sister threw her out, her and the baby," Margaret said.

"So, what is she doing here?" His question was so sensible.

"She's going to work here. Help keep up this big house. The whole third floor is servant's quarters. Seems we need at least one."

He objected. It seemed vaguely scandalous. How could they hope to be accepted into the community if they did something so high and mighty as employ live-in help?

"It's a really big house!"

"We shouldn't be making such a huge decision based on emotion."

She started getting mad. He was accusing her of being emotional. Her face heated up. Her heart was beating too fast. But wait, what else was it he just said? She imagined re-winding a tape and listening again. We. He had said 'we.'

"We can't say no," she countered, faking composure. "This is an emergency. Temporary. The girl and the pastor, they understand this is temporary." She put both arms around his waist and looked into his eyes, like an actress in a movie angling to get her way.

And so, Raki and Josephine moved into the Voll mansion. Just temporarily. Until they could figure out something else to do.

MARGARET PACED. She bit another fingernail. What would Mrs. Voll—was she supposed to call her Mother now? Mom?—going to think about an unwed mother in the house? Margaret looked down at her hands. Her nails were a mess, cuticles, too. Mrs. Voll—Mom—was due to arrive any minute. Her first visit since the wedding.

Of course Mrs. Voll had her own housekeeper, and probably her friends did, too, living in Edina and all, so maybe she wouldn't think a thing of it. But not live-in. What if Mrs. Voll thought Margaret was trying to one-up her? Or worse, that she was so incompetent she couldn't live without help even for the evenings? Maybe it would be better to emphasize the charity aspect. Or was that too goody-two-shoes? The bell chimed.

She grasped the brass door handle, inhaled, and swung it open with imitation aplomb. Mrs. Voll stood in the sunshine, holding a glossy department store shopping bag.

"Welcome."

Mrs. Voll held out the bag by its strings. Margaret took it, peeking inside. Avocado green tea towels and a harvest gold Trim Line telephone, to match the new refrigerator.

"So you will call more often," said Mrs. Voll. "Nobody has ever accused me of being subtle."

"I'll remind Mike." Margaret didn't want to be presumptuous.

"Oh, dear, no! He's got nothing to say worth the long-distance charges. Men. Bah. I want to talk to you."

Margaret motioned her inside, rattling the wooden hangers in the closet before remembering Mrs. Voll wore no jacket, chattering about who knows what, hoping to come off as light-hearted and not inane, although her main goal was to mask the sounds of Raki bustling about in the kitchen. It didn't work.

Mrs. Voll jerked her head to look over her shoulder. "Who is that?"

"Who do you mean?" asked Margaret, stalling. Incapable or bleeding heart, which way to go?

"The girl in the kitchen, of course."

"Oh, that's Rakella Pederson," stammered Margaret. "She's a local girl . . . helping us out . . . getting us settled in."

"And the wee one?"

"Josephine," said Raki, emerging from the kitchen, the baby in her arms. "If you two are all set, I'll just take her out on a carriage ride. To the playground."

"Sure, that's fine," insisted Margaret. "Get some fresh air."

Raki and Joey disappeared out the door. Margaret apologized to Mrs. Voll for not calling more often, not telling her about the live-in help. She explained the whole unwed mother thrown out in the street history. She described the accommodations. She glossed over the part about how and why the pastor made the connection.

"Win, win all around," said Mrs. Voll, settling down at the dining table. "But all these big, empty bedrooms and you stash that poor girl and her baby in the attic?"

"Not the attic," protested Margaret. "The third floor. The servant's quarters. It has a nice view."

"Of the cemetery. Good heavens. This is the Seventies. Give the girl a little dignity."

"Well, I will ask if she would like a different room."

"You should do that." Mrs. Voll lit a cigarette. "I can't help but be amused by the historical irony." She felt around for an ashtray.

How embarrassing to forget to put one out. Margaret leapt to the sideboard to rectify her oversight. Wait, what historical irony?

When Margaret didn't ask the question, Mrs. Voll barged ahead. "You do know, don't you, that this whole Voll family in America was founded on remarkably similar circumstances. Illegitimacy, scandal and all that." She flicked her ashes into the cut glass ash tray, a wedding gift, first time used.

"Really?" Margaret raised her eyebrows.

"Think about it." Mrs. Voll inhaled deeply, then let out a spiral of smoke. "Norwegian guy traipses across the ocean before anybody else and has lots of money enough to buy acres and acres of land. Which he never farms, just buys up and rents out. Clearly plenty wealthy, but he leaves behind a civilized European country to live here, which was, at the time, still is, Nowheresville for sure." She stubbed out her cigarette. "There really are more enticing varieties available these days." She winked dramatically.

Raki had set the table with an urn of coffee and plate of homemade cookies. Margaret passed the plate to Mrs. Voll, who waved her off. Her hand headed to the silver handle, but got waved off again.

"A place populated by Sioux living in teepees, dirty beaver catchers and a handful of daring farmers," Mrs. Voll continued. "No Dayton's department store, no Guthrie Theater. Good grief, not even any roads. And this . . . Aristocratic Ole . . . comes to this?" She swept her arm in front of the picture window, gesturing out to the prairie expanse. "Why might he do that?"

"Because he was thrown out by his family?" guessed Margaret.

"Exactly! Because the mother of his child was, the story goes, a servant. They have to let him 'do the right thing,' but geez, what a scandal, right? And of course they don't want to have to actually accept this scullery maid, or whatever she was, as part of their illustrious Nordic nobility, so they stuff bad son's pockets full of cash and load him and the pregnant girl on a boat. Ta da! Problem solved. But can you imagine—being pregnant on a nineteenth century ship? Poor girl must have spent the entire voyage leaning over the rail."

"Do you know this for sure? Have you researched this?"

"Well, not with academic rigor." She tapped a second cigarette from the pack. "No need for all that. Of course it's true. Every reputable family has a juicy past. If any of us didn't, we'd have to invent one so we'd have something fun to whisper about at cocktail parties. But the Volls, well, that juicy story is true."

IN THE DAYS after Mrs. Voll's visit, it was the mention of a cocktail party that got to rattling about Margaret's brain. Not that she wanted to repeat the Aristocratic Ole story over highballs, but because it would be a way to meet people.

She brought up the idea to Raki one morning. Her 'help' was wiping down the counters. "I keep hearing that the Halcyon Education Association needs a place to hold their annual back-to-school shindig. Would it be presumptuous for me to host? You know this town."

"Oh, my goodness, who cares?" Raki actually sounded excited. "There's not a soul in this town who wouldn't kill to get a glimpse inside this place. I don't know anybody who has been inside. Other than myself. They'll be knocking down the doors to get in."

"I don't want it to seem like I'm showing off."

"It's for a good cause. When I was little, my mom used to host the teachers' union parties. She taught English, like you. We lived in the first Voll house, you know. The one not as grand as this one."

"Would you mind helping?" asked Margaret. "Since you know what goes on at these affairs?"

"Of course. I was pretty young when we had those parties, and mostly stayed cooped up in my room. But I did help decorate and I kind of remember the sorts of food Mommy served. It'll be fun!"

"I'll make the offer."

"If they say yes, we'll buy some *Good Housekeeping* magazines. Get ideas."

THE ASSOCIATION ACCEPTED and the planning began.

"We'll set out the hors d'oeuvres on the sideboard and they can help themselves," Raki told her. "You can't have me walking around with a tray, no matter what you see on TV. That's just not done. Not here, anyway."

It wasn't done where Margaret came from, either. The preparations were making her twitchy. She was grateful for Raki's aplomb.

"Plus, these were my teachers in high school and they're probably all disappointed in me, so my presence would be a distraction. And Joey might be a bother. I'll stay up in my room, just like when I was a little girl."

"I feel bad about that."

"Don't. I'm going to bake rolls from scratch. You know how I like that."

"What about entertainment?"

"Well, you could just turn on the hi-fi. But you know what would be fun? Live music. We should call that Rev. Bergstrom. I bet he knows people."

"Not church music."

"You think those musicians aren't dying to play something that's not a hymn? For an audience not waking up from a Sunday morning nap? Call him."

AND SO, THREE weeks later, a wind quartet turned out, armed with sheet music from the *Peer Gynt Suite*, always a crowd pleaser for the Norwegian set. Teachers in their better than Sunday best tried not to be too obvious about checking out the mystery mansion. The librarian ran her hands over Margaret's gold embossed set of F. Scott Fitzgerald, a graduation gift; the shop teacher ogled the door and window trim; the art teacher lifted a piece of bric-a-brac and turned it over. After a few minutes of marveling, everyone set to drinking.

The last guest came decked out in a black dress and purple satin jacket, a Nikon and flash strobe slung around her neck. Margaret opened the door for this stranger. Did the high school offer a photography class?

"I'm sorry if I'm crashing your party, dear," the woman

apologized. "I'm Miss Dolores Richter, publisher of the *Halcyon Times*. The president of your union insisted I come. To take pictures. He said you wouldn't mind."

"Not at all," said Margaret, wondering if she actually did mind.

"Normally my reporters take the photos and so on. But I think your union president feared my young journalists could not be trusted to clean up sufficiently. He was very persistent."

"It's quite all right. Welcome."

Margaret noticed barely half a dozen flashes before the woman stashed the bulky camera, took a glass of Bordeaux from Mike, who was playing bartender for the night, and wandered into the clutch of teachers Margaret was entertaining.

"Any good new books?" asked the publisher of the librarian. Margaret nodded when the librarian recommended *The Optimist's Daughter* by Eudora Welty over that tripe, *Jonathan Livingston Seagull*. The publisher soon turned left to the man, "I don't believe we've met."

"Our high school art teacher. New, like me," said Margaret, embarrassed that she had been so inept at introductions.

"Call me R.C.," he offered. "Like the cola." He lifted his glass. "Bourbon and R.C.! My drink!"

Margaret worried the man may have had a few ahead of time.

"Stands for Richard Claude. Middle name after my father. God rest his soul."

"So sorry for your loss."

"No loss. He's probably right now hanging out with the guy in the red suit, horns and long tail. Shot in the head when I was a boy. While on a *business trip*." He winked lewdly.

"Oh, my." Margaret and the librarian said it in unison.

Miss Richter's heel seemed to give out. Wine splashed on her hand. Margaret reached to steady her.

"Woman's pistol," R.C. slurred. "Curlicued ivory handle. Very pretty. Police assumed he was murdered at first. By one of his . . . *ladies*." He raised his drink in clumsy salute. "Had a different *lady* . . ." His fingers formed clumsy quotation marks. Margaret worried he'd spill his bourbon. "In every town. But it turned out he bought that prissy gun himself. Gawd." He swilled the last of his drink.

"My heavens, what a story," said the librarian.

"Ruled suicide. Relief for my mom."

Miss Richter's hands trembled. She seemed not to notice the red wine dripping from her hand. Margaret grabbed a napkin and handed it to her.

"Oh, my, I didn't mean to ruin your carpet," she cried, suddenly noticing the mess. "I'll clean it up."

"Don't worry about it. Are you OK?"

"Just woozy." The publisher handed off her glass, grabbing at her chest.

"She's having a heart attack!" blurted the drunken art teacher, too loudly. Other guests began gathering round. The music sputtered as the shouting began.

Miss Richter took a step back, her heel catching on the carpet fibers. She stumbled. "I need to sit down."

"Who's your doctor?" demanded the biology teacher.

"No, no doctor!" pleaded Miss Richter, tugging on Margaret's arm. "I'm so embarrassed," she whispered. "My girdle is a little too tight. That's all."

Margaret took her by the elbow. "Did the art teacher upset you? He seems a little, um, inebriated," she whispered.

"Absolutely not. Just find me a quiet corner. Don't let me spoil your party. I'll be fine."

Mike poured Miss Richter a glass of water and Margaret escorted her to the den. Then she called on Raki to watch over the woman and motioned the musicians to strike up again. Eventually the teachers exhausted their speculations on the publisher's health condition and went back to discussing contract negotiations.

Margaret sneaked into the den to check on her guest. Miss Richter and Raki and the baby were laughing. Everything seemed all right. "You may be having more fun in here than they are out there."

"Your young woman helped me out of my girdle and has been trying to convince me to give it up entirely. She's being wonderfully ridiculous!"

"It's not ridiculous, Miss Richter. It's the Seventies. No need to wear a hair shirt anymore. Or a girdle, especially one with old-fashioned stays."

"Well, I need it to hide my sins. Too many cookies for lunch." Miss Richter patted her own tummy.

AFTER MISS RICHTER and the other guests had driven themselves away, Margaret and Raki collected the dirty plates and napkins and examined the damage.

"I don't think the stain on the carpet is going to come out," said Raki.

"Just move the furniture and put a rug on top of it."

A CARPET CLEANING truck arrived the next day, courtesy of Miss Richter, along with a note of apology and a bouquet of flowers. Red roses, lavender and baby's breath.

18

THE *MINNEAPOLIS TRIBUNE* landed outside the back door with a smack. The privileges of the wealthy, thought Raki. On the farm, they had to go out to the cubby below the mailbox to get it. She kicked herself for being sour-hearted. The privilege was hers, too, now, since she brought it in every morning.

It was hard to stay grateful, squirrelled away in this big house, over a year now, homesick just a mile from home, and still no idea how to make a future for herself and Joey. It was supposed to be just temporary, but temporary was lasting a long time. She didn't know what to do. Taking care of this big house, a growing toddler underfoot. When did she have time to think?

Just three steps out the back door to retrieve the newspaper and sweat was already dripping. The August heat and humidity hadn't let up all night. Central air was another nice perk, but a person couldn't stay cooped up all the time. She took Joey in the stroller every day, but today, the thought of another draggletailed walk down the driveway and over to the playground made her go limp.

Back inside she spread the paper on the kitchen table. Her damp hands came away smudged black with ink. Must have come from the front-page photo, a thick row of dark pines on the shores of a lake 'up north.' A trip to the lake, that would be just the thing. Margaret would be readying her classroom for the First Day of School, so she would be out of the house. Raki washed the ink off her hands with cool water from the tap. It would be wonderful to just get neck deep in a lake, let the ripples lap at her chin.

Margaret came into the kitchen, already outfitted in pressed blouse, schoolteacher skirt and nylons. Raki handed her a cup of coffee. "Can I take one of your cars to the lake? I'm caught up with all my work." That wasn't exactly true, because there was always something that could be scrubbed or baked or some weeds to pull or books to dust. Margaret nodded, but Raki saw disappointment in her eyes. Who was the lucky one today?

Just one day, though. College, buy a bakery, be a business woman, own delivery trucks. Raki's dream had molded like old bread. There had to be something other than mansion housekeeping for her life. She vowed to spend her time at the lake mulling over a plan for the future. She had hidden long enough.

When Mike joined Margaret in sharing the newspaper and drinking coffee, Raki threw on her black one-piece and covered it with shorts and a t-shirt. She tossed a couple beach towels and a bottle of suntan lotion into a cloth bag, plus diapers, a bottle and a library book.

The back-door slammed. Once. Twice. Two car engines revved. Raki picked up Joey, ran down the back stairs, swept the toast crumbs from the table, wiped the counters and rinsed the cups. Done.

SHE DROVE PAST two signs pointing toward public beaches on other corn-fringed lakes before turning onto the back road to Green Lake. She couldn't risk running into Lija and her kids. They never came to this beach. Maybe didn't even know about it. Too far away. It attracted people from other towns. She parked.

Green Lake was fringed with field corn rather than the jack pine in the *Tribune*'s 'up north' photo, but at the end of August the corn was pretty tall. Tree-like, if you had a really good imagination. The scent of algae and fish intermingled with a remote wafting of manure. No matter, she had brought plenty of coconut oil, the smell of relaxation.

She pulled out supplies and found a patch of sandy grass beneath a cottonwood tree. Once her plot was homesteaded, she carried Joey down to the water. The baby sat with her legs straight out, green water sneaking beneath her tubby thighs, retreating, then creeping back. Over and over. Raki backed herself into the water until she was chin deep, her eyes on Joey. When Joey began toddling to deeper water, Raki scooped her to safety. No rest for the wicked. Raki built a sand castle. Joey whacked it down. She poured a handful of lake water over Joey's blonde hair, to cool her down. Joey's shoulders started turning a little pink, so she carried her back to the shade of the cottonwood. The baby fell asleep on a towel.

If Joey napped long enough, there'd be time to read a couple chapters of Jacqueline Susann's *Once Is Enough*, but the handles of the beach bag were pinned beneath Joey's out flung little arms. Not worth the risk. So Raki sat up, drew her knees to her chest and people-watched.

School age boys with sunken chests chased each other, their twiggy arms flapping like chickens. Little girls picked their way out into the water, arms daintily out to their sides, squealing when the cold hit their tummies. Teenagers with strong swimming skills stroked out to the wooden raft, bobbing thirty feet past the beach boundary rope. They dove and cannonballed into the deep water, too deep for their smaller siblings. They shrieked insults and curse words. Free.

That was her own life, not long ago. Now she was an unwed mother, a maid, without family, invisible. No use brooding, but something had to change.

She brushed the sand from between her toes, sighed and leaned back on her elbows. A few yards in front of her sat a youngish man, not a teenager, alone, on a white towel. Something about him looked familiar. She held one hand over her eyes and squinted. Fit enough, but not athletic, straight spine, plain black swim trunks, hair unfashionably short, but scruffy along the neck, like he had missed a couple barber appointments. Night shift? Unemployed? He turned his body half around to grab the can of Bubble-Up planted in the sand behind him. *Oh! That's who!*

She approached from behind. "Afraid the clerical collar would leave funny tan lines?"

He started, set his book and his can back down, and looked up, virtually dumbstruck. "Uhhh. Hello."

"So, Rev. Bergstrom, what are you doing here?"

"Rakella Pederson, I could ask the same thing of you."

She had already baked up a teasing line. "This is where I come when the summer heat feels like too much of a 'foretaste of things to come.'"

"Wow." He didn't laugh, which was disappointing, but it was a pretty macabre joke. "That's heavy. I'm just enjoying the beach."

"I was kidding. Maybe." She pointed at his book. "What are you reading? Something by Martin Luther?"

He hid the cover with his hand and slid it into his bag before she could read the title, but not before she recognized the purple color. The same bestseller trapped in her beach bag. Pretty racy for a pastor. Then he turned off his transistor radio. Pink Floyd, she was pretty sure.

"No theology on my day off."

"Obviously." She squatted down next to his towel, an arms-length away because it seemed inappropriate to get too near a minister wearing a bathing suit. "Why here? You must have passed at least two lakes on your way. With the oil embargo and gas prices so high, I would think a poor minister would want to save a few cents and go someplace closer to home."

"And you aren't interested in saving gas?"

"Heavens, no. My employer pays for my gas, and, as you know, my employer does not really expect me to scrimp too much. Unlike yours."

"I'm less worried about the cost of gas and more concerned about the fact that I can't really relax and enjoy the beach when there are a lot of people around who know who I am."

"Are you girl watching, Rev. Bergstrom?"

"Are you boy watching, Rakella Pederson?"

"I asked you first, and maybe, yes, I was boy watching, until I figured out it was you. Then I had to say a quick prayer for forgiveness."

"You did not." He laughed.

"Well, I probably should now, for lying."

"Yes, I think that would be appropriate." She heard a smile in his voice.

Raki looked out over the swimmers, then over at Joey. Still asleep. "You know what I think? I think we are both at this beach for the same reason, which is the opposite reason."

"Oh?"

"I do not want people I know to see me at the beach because my life is so scandalous. You do not want people to see you at the beach because your life is so . . . righteous."

"I don't think you're so scandalous."

"Well, there you go. I don't think you are all that righteous. You see, our oppositeness makes us the same. We're both wearing black swimsuits, too, another irony, don't you think?"

"Compared to all the little bikinis I see here, your suit is quite modest. More proof you aren't so scandalous."

"So, you *are* girl watching!" She laughed. "You haven't seen the back of it!" She twisted her body around. The black stretch fabric scooped deep and wide down her back, plunging all the way to the rounds of her buttocks. "Quite sophisticated, isn't it? Margaret bought it for herself at Dayton's in Southdale, but Mike didn't like it so she gave it to me. If Margaret were wearing it, it would be pretty racy in the front, too, if you know what I mean."

"I'm too righteous to have any idea what you mean."

"You don't fool me, Rev. Bergstrom. I don't go to your church."

"Since you don't go to my church, you should call me Sam."

"That's a good idea. I will save four syllables every time I say your name. More efficient."

He nodded. The silence felt awkward.

"Would you keep an eye on Joey for a minute? I'm dying of heat stroke." She jumped up without waiting for an answer.

ॐ

THE REV. BERGSTROM watched Raki dash toward the boat dock, running its length and cannonballing off the end. She returned within a minute.

"Sam, would you like a frozen Milky Way on a stick?" Her red hair was dripping on his towel. "I'll pop over to the snack bar and get us a couple."

Instinct made him reach for his wallet, which of course wasn't there. He felt silly, reaching for a wallet when he was wearing swim trunks. It was bound to be empty, anyway. "No, thanks," he said.

"Well, I'll feel all gluttonous and sinful if I eat alone. So I'll buy two and tempt you mercilessly." She was teasing him, but he didn't mind too much. She got up and rummaged about in her bag. A pacifier and a rattle fell out.

"Found a quarter. That'll do it."

He waited until Raki started walking toward the snack bar before he adjusted his posture for a better view. He watched until a grandfather-aged man got in line behind her. He remembered he was supposed to be minding the baby. She was still asleep.

"Here ya go," said Raki, handing him the treat. Of course he had to accept.

He'd never had a frozen candy bar on a stick. She sucked it like a popsicle, licking the sides. He took a taste. Silky sweet, melting against his taste buds.

A few hours later, on his drive back to Halcyon, he vowed to redouble his efforts to convince his girlfriend Claire to marry him. This was getting ridiculous.

CLAIRE JOHANNSEN and Sam Bergstrom had dated off and on since he was in the eighth grade and she in the seventh. They did all the usual things – movies, roller-skating, first kiss, prom. He had never given much thought to the idea that they would marry. It was inevitable, the logical next step. High school, college, seminary, marriage. Actually, he had assumed the last two would be in the other order, but Claire seemed to need more time. She had entered seminary a couple years after he did, one of the first women. He encouraged her. They would be a team.

Claire wouldn't play the organ, true, but she played the guitar. Sensuously. He loved watching her fingers press the strings, strum over the sound hole, caress the curve of the body. The image in his mind led his thoughts astray. Her willingness to wait was maddening, to say the least.

Patience, he counseled himself. He rationalized her marital disinterest the same way he explained away the people who fell asleep during his sermons. This overwhelmed female seminarian was so busy with Greek and Hebrew and Ministerial Leadership, of course she had no time to come down and visit him. Just as the overworked farmer was so exhausted from plowing and milking and slopping that of course he was going to need a snooze. Completely understandable.

Still, even as he saved himself for Claire, the stiff white collar he wore most of the time worked like a force field. New friendships were hard to form. Somehow this Rakella seemed less put off by it. Maybe because she wasn't Lutheran. He rather liked running into her. Some might consider their conversation (flirting, was it?) disloyal to Claire, but Raki was, after all, his 'project.' He had found her and Joey a home and provided Margaret with a means to make atonement. All excellent pastoral work. He felt good about how that worked out.

Of course, as with all projects, follow-up would be prudent. Why hadn't he thought of that before? He had seen the two of them at the public playground. That seemed a safe place to meet up. After the beach encounter, he began choosing it as a lunch spot. For the fresh air.

"ENJOY PICNICS?" Sam disguised his annoyance as best he could as he settled down at the splintered picnic table. Why was that oddball newspaper lady here every time? Raki was holding Joey steady on the springy horse, out of earshot.

"I enjoy dining *al fresco*," answered Miss Richter. "A word my friend taught me when she worked in France." He detected a tiny catch of breath. Miss Richter looked away. "I mean, when she and I worked in France. Together. After the War. World War II." Before he could answer she changed the subject. "We need a young voice for our 'Christianity Corner.' Those old pastors are so stodgy. Interested?"

"Me? Doesn't your generation think my generation is too disrespectful, flouting traditional values? Long hair and miniskirts in church and so on."

She looked him up and down. "You wear neither long hair, nor miniskirts, as far as I know."

He hoped he wasn't blushing. He'd set himself up for that, what an idiot.

"Anyway, don't generalize, Reverend," she continued, "I am not inclined to sugarcoat the past. These older women who cluck at miniskirts, many of them were flappers back in their day. And the crew cuts who hate long-haired draft dodgers? Some of them would have done the same thing if the war hadn't erupted during the depression, when none of them had money for a train ticket. Judge not, and so on, right Reverend?"

He smiled. She wasn't *that* annoying.

"You can't disagree with me. It's in your Bible."

Joey ran up. Miss Richter gave the little girl a banana, handing it over with as much ceremony as the Pulitzer Prize.

Raki sat down next to Sam. "I suppose I should do something about Joey," she said.

"Like what?"

"Get her baptized of course."

Miss Richter smoothed her black skirt, adjusted her amethyst brooch. "This is a discussion for which I am not qualified to participate." She took Joey to the swings, set her on a seat and pushed gently.

"There are things to discuss, first." This was, in fact, turning out to be good follow-up for his project.

"OK, well, let's discuss it now and we can do it next Sunday. I'm not working."

"Not so quick. Preparing for baptism takes a number of meetings." In this case, maybe more than the average, her being Catholic and all. He was looking forward to it.

"Let's start tomorrow." She made a face at his Wonder Bread and bologna sandwich. "Jesus would be appalled at what passes for bread these days. I'll bring a loaf of real stuff."

FOUR O'CLOCK the next afternoon, Raki showed up at his office with a loaf of wheat bread. Joey entertained herself beneath his desk. After that, they began meeting once a week. Raki made a good enough show of listening to Protestant theology, but they spent more time trading funny stories. He told her about the confirmation class pilfering communion wine. She told him about the roach clip in the guest room.

After every meeting, Sam called Claire. The conversations got briefer and briefer. Sometimes Claire didn't answer. Or begged off immediately with a promise to call him back, which she almost never did.

"I've got the 'grace not works' thing nailed down pretty well now," said Raki after a half dozen meetings. "What are we waiting for?" And so they set a date.

It was time to set a date with Claire, too. If she would not speak on the phone or come to visit him or invite him up there, he would drive to her, uninvited.

"OH! SAMMY! It's been too long!" Claire flung her arms around him. "Come in, sit, I'll grab you a coffee. You must be tired after the long drive."

The apartment was cluttered, books and Bibles scattered upon every surface. He chose the Naugahyde recliner, scooping up the *Good News for Modern Man* paraphrase and the *Mastering Biblical Greek* lying together, incongruously. Clouds of stuffing puffed out of the upholstery, like Sunday School pictures of heaven. Claire returned with a cup of barely brown coffee.

"Nice to hear somebody call me 'Sammy' again." He took the cup from Claire's hand. "Nobody in Halcyon calls me that."

"I don't suppose they do, Reverend." She bowed, her hands steepled.

"No need for mocking."

"How are things down there amongst the cows and cornfields?" she asked, pushing aside a raggedy spiral notebook as she settled onto the sofa.

"As fine as ever. The pews are stuffed but the offerings are sparse. Graduate, get ordained and you'll find out."

"If I'm lucky."

"No luck necessary. Any congregation would be pleased to extend a call to you."

"Not true." She wagged a finger at him. "I'm a pioneer and

pioneers have a hard row to hoe, as they say down where you are."

"It's been a couple years since we started ordaining women; people are used to it."

"It'll be decades before they're used to it."

"I hope not." He took a sip; her coffee was both scalding and bitter. "No offense, Claire, but this stuff is church lady bad."

"I'm economizing."

Enough small talk. "How long have we known each other?"

"Why the rhetorical question?" Her eyes narrowed.

"I just thought how nice it is to know a girl long enough, and well enough, that you can insult her coffee and she just shrugs it off."

"I'm not sure we have known each other long enough for that."

She hadn't answered his question.

"All right. I'll answer my own question. We have known each other for twelve years. We met at swimming lessons."

"No, Sammy!" she exclaimed. "We met on the merry-go-round. I puked on your shoes."

"You're spoiling this."

"Spoiling what?" She leaned back, folding her arms over her chest, pulling her feet up under the folds of a very long skirt. Was she taking fashion cues from *The Sound of Music*?

"We memorized the *Small Catechism* together. We life guarded together at bible camp," he continued.

"We sneaked off together to that dance after Good Friday service. Got drunk."

He laughed at the memory. "I miss you, Claire. The small town, it's lonely."

"How so?"

"I have nobody to talk to," he lied.

"Talk? That's what you want?"

"Claire, you were my first kiss."

"Mine, too."

"And the only girl I ever wanted to kiss," he lied again. "I want us to be together always."

"Don't you dare get down on one knee. Because the answer to your question is no."

This was not going as planned. "I haven't asked a question."

"Reverend, you made an oblique reference that prophesies a future that is not going to happen."

"Why not? We love each other. We can help each other." What was the matter with her? They could be a perfect team. Helpmeets.

"No, I can help you. You cannot help me." Claire's words sounded rehearsed. Had she practiced this rejection?

"Of course I can help you," he insisted. "We're a team."

"No, we are not a team. It's not Luther League softball, for heaven's sake."

He wanted to pick out a sparkly diamond, not talk softball diamonds. How had this gone so wrong?

"A few minutes ago you told me any congregation would be happy to call me. But if I'm tied to you? You're in little Halcyon, where there are rarely openings for any pastor, much less a lady pastor. I get a call fifty miles away? A hundred miles? How would that work?"

"We could work together." He struggled to find a word other than 'team.' "A partnership."

"Some of the other seminarians are dating each other. They talk about being co-pastors, a prepackaged senior/associate kind of deal. But the husband will always be the senior and his wife the associate. Women can wear the robes and break the bread, but we're not equal and won't be for a long time. I'm just stating truth."

"Truth changes."

"Not fast enough. I'm not pessimistic, just clear-eyed. You know what else my clear eyes show me? That you, Mr. Romantic, are actually here because you think marriage will solve your problems—loneliness and the fact that being single is a drag on your career."

"It's a calling, not a career."

"Good answer!" She was mocking again. "But you don't deny it." She flung her arms wide and announced in an overly-hearty voice,

"Come on, let's talk about something other than, you know, 'us.' Ask me about my extracurricular activities."

"OK." Stained glass? Calligraphy? Canoeing? That might be helpful for youth ministry. "What activities?"

"I'm working for an abortion provider."

That he had not expected. He put on his almost-poker face, blank except for the raise of one eyebrow, the look he used whenever one of his parishioners said something heretical. He had a lot of practice with it.

"I shocked you!" Her enthusiasm was unseemly.

"What the hell, Claire?" Shock did not begin to describe it. "You think marrying me will hurt your prospects, but wait until some call committee gets wind of this. You won't get a job polishing the brassware."

"For God's sake," she said.

He flinched.

"I mean that literally, not blasphemously. For God's sake, this is not about me and certainly not my . . . career."

First she cares about her career, then she doesn't. She confused him. Her tone was condescending. That made him mad. He had only been speaking openly and honestly, like a friend does.

"And you know," she continued, "that our church's official position supports women's rights in this."

"But that doesn't mean a congregation wants their pastor, you know, directly *involved*."

"It's not like I'm holding the instruments."

"You know that's not what I meant. Many people in the pews, they're not really comfortable with it."

"It's not about being *comfortable*." She spat the word. "It's about *love*, loving the *women*. It's about *caring* what happens to them and their lives and their families, their other children."

He fumed. She was simply refusing to understand.

"Plus, it's legal now."

The fumes exploded. "Never mind legality! What the hell are you thinking?"

"These women are desperate. Rape. Family brutality. Destitution. Drug addiction." Her voice was calm, practiced.

"Yeah, the world is a sorry, sinful place." He didn't like the snide way that came out. If this visit was to be successful, he had to act nice. He took a deep breath. "There are other ways to help."

"You haven't heard their stories. I have, and my heart gets ripped out and bleeds all over the place. This is my calling."

"What about this doctor? Who are you associating with?"

"Doctor believes women are capable of making moral decisions. She provides the service they and their God-given conscience have chosen when there are no good choices available. Doctor does not try to talk them out of it if they want one, but some women don't really want one. Those women she sends to me."

Claire was lecturing, and he still didn't understand. "Why go to an abortionist if you don't want one?"

"The husband or boyfriend insists. Or maybe her family has thrown her out."

He thought about Raki and Joey and Margaret and Margaret's dead sister and Mike and the big Voll mansion and the family money and how that story might have turned out differently.

"I found a home for a girl who was thrown out by her family."

"Goody for you. One?"

"Well, yes, just the one." She made his pastoring seem so . . . puny. "So what do you do?"

"If a woman wants to carry to term and give her baby up for adoption, who pays for the delivery? Laws written to prevent the buying and selling of babies, well-intentioned as they are, prohibit payments to the mother. That's where I come in. I locate a foster home, if she's been thrown out, and then a hospital that will deliver her for free, or a reduced rate."

"But this doctor, she performs abortions."

"Sometimes, yes."

"Why involve seminarians?"

"She used to work with ordained pastors, too, of several denominations. Before *Roe v. Wade* there used to be this 'underground railroad' kind of thing. A pregnant woman would call a hotline and be referred to a pastor. For counseling. If appropriate, he would give her the name of a safe provider."

"I'm not sure that would have been legal."

"Pastoral counseling is privileged. But legality was irrelevant; they were bound to a higher moral law. You had no idea, did you?"

"Um, no."

"Since *Roe*, the Clergy Consultation Service changed mission, but Doctor still appreciates working with us religious types."

"Get a job with Social Services arranging for foster homes and adoptions. Or, at some hospital foundation. Something less controversial." Problem solved. Sam was pleased to offer such a practical solution.

"Christ didn't behave the safe, non-controversial way!" Claire's voice did not sound pleased. "He was a table flipper! Mary Magdalene, Priscilla and Dorcas from the epistles, these women were radicals. I'm radical for women and radical for God."

"You can be radical . . . in other ways."

"I'm *called* to this." She lowered her voice. "But now can you see that marrying me wouldn't be the answer to your prayers that you thought it would be?"

"That's cruel. And unfair. Think about my suggestion."

"You think I haven't thought about it already? For years? My answer is no."

Only a tiny dredge of coffee remained in his cup. It was cold and bitter, but he swigged it down anyway. He handed her the empty cup before heading toward the door.

"Sorry for puking on your shoes again," said Claire.

"May the Lord be with you."

"And also with you."

The door clicked shut. He stood in the hallway, hearing an old Beatles song blasting from some neighbor's stereo: 'Here I stand, head in hand.' He turned his face to the wall.

Now what? He had a ninety-minute drive ahead of him to think. To fume.

WHAT THE HELL? Sam slammed on his brakes. His black Cutlass lurched to a standstill. An immoveable clog of steel trapped him on the freeway. Accident ahead. *Ah, geez, this is all I need.* He reached over to his glove box for a map. Flinging open the folds, he spread it over the steering wheel. The crackle of the paper further grated his annoyance. *I'll never get this damn thing back together right. Like my life.* His fingers searched for an escape exit. No hope. He prayed for a traffic angel to fly him over it. He had to get back for a council meeting.

Come on, God. Then, out loud, "Forgive me, but goddamn this shit." He tossed the map on the floor and pounded the steering wheel. Was there a sermon idea here? Israelites in the desert? Anxious to get home to the Promised Land and stuck until the Lord lets them go? Not a topic that would keep 'em coming back for more.

When he left Claire's apartment he still had a twenty-minute cushion. That was now shot. *Shot. To. Hell.* The cars finally broke free and his speedometer hit sixty-five. Another hour to fume.

SAM BURST THROUGH the door to the council meeting room.

"Welcome, Rev. Bergstrom." Six men raised their coffee cups as if in a toast.

"Traffic in the Cities was terrible," he complained, yanking out a chair for himself.

"You're right on time, and Mrs. Anderson isn't here yet." The council president aimed an indulgent smile at him.

Mrs. Anderson. Not his favorite among God's beloved. It was just like her to make people wait. He smiled to cover his thoughts. "I'm sure she'll be here soon." He hoped she wouldn't be.

When Mrs. Anderson arrived five minutes late, the Christian men were eager to forgive. She had clearly been a beauty in her day, which was a long time gone, but apparently only yesterday to the middle-aged council members fawning over her, admiring the 'twin gazelles' of Song of Solomon fame. What Sam saw were her eyes. The color of lake water. Frozen over. Sam sighed. Forget Solomon, what he really needed was the patience of Job.

Business did not commence until Mrs. Anderson was comfortably seated and presented with coffee. Then Council delved into the spelling anomalies and controversial use of grammar in last month's minutes, before voting unanimously to accept them as written. Then the treasurer's numbers got teased apart, reassembled, and accepted unanimously. This was followed by a procession of reports on the Ladies' Soap for Africa project, new candle holders, and complaints about the heaving sidewalk the city still hadn't been out to fix.

The tedium grated. Finally, Council President reached the last item on the agenda: Other.

"Just wanted you to all know that we're baptizing the Pederson child in a couple weeks," said the Rev. Bergstrom, eager to be done with this meeting.

"Are we all comfortable with that?" Mrs. Anderson's tone was sweet as Cyclamate, with the same bad aftertaste.

A couple council members, probably as eager to get home as Rev. Bergstrom, tried not to scowl.

"It's not a matter of comfort. The Reverend was only providing information," pronounced Council President.

Mrs. Anderson continued anyway. "Well, I for one do think this is an important matter. What is our policy on baptizing babies that are . . . illegitimate?"

"All babies are God's children," explained Senior Reverend Solquist, "welcomed into the body of Christ in baptism."

"Of course, of course," said Mrs. Anderson. "But we should consider doing such privately, so as not to appear to be . . . condoning . . . licentious behavior. Really, with The Pill and now legal abortions and illegitimate births . . . somebody has to make a stand." She sat back and crossed her arms beneath the twin gazelles. Then, by way of exclamation point, "Girls these days."

Sam never regretted what he said next, although he knew he should have. He pulled words from his mouth like a sword from its hilt, galloping heedlessly like a knight defending his fair maiden. Raki? A fair maiden? Why not?

"Girls *these days?*" He paused just long enough for his tone to sink in. "I'm pretty sure Solomon was a bastard child. Seeing as how Mary was betrothed to Joseph and not the Holy Spirit, Jesus himself was a bastard child. That's the word we're all really thinking now, isn't it? Illegitimate, that's just bastard with extra syllables."

"Jesus was God's own son," interjected Council President, his tone conciliatory, "King Solomon, well, I don't know about him."

"My goodness," said Mrs. Anderson. "I'm not talking about King Solomon. I'm talking about proper standards for our youth. I know the world is changing. I'm no stick-in-the-mud. Our own denomination is ordaining women. I never said a word against it, even though I, for one, have little interest in hearing some squeaky voice preach at me."

That she was preaching at them in a woman's octave was an irony lost.

Harking back to high school English class, Rev. Bergstrom dredged up the only literary quote he ever put to memory, "Conventionality is not morality," he said softly. "Self-righteousness is not religion."

"Is that Proverbs?" asked Council President.

"Charlotte Bronte, from the introduction to *Jane Eyre*."

"What is a *man*, like you, doing reading *Jane Eyre*?" Mrs. Anderson stressed 'man' a decibel louder than necessary.

Senior Rev. Solquist shook his head, as if to rid himself of gnats. "I've let this discussion go astray. Our youth are an important discussion for another day. Mrs. Anderson, we look forward to suggestions as to how to instill good morals in our young people. In the meantime, it's been rather a long meeting. Shall we move to adjourn?"

The motion, second and vote were accomplished at miraculous speed.

After Council departed, Rev. Solquist said, "Now what? Sam, you may be theologically correct, and I did a poor job of controlling the meeting. Still, you know this is going to end badly."

"I'm sure I will regret this. But not yet." He never did.

19

PASTOR BERGSTROM WALKED to the pulpit, sweating under his white robe. He sometimes fantasized about wearing nothing underneath but a collar, swim trunks and black socks. The building had no air conditioning. A high ceiling collected the hottest air over their heads. In the winter that high ceiling burdened the budget, now that energy was so expensive.

What he was about to say would have made him sweat regardless, even if it had been forty below. "The Holy Gospel according to St. Matthew, the thirteenth chapter."

The organ surged. The congregation stood to intone the Gospel verse, their noses pointed down. Never mind that most of them had sung these five words thousands of times, they always looked down at the hymnal.

He read from the pulpit:

> "The kingdom of heaven may be compared to a man who sowed good seed in his field; but while men were sleeping, his enemy came and sowed weeds among the wheat, and went away. So when the plants came up and bore grain, then the

weeds appeared also. And the servants of the householder came and said to him, 'Sir, did you not sow good seed in your field? How then has it weeds?' He said to them, 'An enemy has done this.' The servants said to him, 'Then do you want us to go and gather them?' But he said, 'No; lest in gathering the weeds you root up the wheat along with them. Let both grow together until the harvest; and at harvest time I will tell the reapers, Gather the weeds first and bind them in bundles to be burned, but gather the wheat into my barn.'"

The organ surged again, the congregation intoned more liturgy.

"Please be seated," he said, waiting for a moment while the ladies tugged their skirts and shushed their kids. The suited men rested their arms over the backs of the pews. A few loosened their ties.

"Where do I start with all the things wrong with this parable?" he began, secretly hoping that more than the usual number would fall asleep. He liked having a job and figured he was about to get himself fired. If they were paying attention.

"I drive throughout this county and admire the beautiful fields. They produce food to feed the hungry, which is wonderful. They are beautiful. Straight rows, uniform, rising from God's own black earth. Almost never does a weed intrude into this utopia of uniform agronomy. It's because of your hard work that this is so.

"In our context today, Jesus's parable makes no sense. First of all, everybody knows that no matter how clean your seed —and today's seed companies sell cleaner seed than anything in Jesus's day—you're still going to get weeds in your fields. And not because an enemy sows them, unless the enemy is the wind or something stuck in your tractor tires. No farmer in his right mind would blame an enemy for sowing weed seeds in his field. That's just paranoid.

"Then there are these servants, who are so stupid they can't be trusted not to uproot the wheat with the weeds. Who would employ such idiots? Even our teenagers can pull weeds properly. You pay them to walk your beans. You farmers have to be thinking that this householder needs to fire his stupid servants and hire some Minnesota kids.

"Then there's this ridiculous order to let the weeds grow with the wheat. Not a one of you would ever consider such a thing.

"Maybe you're thinking this is just a wheat farmer thing, fine for ancient Israel and modern North Dakota, but not southern Minnesota. Or maybe you're just writing off this farmer as stupid and doomed to have his farm auctioned off in a couple years.

"Or maybe you are thinking that Jesus wasn't a farmer, and so he was just using this story to make a point and it doesn't really have anything to do with farming at all.

"I'm no more of a farmer than Jesus was. You all know that."

Pastor Bergstrom waited for a few titters from the pews. The quiet chuckles were almost imperceptible. Perhaps they were all asleep, or not paying attention. He kept going.

"The School of Agriculture at the University of Minnesota is not going to be adding a course on New Testament agriculture. Even so, Jesus does know something about weeds: Not all weeds are created equal. I can't imagine a use for pigweed, but what about volunteer corn? Corn is a valuable plant that only becomes a weed when it plants itself in the wrong field. But that's some ambitious corn that finds a way to plant itself and grow all on its own with no encouragement. Maybe if you took that corn to be analyzed, you would discover it's a super hybrid that could be patented and make you rich. But volunteer corn does not fit in a soybean field. It wrecks the uniformity. So you yank it out.

"Cockleburs. Now those are useless. Except that it was the cocklebur that inspired Velcro. Its inventor has done very well. But a cocklebur doesn't fit in. It must be yanked out.

"What about a diamond-growing weed? It's probably not worth it to harvest volunteer corn, or meditate on the uses for cockleburs, but any of you would keep a diamond-growing weed.

"Then there's another problem. Some weeds do fit in. Elephant ears, when they are young, look very much like soybeans. It is only when they are full grown that we recognize them for the plant bullies they are.

"In this parable, Jesus is teaching us that God is not a Midwestern farmer. God is willing to let weeds grow on the off chance that there's a diamond tree or a useful invention there.

"We, on the other hand, treat some people like weeds.

"Consider the handicapped kids. They don't fit in, so they get sent to an institution. Or the young mother and her illegitimate baby." He would not let himself look at Raki and Joey, in their usual spot in the back on the left. He would beg forgiveness if he embarrassed her. Was anyone else looking at them? Not that he could tell.

"You pretend there are none, but we all know that they've just been sent to live at homes for unwed mothers, their babies adopted out. Mostly. Who knows what these children could grow to become? We will never know, because we weed them out.

"And what about the elephant ear people? The athletes who grow up to pick fights in bars, or the cheerleaders who grow up to bully people with words."

He did sneak a peek at Mrs. Anderson. She was sitting straight as ever, every hair in place, or at least he assumed, since she was too far away for a detailed look. He couldn't make out her expression, but she wasn't squirming. Should he be relieved, that his veiled admonition missed its mark? Or disappointed, because it proved that his sermons were as big a waste of time as, say, trying to rein in the Luther Leaguers' libidos?

"We are the stupid servants, people. We yank out the people who don't 'fit in.' Then we tend and nourish the bullies because they don't look like the useless weeds they really are."

Calling Mrs. Anderson a 'useless weed' was uncalled for, and, in hindsight, rather judgmental. He had been madder when he wrote the sermon that he was now, but the words had already left his mouth. Mrs. Anderson probably wasn't recognizing herself, anyway. He plowed on to his conclusion.

"I know what you're thinking. We can't welcome unwed mothers and illegitimate kids any more than we can let our fields grow weedy. And it's for their own good, and the good of the family, to send our handicapped kids to be tended by professionals who know what they're doing. There's no such thing as a diamond-growing weed.

"But God calls on us to let the weeds grow with the crops. That will destroy our uniformity. And then we shall rejoice, because that mess is what the Kingdom of God looks like. Amen."

The organ groaned. The congregation mustered to its feet. Pastor

Bergstrom took a deep breath. Drawing on the Gospel of Doris Day he muttered, *"Que sera sera,* whatever will be will be."

MRS. ANDERSON SAT ramrod straight, head high, not fidgeting. *I'll be damned if I'll let that pipsqueak see me squirm. I've had over thirty years of practice. Never show what you're feeling.*

She had been lost in the weed analogy. Mr. Anderson was an insurance agent, like her father, so Mrs. Anderson had scant experience with bean fields. Pigweed plagued her garden, but what was an elephant ear? It was the part about handicapped kids and illegitimate babies that hit the mark.

Did he know, or was he just guessing? Not even her eyes moved as she thought on it. Even Mr. Anderson did not know. Or did he? Maybe everybody knew, and just didn't let on. The only way to know what people know is to ask, and then the question reveals the secret. So she had never asked. If she could have sat straighter, she would have, no matter how much it hurt, and it was agonizing.

ADELINE ANDERSON, nee Huffman, had grown up a good girl. Every grade school report card extolled her eagerness to follow instructions. She dressed neatly, kept her hair combed and yes, as Pastor Bergstrom implied, had been a cheerleader, back when cheering was about wool sweaters and megaphones, not short skirts and pom poms like these days.

Not until she was wildly in love did she take off her lingerie in the presence of a man. Her lover looked like Humphrey Bogart. They met at the university. He was a graduate student, teaching Freshman Introduction to Poetry. On their first date, he showed up at her dormitory lobby carrying a pickle jar of lilies of the valley. He read poets like Dylan Thomas and others she had never heard of. The first time he seduced her he read aloud. The Song of Solomon.

She felt no shame when her satin slip fell to the floor. They would soon be married. They discussed it. Not long afterwards he came to her bearing a beribboned jewelry box. Her heart flipped. She lifted the lid with her eyes closed, so she would see the contents all at once when she threw open her eyes. Which she did.

A silver Star of David. Nestled in the red velvet was a Jewish necklace where the diamond ring was supposed to be. It was 1950.

She cried for three days. Then she went away on a many- months-long vacation to her aunt in Chicago. Her parents were relieved when the protracted labor and forceps delivered her of a damaged child. "No need for all that adoption rigmarole," she heard through the fog of anesthesia. Twilight sleep, they called it back then.

"It's better this way," her mother had soothed, when all her faculties were about her again. "For both you and the baby. It's what any good mother would do. He needs professional care you wouldn't know how to give. As a ward of the state, he will never want for anything. They will always provide what's best for him. You will move on with your life."

And so she had. Armed with a vow that no one would ever again suspect her of being anything but a conventional and upstanding Christian woman, she found herself a blond football star. He was from Halcyon, a Podunk, but safely far from parents and past. She never again read poetry. Her home library consisted of *Emily Post's Etiquette*, the *Revised Standard Version of the Bible* and *Betty Crocker's Picture Cookbook*.

Now this pastor knew something. Or did he?

"ARE YOU ALL right?" Mr. Anderson looked over at her as he drove them home from church. He seemed genuinely concerned.

"Just thinking about all the things I have to do today," she lied.

Her baby, if he was alive, would be a grown man now. All she remembered was the swaddle of blue blankets, a shock of thick black hair poking out of the top. The memory elicited no tears. She had followed instructions; she had moved on.

20

RAKI OVERHEARD the tut-tutting as she sorted through the hamburger packages at the grocery store. Her auburn hair was tied up behind a flowered scarf. It was obvious the ladies hadn't recognized her.

"Uncalled for, I say. We're not as small-minded as all that, plus he doesn't know First Timothy from Timothy grass, so who is he to lecture us on weeds?"

"He made some good points, but the tone, that was too harsh. These are very difficult situations."

Raki fought back a laugh. Last Sunday may have been the first time anybody in town actually listened to a homily—sermon, that is.

She heard more whispering as she perused the New Arrivals shelf at the county library.

"Did you hear about the council meeting beforehand? *Jane Eyre?* Would your husband read such a book?"

"My husband doesn't read anything but the sports section and the grain futures."

The library and grocery store were the only places Raki went to, not counting the playground. She wondered what was said elsewhere.

"The teachers think he's a hero," Margaret told her. "He was at school to discuss Wednesday Religious Release and Principal slapped him on the back and told him, 'Buck up. It'll blow over.'"

"Do you think it will?"

"I don't know. I hope it doesn't derail your plans for Joey's baptism."

ALONE AGAIN in the big house. Joey underfoot and a can of Lemon Pledge in her hand. How many times had she heard: when life gives you lemons, make lemonade. What crap. *Life gave me lemons, and all I got was this freaking dust cloth.* Raki looked through a window, sniffing back tears she refused to cry.

A black Cutlass pulled into the driveway, its windows open and speaker blaring Redbone's 'Come and Get Your Love.' Who on earth?

The associate pastor, Sam of all people, stepped out of the car. He was probably there to break the news that the baptism was off. He could have just called. She tossed the rag and spray can in the cupboard and opened the back door. Joey toddled out, stopping to pick dandelions growing out of the crack in the sidewalk. Raki stood in the threshold. Joey held her yellow bouquet as high as she could, over her head, and Sam hunched down to accept them.

"Patter," said Joey.

"Lovely flowers," said Raki, when he reached the door. "Let me put them in water for you." She found a clean jelly jar in the cupboard. "What brings you here? Is it about canceling the baptism?"

"I'm leaving Halcyon." He sat on a hard kitchen chair. "I'm seeking another call, that is, a job at another church."

"I'm sorry to hear that." Raki pulled out the chair across from him. "It isn't necessary. Joey isn't going to Hell because she can't get baptized at your church."

"Of course not, but we're not calling that off. Just hoped we could do it before I leave. That's why I'm here."

"Were you fired?"

"Not fired. Pastor Solquist advised me to resign voluntarily, before anybody makes too big a fuss. I can seek a new call without a cloud over my head."

Raki considered the cloud over her own head. Would she ever be able to move on?

"It's been a bad couple of weeks. My girlfriend dumped me, too."

"I'm sorry." That explained a lot.

"I always thought Claire and I would be together. She's going to be a pastor, too. We were going to be partners, working together. The day of the council meeting, I drove up to the seminary and proposed. She said no."

He proposed on a day he had to come back for a council meeting? What the hell was the matter with him?

"Is that how you asked her? Like a business proposition?"

His eyes flicked downward. He didn't answer. Joey toddled over and tugged at his black trousers. He lifted her to his lap. She rested her head on his chest and fell asleep.

When he looked up again, his eyes were wet. He was struggling not to blink. She wondered if he was sad or ashamed. Either way, those tears stuck to her heart like water to flour. Her thoughts stirred like dough in a bowl. Maybe something good could rise out of this.

"Can you do me a favor?" She needed a few minutes to think.

He nodded.

"Put Joey down in the playpen in the yard. Wait out there. I'll . . . take care of a few things in here. Then we'll . . . discuss the baptism."

He didn't object. Joey's head flopped as he opened the door. He steadied her with one hand. Raki monitored them through the screen. He set Joey in the playpen then stood, arms akimbo, looking up at the clouds. Cute butt. Not exactly a knight in shining armor, but sweet. And she was sure, surer than she'd ever been of anything, that Sam loved her. Joey too.

He bent down and pulled a blade of crab grass.

Did she love him? She'd been left in the lurch twice, five times including her mom and dad and Lija. Was it worth the risk? To try again?

He stretched the blade of grass between his thumbs, pressed it against his lips and blew. The crabgrass bleated plaintively. He really was sweet.

This time could be different. It could. She looked over the cornfields, to the blue sky above the horizon. Yes, this time would be different.

"I have a business proposition for you," she called through the screen, forcing a lilt into her voice, to cover the quaver of her thumping heart.

He stood on the other side of the screen mesh, leaning against the door frame. His eyes were dry now. The man she saw through the mesh was her friend. That fact would not change. The certainty gave her courage.

"Let's you and me be the partnership." She waited a beat to let that sink in. "You and I should get married." She was almost as startled at the words as he looked to be.

His jaw dropped. "To each other?"

It wasn't a refusal. "I don't know of any other options. You're obviously head over heels in love with me."

He raised one eyebrow. Both corners of his mouth turned up.

It was not quite a smile, but a good sign. "That's why—Claire was it?—turned you down. She knew you were in love with someone else. That being me."

"Are you kidding? How did you know? I mean, I've never said, or done, anything . . . improper." He opened the door.

"Only that you quoted Charlotte Bronte on my behalf. Very chivalric. And that rip-roaring sermon you let loose in my defense. Other than those things, nothing improper."

He leaned over and kissed her on the cheek. The cheek? What was the matter with him? Or was that a friendly way of saying no? "I would like you to do better than that."

His second try had a lot more oomph. He seemed to have the right amount of experience—not too fumbly, not too suave. She smelled his cologne. Musk? Who would have thought?

"Can I tell you something I have never told anyone before?" he whispered into her hair.

"Of course," she said, without conviction. She hoped he wasn't concocting some excuse for saying no. After a kiss like that, a no would be embarrassing.

"I've never gotten a verifiable answer to a prayer. Until now." His warm breath tickled her ear.

"And what was the answer you got?"

"To come out here in person instead of call on the phone."

Then he did a silly thing. He walked to the counter, dipped a spoon into her canister of flour, poured a little into his hands and dusted it over her head. "Like a veil," he said.

"So that's a yes, Pastor-man?"

"As soon as possible. Yes."

"I thought you were never going to say it." She took a step back, two steps, trying to put her wits back in order, before one thing led to another. Too soon for all that. She took a deep breath.

"How did you come up with that quote from *Jane Eyre*, in the middle of a council meeting?"

"I memorized it in high school."

"Margaret was tickled. Proof that literature can come in handy."

"Guess she's right."

"My mother was an English teacher. She left me, died, when I was little."

He took a step toward her, his hands open. "I'll never leave you, Raki."

"That's what I'm counting on. But first I have to tell you something."

NO BRIDE WAS EVER so beautiful was what Sam thought, never mind the brown dress with the matching brown fabric flower. Her bouquet was a dozen red roses, from him, and a clutch of dandelions, from Joey. Instead of white tulle, a wreath of baby's breath encircled her head, a ribbon entwining through her auburn waves. The ribbon matched the peach sheath visible through the brown lace.

"The color doesn't mean anything," Raki told him. "This was my mother's dress, the only bit of family I have here."

Her father had sent greetings, but they were in too much of a hurry to give him time to drive from Arizona. Sam's parents were the only family present, and there were no other guests. Just the Rev.

Solquist, Margaret and Mike Voll to witness, and Joey. Joey's straw blond hair was still wet from the baptism. "Might as well do both on the same day, since we have the chapel reserved," Raki had suggested.

It irked Sam that Mrs. Anderson got her way after all, the baptism private, as if it were something to be hidden.

"Quit doting on the past," Raki admonished him. "Look to the future. Don't you guys have a verse for that?"

After the vows, Sam mailed off his request for a new call.

PART SEVEN

Seldom, very seldom, does complete truth belong to any human disclosure; seldom can it happen that something is not a little disguised, or a little mistaken.

Jane Austen, *Emma*

Suburban Minneapolis
1975 – 1980

21

"YOU REALLY NEED to find something to do with your time. Puttering about that parsonage is driving you nuts." Raki tried to ignore Margaret's schoolteacher tone. "It's 1975. Women don't stay at home anymore." Margaret was persistent.

Raki felt exposed by the bright light of the Crystal Court at Southdale, annoyed by the potted ferns. "Sam tells me the same thing."

Six stringed shopping bags sat propped next to Margaret's feet, teacher back-to-school selections. Joey was going up and down the shopping mall escalator, easy to spot thanks to her multi-colored little jacket and rubber-toed red Keds, the only purchases Raki could afford. "I can't go to college. It's too late, and we don't have the money anyway."

"In the history of the world, very few professional bakers have had a degree. That is your dream, right? A bakery. I can smell Raki's fresh bread and sugar cookies as we speak." Margaret made a big show of sniffing the air.

"I don't have any experience outside my own kitchen, or anybody to care for Joey." Joey reached the bottom and scampered back for a ride up. What annoyed Raki most was that she knew Margaret and Sam were right. She had become too good at making excuses, yet she did it again. "I don't know where to start."

"Try something. Anything. See where it leads. Be creative." Margaret failed to hide her exasperation.

Raki did have an idea. The prior Sunday, like every Sunday, she and Joey were in the front pew at Bethlehem Lutheran. Commonly known as the BBB, for Behemoth Bloomington Bethlehem, the place had five pastors. Sam sat up front with numbers one, two and four. Number three was preaching. A sleeping pill in a white robe. Raki had fought off drooping eyelids as he droned on. *I can't fall asleep, I can't fall asleep.* She repeated it to herself like a mantra. Her head had jerked. *I can't fall asleep, I can't fall asleep.* She had looked for something to focus on.

The dish on the altar. Piled with those dusty little white disks. Communion wafers. An idea woke her up. Surely Jesus wouldn't approve. God would insist on something that tasted better.

"I want to make real bread for communion," she told Margaret. It was the first time she'd said the idea out loud. Margaret wouldn't be bothered by unorthodoxy. "For Sam's church, to replace the communion wafers."

"Those awful things that stick to the roof of your mouth?"

Raki looked over her shoulder, making sure no one could overhear. "It's like you have to pry off Jesus with your tongue."

Margaret guffawed, right there in the Crystal Court.

"The problem is the bread Jesus ate was unleavened. And there would be crumbs."

"Good grief, the place has a two-story organ," said Margaret. "Surely they have a vacuum cleaner."

"Plus, the Chancel Care committee would have to discuss it. And vote on it. And then take it before Council. There'd be a big fuss." There were those excuses again.

"Trick 'em," suggested Margaret. "We women are good at manipulation. Female subterfuge. Without it, Jane Austen would have had no plots for her books."

Subterfuge. The word had the ring of sinfulness, but Raki had practice at it. She never corrected the nice church ladies who said Joey looked just like Sam. A harmless assumption.

"This state is riddled with Lutherans. It could become a really big thing."

Big. Thing. The words scared Raki, even though they described exactly what she wanted. She knew she wouldn't stop at baking a measly few loaves every fourth Sunday. Her heart pounded.

Joey ran from the foot of the escalator, grabbing her mom's hand. "Climb high, Mommy!" she squealed.

"Good advice," Margaret said. "Start small, climb high."

Raki followed her little daughter's tug. She tried out a new mantra. *I'm gonna do it. I'm gonna do it.*

THE NEXT SATURDAY Raki brought a sandwich on whole wheat bread and a thermos of coffee to Sam's office.

"Surprise!"

Sam closed the door and kissed her for a dangerously long time. Joey pulled a pile of books off his shelf. The skritch of ripping paper distracted Raki. She pulled away.

Sam tried to pull her back. "I never read that book anyway."

But Raki insisted this was no place for a small child, smoothed her blouse, took a deep breath, grabbed Joey and left on her true mission.

Glancing both ways as she left the office, Raki sneaked into the Chancel Care kitchen. She scrummaged through the cupboards until she found the stash of wafers, removing them from their usual spot to a different cupboard, then tossing a pile of clean tea towels on top.

"Just misplaced. How would I know where they are supposed to go?" she whispered airily, waving her hands in Joey's direction. "Now, let's go home and bake some real bread."

Sunday morning she stowed six round loaves in a plastic bag in the backseat of the car. Sam had left an hour before. Most weeks she timed her arrival to coincide exactly with the first chord of the entrance hymn. This Sunday she and Joey walked through the door thirty minutes ahead. She took Joey by the hand, wandering aimlessly—or so she hoped it seemed—toward the Chancel kitchen.

"Where are those da . . . Where are the communion wafers?" she heard one woman demand of another.

"I have no idea. There was a huge supply right here, in this cupboard, just last month, the last time we had communion."

"Go ask somebody. Hurry."

"Is something the matter?" Raki inserted a sweet lilt in her voice.

"There certainly is, Mrs. Bergstrom. The wafers have disappeared. Stolen or something."

"I can't imagine anyone stealing communion wafers," said Raki, employing a calculated dose of incredulity.

"Maybe the Men's Bible Study ran out of poker chips," said the woman filling the chalices.

"Don't be blasphemous in front of the pastor's wife," said the first, but Raki spotted the corners of her mouth curl up a bit. The woman continued stomping around, pulling open every door and drawer.

Joey started heading toward the cabinet with the hidden wafers. Raki grabbed her hand. Joey struggled against her, "Mommy!" Raki tightened her grip with one hand while shushing with the other.

"Please, let me help," Raki said, opening the cupboard with flourish. "All I can see are tea towels in here." Not a lie. That was all she could see.

"Where in the world could they have got to?"

The woman sent to ask around returned with no new insights. "What do we do now?"

"Ladies, it just so happens I have a few loaves of bread in the car. I was planning on going to the nursing home this afternoon." The trip to the nursing home had nothing to do with the bread, but each sentence by itself was factually accurate.

"We couldn't take bread from our elderly," one woman objected.

"I'm sure the home has enough bread for lunch." Another true statement.

"Oh, sweetheart, would you let us use it?"

"Of course. It's not unleavened, though." She feigned disapproval.

"Oh, pooh, who cares?" said the woman. "Desperate times call for desperate measures."

During announcements, the senior pastor offered profuse

apologies and insistence that there would be the usual wafers next month. During the coffee hour, a few people complimented the young pastor's wife on her quick thinking and excellent baking skills. Others volunteered that they preferred the taste. The church treasurer revealed the cost of wafers. The Chancel Care woman quizzed the senior pastor on the theological ramifications of eating yeast. He went into a long discourse, at the end of which she said, "So we'll not end up in Hell over it."

"I suppose not," he said, his voice appropriately querulous.

"It's settled then," she announced. "Would Mrs. Bergstrom be willing to bake more of her wonderful loaves?"

"It would be a privilege."

RAKI AMAZED HERSELF. She had managed to get church people to do something differently from what had always been done. Not exactly Martin Luther's Ninety-Five Theses, but revolutionary in its small way.

She told Sam she wouldn't mind if he mentioned her communion loaves to his fellow pastors. He said he was happy to brag on her. She thrust bread on him whenever he went to meetings and conferences. It didn't take as long as she expected for more pastors to ask if she would bake for them. At cost, of course.

One pastor inquired if she could do unleavened. At first she bridled, but then took on the challenge. If she could concoct a biblically-authentic honey whole wheat cracker, one that was edible, those would keep longer and she could work ahead. Joey became official taste-tester. She spat out the first attempt. Raki added more honey. Joey ate a handful.

Raki worried about outgrowing her kitchen. She still wished she'd gone to college. She would have learned about leases and financing. Her fears battled against her dream every night while she was asleep. Awake she worried over the next step.

A dozen churches later, Miss Richter showed up. Margaret had tipped off the newspaper publisher to the 'hometown girl makes good' angle. A photographer, the same one from the snowman day, snapped pictures. Miss Richter marveled at how big Joey had grown. After the article was published, the *Minneapolis Tribune* came calling.

Orders started in from all over the metro area. A few rural churches called, too, but Raki had to turn them down. No way to deliver. No trucks.

๛

SAM HEARD WAILING as he got out of the car. Then screeching, a bang like a cymbal crash followed by high-pitched clinking. He ran to the door. This was no church concert. And the burning smell was not incense.

Raki burst through the door, almost knocking him over, Joey clinging to her hand. They were both coughing.

"It's NOT a goddamned fire!" she shouted. "Just six burned-up loaves!" She collapsed on the steps. Her wailing grew louder. Joey ran to him, hugging his legs, burying her face against his side. The wet from her tears soaked through the fabric of his trousers. He knelt down so the little girl could cry against his shoulder.

"What happened, Raki?" He reached over to touch her.

She slapped him away. "Go look!" She buried her face against her knees. He opened the door slowly.

Flour covered the floor, like the aftermath of a blizzard. Flour dust mixed with the ash in the air. An empty twenty-pound bag sagged in on itself in the middle of the floor. Six blackened loaves, still spewing smoke, sat atop the stove. A dozen cracked eggs made a gooey mass in one corner. Shards of a glass canister lay in a pile in another corner. Crumpled notebook paper clotted on the counter. A paper carton sat in a white puddle, milk dripping down from the impact zone overhead.

A picture worth a thousand words. This was no accident.

"What happened, honey?" Sam employed his best pastoral palaver as he sat next to her. What on earth had made her snap?

"I'm an incompetent amateur! That's what happened!" She was shouting. He had not seen this coming. If there were signs, they had gone right past him. Or he had ignored them. The tossing and turning every night, the far away looks and sighs, he had written all that off as just woman things. Maybe those were worry things. And he hadn't done a thing to help.

"I'll clean it up," he offered.

"No! I made the mess. I'll clean it up!" She jerked herself off the steps, stormed into the kitchen, grabbed a broom and began flailing. He and Joey followed, flour dust choking them. Joey fled to a corner.

"You're scaring Joey, Raki." He held her wrist until she quit sweeping. "Go somewhere quiet. I'll take care of this."

It took an hour. When order was restored, he found her in their bedroom, lying on the bed, staring at the ceiling.

"It's my fault," he whispered. "It was all my bragging that brought this on you. I didn't think about what it meant, in terms of work for you."

She turned to face him. "It's not that. I lost it, because I'm scared."

"Scared of what?"

"I want so much to make a success of something, on my own, but I don't know what I'm doing. I want to be a real business woman, and yet I keep track of my expenses and reimbursements in a spiral notebook. Like a school girl. All those years seeing the green ledgers in my dad's office, and I have no idea how accounting works. If some church auditor or, heaven forbid, the IRS, came calling, what would I do?"

He hadn't thought about that.

"Not to mention that I'm probably breaking the law. What if the health inspector reads the *Minneapolis Tribune* and comes and arrests me?"

He hadn't thought of that, either. "I doubt they'd handcuff you. Bad p.r. to arrest a pastor's wife."

She didn't laugh at his joke. "One of the few perks of this gig."

That stung. "How can we make it not scary, Raki? What do you want? Do you want to quit? What do you really want?"

The way her mouth quivered, he could tell she had the answer, but she was hesitating.

"Whatever you want, sweetie."

"A real business. I want a bakery with giant mixers and stainless steel bowls. Bakers in white aprons. Some of those long paddles, like you see on TV, for reaching into really huge ovens. And a delivery truck. With a picture on the side."

FROM THE SANCTITY of his den, Sam remembered the brash young woman in the racy black swimsuit at the beach. The girl who cannonballed off the end of the dock, dripped on his towel and bought him a candy bar. Scared of church auditors and the health department? It didn't fit.

She wouldn't have jumped with such aplomb if she hadn't had some experience with swimming. Everybody panics the first time they get their head under water. Even future Olympians start with lessons.

He dialed two long-distance numbers, in-state to the newspaper publisher's office in Halcyon, out-of-state to his father-in-law in Arizona. Expensive calls, but necessary.

A week later Miss Richter showed up at the parsonage with a load of books and catalogs. Raki answered the doorbell. Sam leaned against the wall by the front window, pretending to have no idea why she was there.

"There's word on the street that you dream of owning a bakery." The older woman marched right past Sam, taking Raki by the hand and setting her load of books on the dining table with a thud.

The woman didn't waste time with pleasantries. Where was Lawrence?

"Yes, but . . ." said Raki. Miss Richter cut her off.

Sam listened, now and again glancing behind the curtains to the front sidewalk.

Miss Richter patted Raki on the back in a 'go get 'em' manner. "No buts. You have the most successful non-business I have ever seen. You are only a step away from your dream."

"But, I . . ." Raki looked like a drowning swimmer afraid of grabbing the lifesaver ring.

"No buts!" Miss Richter interjected, sweeping her arm over the books on the table.

"I'm listening," Raki said, sitting down in front of the books.

She was grabbing the ring. If she would just sign up for the lessons.

"I've brought books on business and a course catalog from the community college," said Miss Richter. "There are night classes in business management, food science, you name it."

"But, I don't know . . ."

"You think I knew the first thing about publishing when I started out as a proofreader? It doesn't matter what you don't know; it matters what you can learn. And don't forget, mistakes make the best teachers."

"Listen to her, honey. She knows what she's talking about," said Sam, adding a dash of no-nonsense to his usual pastoral timbre.

"In addition to classes, you need a space." Miss Richter stood, pointing into the cluttered kitchen. "This. Will not do."

Raki sat up straight, like an eager student. "I know, I know. I've been thinking about this for months. But without money . . ." Her voice trailed off.

"I'm giving you a loan. If it's not enough, we'll go to a bank."

"How will I pay you back?" Raki was reading Sam's mind. The loan offer had made him nervous, too. They didn't have much money in the bank, and probably never would.

"Now we're getting somewhere," said Miss Richter. "I'm not worried about that. Your success will pay me back. Learn first. Grow slowly. Start charging enough to grow the business. Blame inflation if you get complaints from penny-pinching church councils." She nodded at Sam. "No offense, Pastor."

"None taken." He peeked out the window again. A pickup truck pulled up to the curb. It was about time. A big man stepped out, hauling green ledgers and an adding machine. Sam opened the door before Lawrence got to the front steps. He jostled his load to shake Sam's hand. Sam, a connoisseur of handshakes, found Lawrence's bear paw grip reassuring.

"I hear my baby wants to learn bookkeeping!" the big man boomed, unloading the paper and machine next to Miss Richter's books and catalogs. His sunburned arms enveloped Raki in a hug.

"What are you doing here?" Raki cried.

"First things first." He turned to shake Miss Richter's hand. "How do you do?"

"Fine, sir. I was just telling your daughter that she needs to take a salary."

"You did not . . ." Raki started, before her father interrupted.

"Damn right, she does."

"Nonprofit. Churches. I couldn't," Raki stammered. Sam had anticipated this objection. He was ready.

"No need to become a Howard Hughes, but everyone deserves fair pay." Miss Richter threw Sam a look.

"Romans 4:4," said Sam, as if he had just come up with it off the top of his head. He had looked it up in his concordance after his phone call to Miss Richter. She had ordered him to find justification.

"Like a real career," breathed Raki.

"Is that what you want, honey?" Sam wanted to make sure.

"It's what I've always wanted." She grabbed Miss Richter's hand on one side, and her father's hand on the other and looked straight into Sam's eyes. "I can do it," she said, her tone laden with conviction. "I'm gonna have faith in myself, like you have faith in me. No more messing around."

Sam felt like a lifeguard saving a future Olympian. In his head, he heard the cheering.

"I HEAR YOU like Scotch on the rocks, in a crystal glass," said Sam to Lawrence later that evening. Sam had taken Joey to a *Winnie the Pooh* matinee while Raki and Miss Richter and Lawrence plotted a preliminary business plan. When he returned, Miss Richter had gone. Raki set to putting Joey to bed. Lawrence looked thirsty.

"Praise God," said Lawrence as Sam handed him the glass. "Nothing sacrilegious intended."

"Of course not." Sam took a sip. He enjoyed the chiming of ice against the glass, the ashy bite of Scotch on his tongue.

"Thanks for inviting me. And letting me bunk here, while I teach her the ropes. About time I made some amends."

The last comment didn't seem to need a response. Sam took another sip.

"This whole mess with my daughters," Lawrence continued, "it was recently pointed out to me that it was my fault. Apparently I doomed them."

That comment, on the other hand, begged a response. "How so?"

"With the names, of course."

Sam lifted one eyebrow.

Lawrence chuckled and slapped his knee. A little booze splashed out. "You, of all people, should have figured it out."

"I don't understand."

"I thought I was so clever, picking Norwegian names out of the Old Testament. Names of sisters even. All these years, and I never read the story. One of the other geezers in Arizona, when I told him all that happened with my daughters, dragged out his Bible and forced me to read it."

"Read what, Lawrence?"

"Genesis 29. Rachel and Leah and all that."

Rakella and Lija. And James, like Jacob, working the father's farm. Married to one, loving the other. In those few days between the proposal and their wedding, Raki had revealed the whole story. A coincidence of biblical proportions, but the parallel had never dawned on him.

"Nothing new under the damned sun, now is there?" said Lawrence, draining his glass. "Story is ending differently, though. Thanks to you."

SAM COULDN'T GET enough of Raki's enthusiasm, watching her trade in cups for buckets, bowls for bins and potholders for paddles. She legally registered the name, 'Blessed Breads,' with the Secretary of State and framed the certificate. She came home with flour streaking her hair. *Like when I proposed.* He corrected himself. When she proposed, that is.

He was never sure whose idea it was to ask Social Services to send over unwed mothers who needed jobs and training. Raki said it was Miss Richter's idea, but he didn't believe her. The young mothers took turns watching each other's babies while the others baked.

Few of these young women had ever made anything but cake from a box. The loaves they turned out were inconsistent. "We can't afford to throw out all the lumpy ones," Raki told him, "but an idea came to me during my class on marketing."

"What class on marketing?"

"The one you teach on Sundays." She punched him in the shoulder. "Our loaves are like people, all messed up, but essentially good. Worth saving. That's how we market it."

❧

RAKI PONDERED the green ledgers. She rubbed her eyes. The columns blurred. Her costs kept going up. Flour, electricity, rent. Inflation.

She called Margaret. "I can't bear to ask Miss Richter for more money. My customers are already complaining about the price increase. I couldn't possibly lay off the girls. I'm so frustrated."

"Benefactors," said Margaret. "That's what you need. A fancy fundraiser. One that attracts people with real money."

"I wouldn't know the first thing about any of that."

"My mother-in-law would help," said Margaret. "She admires you. She's still mad at me for making you sleep on the servants' floor. Her social circle includes lots of people with money, and they know all the party planners in the Cities."

THE HANDWRITTEN NOTE came in the mail a week later, addressed to Mrs. Rakella Bergstrom on Mrs. Voll's embossed stationery. Tucked inside was a business card:

Inspiring Events.

The place for prestigious party planning

An appointment was scribbled on the back:

3:00 Wednesday

Raki pulled up to the address at precisely fifty-nine minutes past two o'clock on Wednesday. She parked, leaned over the passenger seat and squinted at the number above the door. *An art gallery?* She climbed out of the car, tugged her skirt, smoothed the front, pushed a couple nickels into the meter. Pretending to be poised, and doing quite well at it.

A large watercolor on an easel greeted her inside the door, an abstract wash in shades of purple. She focused on it for a second. The violet swirls suggested shapes. Three spoons, a trio of keys.

"Look familiar, Raki?" A woman walked up behind her.

Raki turned. The woman looked wise beyond her years, and weirdly familiar, like the painting. A member of BBB? Nothing was more embarrassing than not recognizing a congregation member.

"Carol. Remember? I knew it was you as soon as I heard the name. Unique. It's been a long time. Five years? Six? Maybe longer?"

"Of course I remember you, Carol." Memories crashed through Raki's brain. The commune with the rickety steps, pot on the porch, a flour-covered boy in a diaper. Raki turned back toward the painting. Carol's hand traced the shapes into the air in front of the art. "Recognize the theme? From the cement shrine in front of the house on Nicollet Island? Did you ever notice it? The spoons and the keys?"

"Yes, I remember that."

"I can tell from your last name that you and Luke didn't make a long-term thing of it."

"No, just that summer."

"Do you know what happened to him?"

"No, I don't. I moved on. How's, um . . ." She searched frantically for the little boy's name. "Owen?"

"Thanks for asking. Very well."

"This is your gallery? I came to meet with a party planner. A specialist in fundraisers."

"My gallery and I'm the party planner. Art doesn't pay the bills some months."

Raki nodded.

"To supplement, I call upon my other talent and passion." Carol took a deep breath and clasped her fingers together in front of her chest like a student reciting a poem. "Inspiring those blessed with material advantages to create a lasting legacy through donations that benefit their local community and greater humankind." Then she leaned in close and whispered, "That is, extorting money from rich people."

Raki laughed.

"All right, then," said Carol. "Enough small talk. I have ideas for a theme and have cobbled together an invitation list. Mrs. Voll loaned me her Rolodex. Let's get to it."

Raki hadn't yet made it to a chair before Carol started throwing out questions. "Venue?"

"Sam's church will let us use the fellowship hall."

"Hmmm" said Carol, placing one finger on her chin. "No."

"It's free."

"We're not going for dollar bills and five dollar checks. I'm thinking the Leamington Hotel ballroom."

Raki's heart fluttered. This was no Halcyon PTA kind of thing. She was in way over her head.

"Wine, beer or full bar?"

Raki raised her eyebrows.

"You have to have alcohol to get the ink running out of those fancy pens onto those big checks."

Way over her head. Sink, or swim. "Full bar."

"That's the spirit! And speaking of spirit, we need somebody to offer a prayer, since this is a Christian kind of thing."

"My husband can do that."

"Hmmmm."

Raki recognized the finger on chin charade again, but Carol meant to be nice.

"No. We need a name. Local celebrity. Pastor Claire Johannsen is big into social justice, women's rights, reproductive issues, sexuality. She gets her name in the paper all the time."

"Claire? Oh, no. She used to date my husband."

Carol squinted at her, funny-like, before clapping her hands. "All the better. People will come to watch the cat fight. Or the burying of the hatchet. Or whatever." Then she laughed. What was so funny?

Raki could not believe she was agreeing to all this. Her eyes flitted to the painting.

"Oh, and that painting is yours," said Carol. "For Blessed Breads' new offices. It belongs there. But don't forget my fee."

THE LEAMINGTON HOTEL churned with Raki's friends, others she knew only by sight and a whole lot of people she had never seen before. Raki marveled. All this? For her little organization? The months of nightmares of her and Sam rattling around an empty ballroom now seemed foolish. Everyone seemed to appreciate the champagne, lemon chicken, twice baked potatoes, chocolate cake and the rolls from Blessed Breads.

Raki headed to the ladies' room as the waiters cleared the dishes. Who was that by the door? She peered intently. The infamous Mrs. Anderson, from Halcyon. What would she be doing here? Not to make trouble, at a charitable fundraiser, surely. Deep breath. It will be fine, she repeated to herself, it will be fine. Still, she veered away toward the other exit.

The band struck up, playing current pop songs in a big band style. The women shimmered under the mirrored ball, their diamonds twinkling, skirts of teals, reds, golds and florals swishing and swaying over the dance floor. Raki's gown, borrowed from Margaret, featured a stylish macramé bodice. Sam had rented a tux. No blue or peach, she had insisted. Black, no matter what the guy at the rental store says. Fresh haircut, shiny lapels, he looked like a movie star. And eyes that turned her knees to jelly when he looked at her. *No cat fight tonight. Because I totally won.*

Talking over the beat was impossible. Sam guided her to the dance floor. When the band took a break, Mrs. Voll, Honorary Chairwoman, hiked up her long skirt and climbed the stairs to the stage.

Sam and Raki rejoined Margaret and Mike at the head table. Raki felt a hand on her elbow. Mrs. Anderson whispered in her ear, "Thanks for not throwing me out."

"Of course." Raki was embarrassed.

"I came to make amends." Mrs. Anderson was still whispering. Raki leaned in to hear. "Because I'm sorry for what I said about you and your daughter, and how it all ended up with Pastor Bergstrom leaving town."

"Everything turned out all right," breathed Raki. It had.

"Tell your husband I wish only the best for both of you."

Raki squeezed her hand.

By the time Mrs. Anderson swished away, Raki had missed Mrs. Voll's first words. On stage, her best friend's mother-in-law was waxing lyrical about some saint with an organization capable of improving the lives of every mother and child in Minnesota. Carol should have reviewed Mrs. Voll's speech beforehand. She should be talking about Blessed Breads. That's what everybody came for.

Raki gestured palms up at Sam, mouthing silently, "Who's she talking about?"

Sam pointed back, perplexed. "You," he mouthed.

Me?

When the clapping died down, Claire ascended to the lectern, her black pumps clacking across the stage. She wore the regulation lady pastor knee-length black skirt and black blouse, but it was sort of— spangly. Could those be—sequins? Based on Claire's reputation, Raki had half-expected Birkenstocks and a protest placard.

After her introduction by Mrs. Voll, Claire ran her finger under her white collar, leaned her elbows over the lectern and glared at the crowd. Her hellfire and brimstone eyes seemed very un-Lutheran.

"I want you all to think back on your last sin," she started, her tone matching her eyes. The ballroom echoed with guilty silence.

She slammed her fist on the lectern. "And how much fun it was!" She threw her arms in the air. That felt really un-Lutheran, too.

Claire waited for the smattering of chuckles to die down. "I don't know what all of you were thinking about." She wagged her finger at the crowd, winking lewdly. "But I was thinking of the embodiment of evil we just ate. That chocolate cake."

The chuckles grew a little louder.

"My problem is, when I say 'Get behind me Satan!' it literally happens!" Claire turned forty-five degrees and swatted her own sequined black-skirted behind. Mrs. Voll snorted champagne out of her nose. The audience was rollicking now. Claire had a routine like

Joan Rivers, or Phyllis Diller, with a collar.

As the roaring subsided, Claire slammed down the clear contents of a water tumbler, swabbing her mouth with the back of her hand like an old sot at a saloon. "That was water." Another suggestive wink. "I swear." Pause. "But you'll never know for sure now, will you?"

From there Claire launched into an endorsement of Blessed Breads, chockablock with feminist scriptural references, as funny as a Johnny Carson skit. Raki had no idea there were so many women in the Bible. And that they were all so . . . cool. Margaret laughed so hard she had to wipe her eyes to keep her mascara from running. Mike handed her a glass when she started to hiccup. Sam put his head in his hands, chortling so hard his shoulders shook. He leaned over to Raki, "I never expected her to be so funny, or so sparkly."

The applause at the end would be described as 'shaking the rafters' the next day in the *Minneapolis Tribune*.

Everybody quieted down for the prayer, then Raki joined Claire on stage. They put their arms around each other's shoulders, smiled in unison and the camera flashed. Raki thanked everyone for coming, Mrs. Voll returned on stage to urge everyone to be generous, and the band started up again.

Eventually two dozen breadbaskets were heaped with checks in envelopes stamped 'Blessed Breads Co.' One envelope was of fine linen stationery, addressed formally in flowing cursive: *Confidential to Mrs. Samuel Bergstrom.*

Inside was this:

Dear Mrs. Bergstrom,

I came here to express my gratitude. After you left Halcyon I did something I never thought I could do. I went to visit my son. It was you, and your husband, that inspired me to do it. Charles, as I called him, was born illegitimate and handicapped. My parental rights were terminated so he could be sent to live in an institution. By the time I got the courage to seek him out, he had already passed away. The staff were kind. They told me he had grown into a fine young man and he liked to help out in the kitchen. He lived there 29 years. They even found a picture. I framed it.

My son was a secret I kept for decades. There are many of my generation, and older, who hide behind flowery aprons, terrified that we will be found out. When I finally told my husband, he did not disown me as I had been led to believe he would. How awful was I for not trusting him? I am glad to be free now.

Recently, my parents left me some money. I sent it to the institution as a gift. They returned it. The institution will be closing down, because people like my son are better off living within their own communities. Deinstitutionalization is what they call it.

In memory of my son, I am donating the money to your cause.

Sincerely,

Adeline Anderson

PART EIGHT

Forgive us our trespasses,
as we forgive those who trespass against us.

Suburban Minneapolis
1985 - 1986

22

Minneapolis Tribune, October 2, 1985

'Halcyon Man Dies in Tractor Tip'

James Isaksen, 39, of rural Halcyon, died Tuesday after the tractor he was operating overturned.

His eldest son, Randall Isaksen, discovered the accident when his father did not return home as expected. Neighbors responded to calls to free him from beneath the tractor, which weighed several tons. He was taken by air ambulance to the Mayo Clinic, but died en route from injuries to his skull.

Tractor rollovers are a leading cause of death on family farms. Seventy percent of agricultural fatalities are caused by tractors, half of those by rollover. This year, manufacturers began voluntarily fitting new tractors with rollover bars.

Mr. Isaksen is survived by his wife and four sons.

Raki's tears smudged the last two words. Margaret and Miss Richter had both called to let her know what had happened. Still, the words in black and white came as a shock. Not even forty.

She remembered that evening so long ago, sitting beside him on the Ferris Wheel. The night that changed everything.

"Survived by his wife and four sons." Four sons. Of course that is all it would say.

23

DRIVING HOME from work, Raki struggled to recall the innocent sparkles that fell back in Advent, hard to do now, in March, with filth scumming the snowbanks. It had been a trying day. Blessed Breads' new accountant wanted to computerize the books. A delivery truck driver came down with chicken pox. The retail store lost power. One of the ovens went on the fritz.

City plows had taken one last swipe down her street. Left exposed were winter's historical strata of snow and dirt, snow and dirt crowned with black sludge. Just like her day.

She passed an unfamiliar pickup truck parked across the street. Tina Turner's 'What's Love Got to Do with It' blared from the radio. She snapped it off as she pulled into her driveway, the Civic's tires furrowing the thick mush.

She hopscotched from garage to porch, slopping into a puddle anyway. *Damn it.* But there by her squishy shoes was hope: a purple crocus poking up from a sunny spot. Maybe things could be looking up.

She reached the side door and kicked off her shoes. The front doorbell chimed. Wet-footed, she jogged to the living room and opened the door. Lija stood on her porch. Stout legs, corn silk hair, thick coat, waterproof boots, a potted plant in her hands. The same as always, just older. Much older.

Why today? When things were already crappy enough. Anxiety burned deep in Raki's gut. She didn't want a confrontation. The burning spread upwards to her heart. She searched for something to say.

"Long time, no see." Raki's tongue felt too big for her mouth.

"Fourteen years, I think."

"Yes, right." As if she hadn't kept count of every year, every day.

Lija held out the plant. "Basil. From my windowsill garden. For you."

Peace offering? Raki's heart settled down. She held the door ajar. The last of the day's sun inveigled through the chilled breeze. "Come in," she said. "We don't want to let all the cold in."

Raki's brain buzzed, like a bee searching for a flower. What should she say? What should she do? Act all serious? Be casual or get up a big to-do? Go through confession and forgiveness or just forge ahead? What to say about James? And the accident? How to bring up Joey? The weather! That would be safe. Before she could say anything, Lija found her own safe topic.

"Nice home," she said, steadying herself with one hand against the foyer wall, pulling off her boots, shrugging off her coat, hanging it on the hook by the door.

Raki's damp socks brought her mind back to childhood, when Lija scolded her, always gently, when she forgot sensible things, like boots. But this day Lija paid no attention to Raki's wet feet. She walked into the living room, heading straight to the family photos on the wall. She hesitated in front of Joey's school photo.

"That's my daughter," said Raki. "She's fourteen now."

"Of course she is." Lija moved closer to the picture.

Raki wished Lija wasn't studying that picture quite so closely. What was she looking for? Some resemblance to her boys? A feature that proved they were closer than cousins?

"She's beautiful, Raki." Lija paused. "My boys are handsome, too, but . . . well, they are boys . . . good ones."

"Of course. Tell me all about them. Sit down, I'll make us some coffee."

"Thank you." Lija eased onto a chair at the dining table as Raki fumbled in the kitchen.

"Nice day, isn't it," Raki called out above the whoosh of the water streaming from the tap.

"Certainly is. The boys are eager to get out in the fields, but it's too early and wet. Sunny days like this help, though."

Raki wondered how teenagers could plant a whole farm by themselves. A question along those lines seemed too dangerous to ask. The coffee pot burbled. She was grateful for the noise filling the nervous silence.

"I was very sorry to hear about James," she finally blurted, setting the coffee cups on the table. After she got the news, Raki had lost a week of sleep praying over what to do or not to do. Send flowers? A sympathy card? She worried flowers or a card would prompt the boys to ask questions Lija didn't want to answer. Donate an 'in memoriam' somewhere? Where? Her prayers had received no answer, so she had sent nothing. Too late now.

"I appreciate that." Lija was gracious, accepting the hot cup from Raki. "It was a very hard thing to deal with, but I'm much better now."

"He was a good man," said Raki. *Uh, oh.* That could be taken the wrong way.

Lija didn't seem to read anything into it. "Yes, he was," she said, pouring cream and a teaspoon of sugar into the coffee. "It's hard without him. We had a good life, but I also missed you. That's why I'm here. To tell you that."

"I missed you, too, Lija."

A few moments, seconds that felt like hours, elapsed. They blew on their coffee, staring through the steam, as if the swirls might form themselves into intelligent sentences.

"He was a very good father," said Lija. "Even a pretty good farmer, considering it was dad who taught him."

Raki caught a laugh in her throat. "Well, he had more passion for it than Dad did."

"Yeah, he had passion, for sure."

Without the cream and the stirring, Raki's coffee was still too hot to drink. She tapped her fingernail against the table. Lija wasn't talking about farming, but it was safer to pretend that she was.

Lija changed the subject. "Do you see him much? Dad I mean?"

"Sometimes. Probably as often as you, but I'm sure he stays longer at your house."

"Trust me, he doesn't stay long at my house. Not a fan of teenagers. But you know that." Lija took a deep breath. "If Dad hadn't left when you were still in high school, would things have turned out differently?"

Raki fidgeted, cleared her throat. "Who knows?"

"Dad's leaving was harder on you than me."

"You already had your own family. I did feel . . . abandoned." First their mother died, then their dad left. Raki fell in love and he left, too. Her girlfriends abandoned her. The boys stole all of Lija's attention, then Lija kicked her out. Not that Raki blamed her, anymore.

"Your leaving. That was hard on me," continued Lija. "James was my only friend." A tendril of her corn silk hair strayed over her cheek. "He was everything to me—friend, husband, father, provider." She peered through the steam straight at Raki.

The conversation threatened to explode and collapse, like dough with yeast and no salt, so Raki measured in some safer topics. She questioned Lija on the minutiae of family life. Which child was on what team, coming home with what grades, looking forward to what goal?

The boys would not be planting the entire acreage this year. What they couldn't handle she would lease to neighbors. Eventually Randall hoped to work the entire farm, and buy up even more. A thousand acres was his goal. He needed his brothers to pitch in, but only Lance showed interest, and only if his football career didn't pan out. Sandy played guitar and dreamed of becoming a rock star. Jimmy Jr., the youngest, was thinking along the same lines.

"Even athletes and musicians have to eat," said Lija, "so it might work out in the end."

Raki talked about Joey's love for reading, argumentative nature, and busy schedule of school, debate team and Luther League.

"Sam is picking her up," said Raki, as the update on children began petering out. "Would you join us for dinner?"

"Thank you. I would like to meet Sam. And Joey. I always imagined her as a little girl version of my boys." Lija's hand started toward her mouth, like she was going to stuff the words back in. "Please, let me contribute." Lija sprang out of her chair. "Is there anything you need from the store? I passed one on the way. I could pick up whatever." She headed for her boots even before Raki could answer.

"You don't need to do that."

"Nobody ever has an empty shopping list. I insist."

Raki walked back to the kitchen and reached into the junk drawer, extracting a scribble pad jotted with shopping notes. She felt a little embarrassed, sending Minnesota's greatest gardener to the grocery store for canned vegetables.

As Lija shrugged on her coat, Raki noticed that she no longer wore a girdle. When had Lija given up on that? Did anyone wear one anymore? Lots of things had loosened up in the past fourteen years. She watched Lija walk to the truck, past the crocus in the sunny spot.

Can forgiveness sprout like that? From a dirty and buried bulb? Years of listening to Sam's sermons made her think in metaphors. Even if we keep the hurt buried? Crocus. Purple, like a bruise. No, the color of Lent. Repentance and forgiveness.

Raki shook out of her reverie. What was she going to tell Joey? That Lija, an aunt she's never heard of just happened to pop by for dinner? There was no sensible explanation.

Joey came in the door an hour later, laden with textbooks, too preoccupied to ask why a strange woman was unloading groceries in her mother's kitchen.

Sam's eyebrows flew up and his head snapped back a bit. He recovered quickly. He grasped his sister-in-law's hand and blurted, "So good to see you. This is wonderful! What brings you by?"

How did he recognize her? If he had ever laid eyes on Lija, it was over fourteen years ago. Did he interfere again, contact her, like he did way back when? Did it matter? "She's staying for dinner."

"It looks like she's cooking it." He reached his arm around Raki's waist and squeezed, leaning over to put a kiss on her forehead. "So good to see you two together. Peas in a pod."

Lija sliced cucumbers, whipped dressing and seared the chicken breasts in butter. It smelled like the kitchen at the farm. Raki plopped canned cream of mushroom soup into the skillet.

Dinner conversation was oddly scant, considering the decade plus of news they all had to catch up on. Joey's contribution was recounting the antics of the *Family Ties* kids on TV. She seemed confused about her own family ties. "They're my cousins because you're mom's sister?" she said. "And my grandpa is their grandpa, too?"

After the dishes were cleared, Joey escaped to her room. "Homework! Debate prep!"

Sam excused himself. "I'm sure you two have a lot to catch up on."

"You need coffee before you hit the road," said Raki when they were alone again.

"I had plenty this afternoon."

"That's worn off by now. Just to keep you awake. There's time for that." Raki pointed back at the table.

"Your husband seems nice."

"Well, it's kind of his job to be nice."

"I see the way he looks at you. Like every glance is a treat. And the little touches here and there. Affectionate."

"It comes natural."

"I always worried a little, that the two of you had some 'arrangement' or something."

Raki didn't know what she meant; she must have shown it on her face.

Lija stammered, "I mean, you left Halcyon so suddenly, and he . . . well, he wears a collar. I know it's not the same for pastors as priests; for heaven's sake, the Lutheran PKs monopolize all the solos at the school concerts. But I heard you had no more children." Lija's voice trailed off. "So I worried."

"No cause for worry, Lija."

"That was silly of me."

The follow-up question hung in the air, unasked.

"Mumps. Sam had mumps as a kid. That's the reason."

"None of my business."

"Infertility is a common enough problem for men born before the vaccine. Sam loves Joey, and Joey's a daddy's girl."

"James and I built the life we bargained for. But he had lots of loves—the farm, the boys." Lija paused. "I was one of his loves, I guess, but not the biggest one."

Please don't go there. If you dig up the bulb, the flower won't sprout.

Lija continued, "When you were pregnant, before I understood what had gone on, I vowed to make sure that everything would work out all right for you. I didn't keep that vow."

"Lija, everything did work out. Forgiveness all around, right?"

Lija nodded, a tear coming from one eye. She pushed herself away from the table. "Well, it's time to get back."

Raki forced herself to ask the question that had gnawed at her all these years. "Lija, do people in Halcyon, do they gossip about us?"

"Not within my earshot," she said. "A baby out of wedlock is a pretty everyday scandal these days. Too boring even for Halcyon. Plus, Miss Richter's feature stories have made you out to be some kind of saint. If they're still whispering, it's about me."

"You didn't do anything wrong."

"Doesn't matter. I came here to make it right."

"Thank you."

"You and Sam and Joey come see me and meet my boys. We'll be the most normal family in the county, a regular Hallmark special."

Raki's heart stopped pounding. "It will be wonderful to see them grown up. No diapers and all."

"It's settled then. Sandy's graduation is in a couple months. You must come. All of you. No more Minnesota good-bye, I really do need to hit the road."

LIJA FUSSED with the graduation cake, silver icing spelling out 'Congratulations, Sandy!' She counted the plates, lined up the silverware and straightened the napkins embossed 'Class of 1986.' Sandy had talked her into a picnic party. He was still in his graduation robe, unzipped, the sides flapping in the spring breeze. The ceremony in the gym had gone off with no untoward excitement. Lija hoped Raki's homecoming would be as easy. There was no need to explain too much; the boys got bored with history anyway. Normal. She vowed to act completely normal.

"Well, I'll be goddamned to hell!" Lija heard her father's bellow from across the farmyard. Sam and Raki's white Civic was pulling into her driveway. Raki climbed out of the passenger seat, followed by Sam. Lija had spent a week thinking how she would greet them. Throwing open her arms and running across the yard like TV would be ridiculous. She couldn't stop her dad's drama, but she would act normal. Like this happened every day.

He pulled himself off his lawn chair and ambled to the car as fast as ambling could take him. Her boys trooped behind him. Lija had told them her 'long lost' sister and husband were coming, but they still looked confused. Dad threw his arm around Raki and thumped Sam on the back. Joey stayed in the backseat, surveying the farmyard through the window. Lija could see the teenage nervousness, confusion about new people and a new environment, worry about fitting in. Lija opened the rear door and leaned in just a little. "Good to see you again, Joey," she said, extending her hand. Joey accepted the invitation and climbed out.

Joey winced as her grandpa ruffled her perfectly poofed hair do, but in a direction so he wouldn't see. Then she teased it back into place and kissed him on the check.

"Welcome!" said Lija, making introductions all around. Her sons stuck out their hands as trained. "Sandy, greet your guests as they come. Everything else is ready." She turned to Joey. "Let me show you around. Where your mom grew up. You, too, Sam."

Lija was proud to show off the wide lawn, prodigious garden and neatly tilled fields. She hadn't noticed the milkweed growing behind the freshly-painted barn, tall as a teenager. That was a little embarrassing, but she decided not to stop and pull it. Instead she kept on walking, telling stories of 4-H and school events from the Sixties. Raki trailed behind. Every now and then Lija threw a look back at her, seeking confirmation. "Yes, yes, that's how it was," Raki repeated. Normal. They were a normal family again. Sisters together again. Only one subject off limits. Every family hid something in the closet.

When the tour was complete, Lija found Dad in his lawn chair, the nylon webs straining to contain him. She squeezed his shoulders. The lemonade in his glass was bronzer than everyone else's and it was making him happy. He was acting the lord of the manor like the old days.

"The land is in good hands. Your great-grandsons' hands, Old Man," he said, shaking his fists at the sky. "I did the deal."

Raki walked up and stood next to Lija. Their father opened up his hands, continuing to gaze at the sky. "Laura, Sweetheart," he continued. "Tell the Big Guy, God that is, that I don't blame him anymore. It was just that kid. A teenager. They're all trouble. Anyhow, tell the Big Guy I'd like to join you up there, if he'll have me."

Of course Dad was in no particular hurry. He lived for another ten years.

PART NINE

The bison is gone from the upland,
The deer from the canyon has fled,
The home of the wolf is deserted,
The antelope moans for he is dead,
The war whoop re-echoes no longer,
The Indian's only a name,
And the nymphs of the grove in their loneliness rove,
But the columbine blooms just the same.

A.J. Fynn, *Where the Columbine Grow*
A Colorado State Song

More Letters
Denver, Colorado, 1951
Read in Halcyon, Minnesota, 2016

24

January 4, 1951

Denver, Colorado

Dear Katherine,

I am both elated and stricken. Elated that my ruse is working so well. Stricken for the same reason. Mommy and Daddy seemed quite proud of my decision to abandon them for a do-gooder adventure. They helped me dis-enroll and get my tuition refunded. They presented me with a very generous sum to avoid any untoward 'deprivation.' They even waved good-bye at the train station. And I was lying the whole time. Who knew I was capable of such depravity?

Judge me as you will, but it's working very well. As you can tell from the postmark, I headed west. Once I got to Union Station in Chicago I looked up at the Departures board and decided to see mountains. Halcyon doesn't even have any hills! The travel west itself consisted of nothing more than Great Plains and more Great Plains. Fields and cattle and cattle and fields. Plus horses. It resembled my life until lately—boring, wholesome. I expected to see some town ripped apart by a tornado, because my own heart still feels ripped up. Alas, if there were any storm damage, the people had already buried the debris and moved on. As I hope to as well.

I arrived at Union Station in Denver, an architectural twin to its namesake in Chicago. Both have gigantic halls, oversized benches, immense windows, impressive chandeliers and much hustle and bustle of business travelers and tourists.

The Colorado sky is a blue such as I have never seen before. The contrast against the craggy, snow-covered peaks is breathtaking. The downtown, however, feels quite like Minneapolis. Rather than Dayton's they have Denver Dry Goods, but offering the same pencil skirts and feathered hats. Nothing as haute couture as you see in Paris, I'm sure.

For the time being I have found myself a room in a small boarding house for young women. I can expect to pay $1 to $3 per day depending on how fancy I intend to live. Although I have a comfortable sum stashed away, the idea of spending it makes me feel even guiltier than I already feel, so my first task is to find myself a job.

By the way, how is your French beau?

Your trusting friend,

Dolores

January 5, 1951

Denver, Colorado

Dear Katherine,

I spent all day today reading the Want Ads. Am I a young, attractive woman? If so, there are a plethora of jobs for me: typist, airline hostess, stenographer, keypunch operator. I am young and a woman. The jury is out on the attractive verdict. Even the 'radio telephone operator' ad required applicants to be attractive. How would anyone know??

I am most hopeful for the possibility of being hired as a proofreader for the Women's Section of the Rocky Mountain News. *I have been proofreading Daddy's legal opinions for years, so that is a position for which I am perfectly qualified, provided they don't insist upon references.*

The news story of the day here is the sad tale of the young veteran/student/father caught stealing children's clothing from a department store. He was nabbed by police holding a dozen tiny suits and dresses for which he had not paid. His GI Bill stipend was not sufficient to feed and clothe five tykes, so now he's in a cell instead of a classroom. On the other hand, he left a trail of footprints in the snow, so perhaps his mental intellect isn't really up to university standards.

But when it comes to stupid moves, I have not earned the right to pass judgment. I hope only to cover my tracks better than he did. Which reminds me to say again: Thank you, so much, again and again, for abetting me in my 'crime.'

Your friend,

Dolores

January 20, 1951

Denver, Colorado

Dear Katherine,

It is good to hear your workload is so much lighter you have time for fun. Your weekend on the Riviera sounded delightful – sunny and cool.

Oh, the irony, to escape from little Halcyon only to find myself in a metropolis where the biggest event of the year includes a Rodeo, Sheep Dog Act and 4-H Pigeon Show. The National Western Stock Show is such a big deal the City of Denver spent $3 million on a Coliseum to house it, and this castle for cattle isn't even done yet.

Busy, you say? Indeed! Henceforth should anyone find an error of spelling, grammar or punctuation in the Women's Pages of the venerable Rocky Mountain News, *the blame shall be placed squarely upon my shoulders. I make sure the funeral directors have placed all the commas and semicolons correctly within the lists of survivors of the deceased. Once that task is squared away I proofread feature stories. Today's treat? The Martin family, every member having a first-name starting with M: Mabel and Martin (that's right – Martin Martin) are the parents of Morris, Muriel, Mary, Michael, Mervyn, Manfred, Melvin, Marilyn, Myrna, Murray, Major and Melissa. I'm not kidding!*

I am very happy that the Carnegie Library is very close to the newspaper office. Without friends here, I need the company of good books. Also, the research department is an excellent resource. There is so much I don't know that I need to learn.

Do keep up the good work. And be glad the Red Cross has not sent you to Korea.

Your friend,

Dolores

February 5, 1951

Denver, Colorado

Dear Katherine,

What great things I could be accomplishing if I were really working with you, instead of proofreading the Society pages. Misspell the name of one Aspen socialite and your job is on the line.

Working for our local advice columnist, Mrs. Mayfield, is more entertaining. I protect advice-seekers from the embarrassment that would be caused by seeing their sloppy grammar and incomprehensible syntax in print, even as they publicly reveal their stupidity. Every day I get to feeling superior to these idiots, only to remember I was stupider yet. If only I had thought to write to Mrs. Mayfield: 'Why hasn't my boyfriend ever invited me to his home?'

I have become very fond of the hurly burly in the newsroom. It is so different from the decorum of Daddy's courtroom. I will miss this place when I go home again. When will you be coming stateside?

Your busy friend,

Dolores

May 10, 1951

Denver, Colorado

Dear Katherine,

I was looking forward to seeing you, and now you are heading to Korea. It cannot be!

I can't go home quite yet, but I will in a few more months. Then I will happily re-devote myself to my parents and to a career—in journalism. I have decided to drop the study of law. I need more time here to learn the ins and outs of newspapering.

In the meantime, enclosed are several pre-written letters addressed to my parents. Could you please prevail upon a French acquaintance to occasionally slip one in the mail on my behalf?

Good luck in Asia. Keep yourself safe.

Your ever-demanding friend, who fears for your safety,

Dolores

৽

COLORADO. That explained the souvenir spoon from Denver and nothing from France. Was this Miss Richter's big secret, an affair followed by a deceptive adventure? Surely not. The secret was bigger than that.

Still, why had Dolores never told her this story? She and Raki had been friends for forty some years. By the time they met, Judge and Mrs. Richter were long dead and the man long gone, too. What had stopped her?

Dried lavender on every shelf. Pale purple sheaves dried and dead visible from every window. What had Miss Richter kept buried beneath all these flowers, her black dresses and purple accessories?

Was it even worse than what Raki had done? She was pretty sure it was, and no longer sure she wanted to find out.

Part Ten

No one I know of has ever had this experience—where you had to sit and wait and wait for a DNA test to come back just so you can write the last page of the book.

Joseph Wambaugh

Halcyon, Minnesota

2016

25

RAKI AWOKE in her childhood bedroom, more recently occupied by her youngest nephew, although even that was a long time ago. The digital clock read '3:30.' Her foot searched the sheets for a cool spot. Oh, to be young enough to get through a night without waking up in a surge of heat. She had never understood how twenty minutes could be called a 'flash.'

She threw off the covers, stared at the ceiling, yearning to be home, entangled in Sam's arms no matter the heat. She wanted to be planning her day at the bakery office, not another day sorting through that old house.

She searched for something to read, the best way to fall back asleep. Moonlight highlighted her nephew's old textbooks. She padded to the bookshelf, chose *History: The Twentieth Century*, propped up some pillows, switched on the table lamp and turned to the copyright page: 1990. Apparently the century had ended early.

So many familiar photos. She had lived through half of it, half of a history textbook. The iconic picture from the Kent State shootings, the girl weeping over her friend's body.

Raki's lie, if it had historical significance, would be on the next page, spring semester reading, when nobody cared anymore. She looked up from the book. Nobody cared anymore. It happened so long ago. She was the only person burdened. What day was a good day to confess?

Today would be a good day.

The clock now read '4:30.' Too early. She laid the book on the nightstand and closed her eyes. Words and phrases tumbled about in her mind. She turned the light back on.

The chapter on the Sixties and the Vietnam War took her to five o'clock. The house remained quiet. On to Nixon and Watergate. Then, there it was, the soft tapping of footsteps below. Farm women get up early, even those without animals. Then the whoosh of water from the tap, followed by the earthy scent of brewing coffee. No worry about waking up Lija.

Raki walked down the hall and tapped on the door to Lanny's old room, where Josephine slept.

HERE GOES.

Raki put her ear against the door, listening for the rustle of bedcovers. "Joey, are you awake?"

"I am now," came a sleepy voice. "What the heck, Mother?"

"It's important. May I come in?"

"Sure." The word ended in an upsweep.

With all the blood pounding to her head, she was almost too weak to turn the door handle, but somehow managed. Inside, a thin sunrise filtered through the curtain.

Joey sat up, patting the edge of the bed in invitation. "What on earth is the matter?"

"There's a story I've meant to tell you for a very long time. I couldn't sleep."

"Mom, are you all right?"

The speech she'd rehearsed in her head a thousand times tumbled out. "Your grandpa was a fine Dad, but after Mom died, it was Lija who raised me. She told me stories about our mom, took me to the Five & Dime for barrettes, taught me how to weed a garden. Not a skill I've used much through the years, but still, she loved me."

Raki paused for breath. The thin light made it hard to interpret Joey's facial expression. Bemused? Confused? The barrettes thing was stupid, but she couldn't rewrite the script on the fly.

She continued. "It was thanks to Lija that I met your father. The first time I met him I didn't think of him romantically at all. He was a pastor, for heaven's sake. Who wants that? Anyway, I was in love, but not with him. I had a 'green apple' love – tempting but it makes you sick. Your dad was more like a baking apple, sweet but boring, or so I thought."

"You woke me up to talk about apples?"

The apple thing was as dumb as the barrette thing. Raki took the deepest breath she had ever taken in her whole life, held it for two seconds, discarded the rest of her speech and blurted it out. "Your dad is not your biological father."

Joey burst out laughing, then covered her mouth. "Of course he's not."

What?

"'Bout time you told me, though."

"Of *course* not? What do you mean? How long have you known? What do you know?"

"I'm not having this conversation without caffeine. Stay here." Joey ran fingers through her blonde hair as she scooted through the door.

Waiting for Joey's return, Raki watched the sunrise illuminate the farmyard. There was the gas tank, a newer one, but in the same place as the one she had used to fill the lawnmower as a kid. Wild roses in the ditch, growing now just as they had when she was a girl. There was the spot where Randy got hit, and the place the family had built the snowman.

Joey nudged the door open with one foot, carrying in two steaming cups. She got right to it. "I've known forever," she started, handing over one of the cups. "I'm not an idiot. Aunt Lija and all my Isaksen cousins appear out of nowhere when I'm a teenager? You didn't think I'd be curious?"

"You never asked."

"A girl doesn't want to hear her mother's tawdry history. At least not directly from said mother."

Raki raised the cup to her lips. Too hot. She took a sip anyway.

"What made you think it was 'tawdry'?"

"Because you kept it secret."

"What exactly do you know? And how did you find it out?"

"I was gobsmacked when Aunt Lija came for dinner that day. Even an only child knows that sisters don't go years without talking unless something big, really bad, happened. I started snooping around, whenever you and Dad weren't home, rousting in the attic for evidence, looking for anything incriminating. I used to listen for little hints, maybe you would slip up and say something. About why Aunt Lija had been so mad at you, or why you were mad at her.

"Anyway, when I did junior year abroad I had to get a passport. For that I ordered a copy of my birth certificate. The name on the father's line was not one I recognized."

The birth certificate. Of course. "That was, what, over twenty years ago, and you never asked about it."

"Would you have told me my biological father was an army medic who got killed in Vietnam? Somebody named Luke?"

"Maybe."

"Well, that's why I didn't ask. I didn't want to hear you lie."

The secret kept wasn't hers at all. It was Joey's. She had found the truth and never said.

"How did you know the man on your birth certificate was an army medic? That wouldn't have been on there."

"Because I met him. He's alive and well."

Raki's mouth dropped open.

"I found him online. He's a surgeon. Lives in a very posh renovated Victorian on Nicollet Island."

Posh? Of course she knew the island had gentrified a long time ago. "You found all that online?"

"I also went over there and knocked on the door."

"He must have been shocked."

"No, more like amused. He asked if I was looking for a DNA test. I said no, but he offered to do it anyway. He was pretty sure it would come back negative."

"Did he do it? Get the test?"

"No, I couldn't feel any connection, see any resemblance. I told him if I ever wanted that done, I'd be in contact. He was very nice." Joey looked into her mother's eyes. "You knew, all along, that it wasn't him?"

"Not for absolute certain, of course. Putting his name on your birth certificate was the hardest part. I wasn't raised to lie, especially not to the government. I told myself it wasn't so much a lie as a poor guess."

"So, anyway," Joey continued, "I was pretty sure it wasn't him, but I didn't know who it was. Eventually Margaret spilled the beans. Don't be mad. She thought it was my right to know."

"Damn that Margaret." Raki's lips trembled. Relief? Sorrow? Embarrassment? Or all three?

Joey reached over and squeezed her hand.

"Isn't it funny?" said Raki, sniffing back the tears. "I don't mind she told you. I'm mad that she didn't tell me she told you." Then she started to laugh, which didn't stop the tears.

Joey hugged her about the shoulders. "The thing I kept wondering about, Mom, was how you knew." She waited for Raki to compose herself. "That it was Uncle James and not your boyfriend."

Raki swabbed her cheeks and exhaled sharply. "It was the Seventies," she said. "All evidence to the contrary, I did know about birth control."

BEFORE THAT ILL-FATED *trip to Mankato for The Pill, she had taken another, shorter drive, to the tiny General Store at Gore Corners, just up the road from Halcyon. She sauntered inside, acting cool.*

The clerk behind the counter called her "ma'am," which was how she was sure he didn't recognize her. If he had, she would have driven elsewhere. She picked up a box of condoms, jar of peanut butter and bag of chocolate kisses. Her hands were so sweaty and shaky she worried she'd drop it all on the way to the cash register. Making it to the counter without incident, she paid, drove home and baked a batch of cookies for Luke. The kind with the chocolate kiss in the middle. When they were cooled, she slid all the shiny little square packets onto a plate, then covered them with the cookies and plastic wrap. Kinda corny, but also clever.

"I MADE SURE Luke used protection every time," Raki explained. "I knew from reading that it wasn't one hundred percent effective, but it made more sense that Uncle James was your father, because with him, well, with him it had been . . ."

HOW HAD IT BEEN?

Like two people dying of thirst falling into a well. Without that water, neither could have survived, but there they were, covered in muck and stuck on the bottom with no means to get out.

So she had taken water and love, mud and algae and used it to paint a lovely picture of dry land—butterflies and flowers, peace symbols and moonbeams—and that was her plan. She heard James proclaim undying devotion and imagined he could turn her painted fantasy into reality, which of course he could not do.

". . . UNPLANNED. James and I, we were not prepared."

THE LITTLE DITCH rose bouquet, the one James gave her the day they met. That's when the not-planning began. When she was just a tween, as they say now, and he a grown man, when such thoughts were not thinkable and so were not thought.

Seven years passed and then she was a young woman and he a young man. Both abandoned. Then the ride on a Ferris Wheel, colored lights reflecting from his eyes. Cotton candy on a stick, pink as those ditch roses. Two people not thinking straight. The oldest story in the world.

"AFTER YOU were born, and Lija saw you in the hospital nursery, she told me I couldn't come home. I figured she saw the resemblance, and that was about all the proof I needed."

"She made you homeless, with a newborn, me. I can't imagine what that was like."

"I betrayed her. After all she did for me. And then I pretended it didn't matter. Of course it mattered. Lija had four little boys to feed. She did what she had to do."

LIJA THREW DOWN the rope that dragged everyone up into reality. Raki had been delusional. James too. May as well have been high on acid. Seventies free love commune bullshit. Love is never free and it's not peaceful, either.

"WE WEREN'T HOMELESS for very long," said Raki. "Thanks to your dad, your true dad, racing around town to rescue us."

26

ALMOST DONE. Raki and Margaret and Joey finished cleaning out Miss Richter's house. The letters, all read, lay in a blue heap on the floor. Raki raked her fingers along the bottom of the box, pulling up the bottom flap. *I gave up my secret, damnit, now what was yours, Dolores? What was yours?*

"Looking for a secret compartment?" asked Margaret. "Ala Nancy Drew?"

"What about her secret? What was the point of making us read these letters? Where's the clue?"

"It was just the affair, and the trip," said Joey. "That would have been plenty scandalous, especially back then."

"Those were secrets, not *the* secret," Raki insisted.

Joey sighed. "I'm relieved we didn't find out anything too awful, and I don't care anymore. It's time to call the liquidator or an auctioneer."

"We haven't cleared out the shed," said Margaret. "The garden shed. Maybe it's in there, like in an Agatha Christie mystery." Margaret turned to Raki. "Remember that party at my house way back when? How Miss Richter swooned when that man mentioned his father, Claude?"

That was it. That was how she remembered that name. Claude.

Years ago, when Joey was a baby. "Yes, I remember. We thought she was having a heart attack, but she wouldn't let us call a doctor. Said she got light-headed because her girdle was too tight."

"That's what I remember, too."

"What are you suggesting? That she poisoned Claude and stuffed his body in the shed?"

"Of course not," said Margaret. "The man said his father was shot. I'm just guessing, but I think there's something having to do with Claude in the shed."

"Nothing for it but to have a look," said Joey. "Probably nothing but clay pots and bags of fertilizer, but we have to clear it out anyway."

They walked out the back door together, traversing the yard at an unnaturally slow pace. Margaret creaked open the hatch to the shed. For a few moments, nobody moved. Oh, for heaven's sake, thought Raki, somebody has to be brave. She stepped in first.

Dried stems crisped beneath her feet. Thick layers of faintly fresh to ancient lavender carpeted the floor. A pair of mullioned windows, frilled with lace curtains, let in daylight. A lantern hung from a hook. Tucked in a corner sat a small table set with two chairs, a cribbage board and pack of cards. A wrought-iron bed was covered in a crocheted white bedspread. A mirror and antique basin and ewer stood upon a white bed stand. A bookshelf nailed to the wall held a wooden box and a copy of *Let Love Come Last* by Taylor Caldwell. A green dress on a padded hanger hung from a hook. Watered silk.

"It's a She-Shed," said Joey.

"Don't be ridiculous," said Raki. "That's a new fad. This goes back decades." Raki ran her finger across the top of the bed stand. "Not decades of dust, though. She must have come out here to clean."

"What's with all the weeds on the floor?" said Margaret, toe-ing the purple flowers. "You could bury somebody underneath all this."

"Not Claude, though?" said Raki.

"No, but I bet he, more likely they, spent some time here."

Joey pulled the wooden box off the bookshelf. She slid her finger under the latch. Inside was a stainless-steel safety razor and a brush.

"Well, that's evidence," said Joey.

"Why keep this room so tidy? Claude was already dead before the Eighties."

Raki swept her toe through the petals. *Clink.*

"There's something metal under the bed." Raki toed away a few inches of lavender. The brass handle of an old suitcase gleamed dully. The secret was in the suitcase. She just knew it. She considered turning away, but if she did, she would never sleep again.

"Claude's overnight bag?" guessed Joey. "There's a train tag attached," said Raki. "Denver to Minneapolis." She pulled it out from under the bed. "It's very light. Who wants to open it?"

Margaret fumbled with the clasp, unlocked but immobile from age. "Find something to pry this open with," Raki said.

Joey volunteered for the errand, returning with a butter knife. It worked.

The inside was packed with lavender, like Miss Richter's funeral casket, the floor of the shed and the deck of the house. Nestled within was a tiny skeleton. So tiny. Finger bones as delicate as filigree, curled around a beribboned scroll.

Joey gasped.

Margaret put her hands to her mouth.

Raki rushed for the door.

Joey and Margaret scrambled out behind her. Raki hipped it shut, gently. "Oh my God, now what?"

They stared at each other.

Raki bent over, putting her hands on her knees. She retched, but nothing came out. She stood up again, trying not to hyperventilate.

Joey squeezed her eyes shut and twisted her hands, over and over again. She risked wearing the skin right off.

Margaret put her hands on her hips, staring at the ground, breathing deliberately. She seemed the most composed.

Raki imitated her. So did Joey. In and out. In and out. In and out.

"She meant us to find it," Margaret said, after an eternity had passed.

"Of course she did."

"I didn't mean 'it.' I meant him, or her."

"Who knows about this?" asked Joey.

"Lord, I only hope nobody knows about this." Raki started breathing fast again.

"Are we supposed to call the police? Hold a funeral? Bury it in the yard?" Joey was starting to hyperventilate too.

"Calm down. Breathe slowly, or I'll need to get paper bags for both of you," said Margaret. "Let's go in the house and get our heart rates down."

Once inside, Joey went to the coffee pot, but Margaret pushed a twenty into her hands and told her to get something stronger. Joey returned ten minutes later with two bottles of pinot grigio. "Quantity over quality," she said, pouring three glasses.

The three drank. Lift the glass, drink, put it down. Lift the glass, drink, put it down.

Raki waited for somebody to say something. She didn't trust herself to make sense, but somebody had to say something. Her glass was dry. She had nothing else to do with her mouth. "How the hell did she manage to keep *that* a secret? Never a hint."

"I disagree," said Margaret. "The black clothes. Always in mourning. The accessories? Her badge of shame, like Hester Prynne's scarlet letter."

"All the charity," said Joey. "The way she befriended us, Mom, and gave you a loan and got you on your feet in business. All the gifts and scholarships. Every one to a single mom or illegitimate child."

That was the pattern Raki had missed.

"But why me?" asked Margaret. "Why am I here?"

"Because you did for us what apparently nobody could do for her." Raki's head was clearing. She grabbed her friend's hand, and then her daughter's. "Let's let the spirit guide us. We aren't nearly wise enough to know what to do by ourselves." They bowed their heads.

THE SPIRIT FAILED to provide any wisdom before the sun began sinking behind the shed.

"We need to know what's on that paper scroll," said Raki.

"None of us wants to go out there when it's really dark." Margaret got up and slipped on her shoes. She got halfway out the door and turned, "You *are* coming with me, aren't you?"

Guilt propelled Raki out of the chair. Of course they couldn't let Margaret go out there alone. Joey got up, too.

"Turn up the lights. We don't want to come back to the dark."

The suitcase clasp opened freely this time. Raki deftly retrieved the scroll, pushing the suitcase closed as efficiently as she could. The three hurried back to the bright light, circling the kitchen table, smoothing the tiny scroll flat. The paper cracked, startlingly loud. The ink was so faint they had to bend close to decipher it:

"Dear Baby, You are perfect. Every finger, every toe, every hair on your head, the product of love so deep that we have both drowned in it. I did not mean for you to die, dear little one. But we were all alone, you and me. In spite of all my reading, all the details I studied from the books I read in the library, I didn't really understand what to do.

I imagined I would be delivered of you deep in the night, swaddle you lovingly and slip out to a convent. Kindly nuns would discover your perfection and find you a perfect mother and perfect father who would hold you to their hearts and make you their own. Your new mother would wear a pretty apron. Your new father would sport a bow tie. But this was not to be. I didn't do it right or it didn't go right. All I managed was a mess in the bathtub, shame for us both.

You must have drowned in all the fluid, as I am drowning in this sorrow. Yet, I still breathe. It is very, very unfair. You will never slide down the slippery slide, or ride the merry-go-round or eat a banana or hold your mommy's hand to cross the street. You are going to a special heaven for perfect babies. I shall hold you forever in my heart, but not in my arms. Love, Mommy."

"SHE ESCAPED," said Raki.

"Escaped?" said Margaret. "She didn't escape anything."

"She escaped prosecution," said Joey.

"She didn't do anything to be prosecuted for," said Raki.

"Oh, God, Mother," said Joey. "There's a body in a suitcase."

Was it the legal training that made Joey so judgmental? "This was a tragedy, not a crime. All I meant was she escaped disgrace."

"She never let herself forget," said Margaret. "She wore the disgrace on her sleeve, literally."

"Unforgivable." Joey shook her head.

"Nothing is unforgiveable," said her mother.

Joey opened her mouth, then closed it again.

"Anyway, the evidence is, how do you lawyers phrase it? Inconclusive."

"The thing to do is call the police," said Joey. "Cold cases division."

"What good would that do? She's dead." asked Margaret. "And which police? Halcyon? Denver? The FBI?"

Joey ran her fingers through her hair. "I'm imagining the headline if we don't. 'Aide to the Governor Covers Up Baby's Death.' It would go viral."

That's what she's worried about? Publicity? "We are definitely not calling the police." Raki looked to Margaret for reinforcement. "She entrusted her reputation to us. She entrusted this baby to us."

"Let's take a walk."

Margaret could always be counted on for a practical suggestion.

They trekked down the front steps, along the sidewalk, into town, past the playground with its rusted slide and the faint circle where the merry-go-round once twirled, ending in front of the newspaper office, the route Dolores had walked every day. Then they turned around and retraced their steps.

The playground stood deserted. Raki detoured to the old picnic table and sat down, taking care not to get splintered on the old wooden bench. She motioned to her daughter and friend. "This is private enough."

"Somebody had to know something," said Joey. "Somebody in Denver, somebody knew. There would have been blood in the bathtub."

Margaret gasped. Raki reached for her hand.

"Unless she cleaned it up, before she escaped," said Raki.

"How could you clean up something like that by yourself? After giving birth? Alone? That's not humanly possible."

"Keeping a secret like this for sixty-five years, that's not humanly possible, either, but she did it," said Raki. "And the baby's body. It was carefully packed. In flowers. Somehow she managed that, too. If she left evidence, nobody pursued it. She wouldn't have been hard to find."

"Why didn't she bury it? Before she left? Like a normal person would do? Why carry it on the train, and keep it, only to set us up to find it?"

"She wanted to be forgiven," said Margaret.

"We're not God," said Joey.

"She was such a good person," said Raki, "but I always knew something was wrong. I need forgiveness for never pursuing it, never offering comfort when she was alive."

"What would you have said, Mom?"

"I don't know. Maybe that good comes out of bad. Like yeast, fungus that makes bread rise. Or maybe that good girls do bad things because they are good girls. And bad girls do good things because they are bad girls."

"That makes no sense."

"Sure it does," said Margaret. "Dolores saved her parents from shame. And when it was over, she came back and did good deeds."

Joey shook her head.

"Times were much different then, Joey," said Raki. "Hers was not a time or place where she could go to her parents and say, 'Look, Mom and Dad, I'm pregnant out of wedlock by a man who already has a wife and kids. Help me out.' That was not a choice available to her. An announcement like that would have devastated everybody. Dolores, her parents, the man, his wife, his kids, even the baby she was carrying. No good would have come from it. So the good girl ran away and hid, because that's what a good girl had to do."

"And what bad girl did a good thing?"

"Me, I suppose," said Raki. "Virtue shmirtue, didn't matter to me. I didn't intend to betray Lija, but I did. If I had stopped to think, maybe I wouldn't have done it. But it's like when you're at the county fair, standing in line for the Tilt-A-Whirl. You don't stop and think about how some high school drop-out with a hangover bolted the ride together in an afternoon. And even if you did, it would just make the ride more exciting. You wouldn't step out of the line."

"You're comparing my conception to a carnival ride?"

Raki laughed. "Yeah. Exactly."

༅

MARGARET LED the way back to Miss Richter's house. She was determined to do what they had to do. May as well get on with it. But then wine came out again. More talk. They were like a three-headed Hamlet, dithering when they really needed a course of action. Joey seemed especially determined to hash to pieces the moral and legal implications.

Margaret searched for a different literary reference to help Joey come to grips. Eventually she settled for pop culture. "The Fifties were not 'Leave It to Beaver' and the 1970s were not 'The Brady Bunch,'" she lectured. "You younger women look at these black and white photographs and see the pressed blouses and the perfectly coifed hair and you assume we were all tied up in virtue, but what you can't see are the hormones we had pepsquadding through our veins."

Margaret took a breath for dramatic effect, and because she needed it. "Hormones, love, whatever, that's what killed my sister, and your grandmother, too." She screwed up her eyes like she was crying, but she had long ago run out of tears.

"What?" said Joey. "Now we're talking about my grandma?"

"That's my secret. Only your mom and dad ever knew, not counting Mike, and my parents—but they're long dead."

She told Joey the story she had confessed to Sam in his office so long ago. Of the older sister, the secret marriage, the pregnancy that wasn't, the coat hanger that killed her anyway; the boyfriend/husband flying hell-bent-for-leather down the highway. The crash. No seatbelts, of course, it being the Sixties. Both drivers dead, the teenage boy and the mom of two daughters.

"We didn't put our two stories together for a long time. You see, I could have saved not just my sister and her husband, but your grandmother, too. I just didn't know how. Fate brought your mom and me together. So I could atone."

NOT FATE, thought Raki. Sam. But she didn't correct her friend.

"How did the bad girl end up marrying the pastor?" asked Joey, turning to her mother.

"I took advantage, in my bad girl does good way. He wanted to marry this other girl, Claire. Chaste and all, a seminary student. She dumped him. So there was my opportunity."

"What happened to her?"

"We have seen her at church things many times through the years. She spoke at my first fundraiser. Works on social justice. There's not a homeless person she hasn't given a sandwich, a legislator she hasn't lobbied or a protest she hasn't marched in. Everyone loves Claire."

"But Claire didn't love Dad?"

Raki steepled her hands under her chin. "Not in that way. We were all such idiots back then, couldn't see the rainbow in the sky."

"What?"

"Claire is gay. She's married now. To a very nice woman."

THE NEXT DAY, after more discussion, the three women decided to quietly bury the tiny body beside the shed.

Margaret located a spade in the garage. They hoped the soil would be loose, so the digging would be easy. It was not to be. Raki drove the spade tip toward the earth. Chunk. A teaspoon of dirt sprayed from the tip of the shovel. She did it again, harder. A tablespoon came up.

"Let me try." Joey took the handle of the spade, placing the tip into the tiny indentation left by her mother. She pushed her foot hard against the back of the blade. Up came a quarter cup. "This is going to be harder than we thought."

A voice came over the back fence. "What are you ladies doing over there?" The old woman from the funeral. The grumpy gossipmonger. Whose suspicions were well founded, as it turned out.

Joey jerked her head up. Raki swung her head to look at Margaret. "Gardening," Margaret hollered back.

"Aren't you selling the place?"

"The realtor stressed the importance of staging the house for the best price. We're prettying up the yard," answered Margaret, her voice rich with school teacher authority.

"It's going to take you forever with that little spade." They could see Gossipmonger's eye peering through a knothole in the fence. "I've got a rototiller if you ladies want to push it over."

Raki's face flushed. Joey's mouth opened. Margaret turned to hide her own dismay. "That would be a big help," Margaret called over her shoulder, then whispered, "She thinks we're digging something up, not putting something in. The rototiller is a good idea."

They three women brought over the machine. The old woman accompanied her tool, apparently to supervise.

The blades bucked at first, but soon began chewing. Joey pivoted the tiller.

"That all? Such a little spot?" shouted the old woman over the roar of the motor.

"We just want to plant a few flowers," Raki shouted back. Joey cut the engine.

"Something better than all this damn lavender, I hope." The old woman grabbed the spade from Margaret, poking here and there. She jumped like a cheerleader when the metal chinked against something hard. "Lookee here!" The tiller had churned up a glacial era rock. "Oh, never mind. Thought it was . . . buried treasure. Put my tiller back when you're done." She turned on her heel and headed to the other side of the fence.

They heard her screen door slam. Joey looked to Margaret. "Do you think she will come back over here and start digging?"

"I'm positive of it," said Raki.

"So what's Plan B?" Margaret's voice had lost a bit of its authority.

Joey leaned in close and whispered, "The dirt over Miss Richter's grave will still be loose."

"You're kidding," said her mother. "Counselor to the governor wants to sneak into a cemetery and bury a suitcase? Now that's a story bound to go viral."

They went silent about it for a few minutes. Margaret finally said what they were all thinking.

"Not if we don't get caught."

In the shed they tucked the scroll back under the tiny fingers. Raki carried the suitcase to Margaret's car. Margaret loaded the spade. Joey returned the tiller.

They brainstormed strategy over lunch in Miss Richter's kitchen. One would barely finish speaking before another would throw out another concern, tactic or question.

"What if somebody sees us? What's our cover story?"

"Does anybody know what the caretaker's hours are?"

"We can't ask. That would create suspicion."

"What's the maximum sentence for disturbing a grave?"

"I'll Google that."

"Even if the caretaker doesn't see us digging, he's bound to notice freshly turned soil."

"There's no explanation for being in the cemetery in the dead of night."

"Tell that to the local hormonal teenagers."

"We may be hormonal, but we're not teenagers."

"If we sneaked out, Mike would surely notice, and probably Lija, too."

"Pray the police don't arrest us."

"Never mind the police, God will smite us for sure."

"Not if our hearts are pure."

Their hearts thumped in unison, and nobody backed out.

In the end, broad daylight seemed the safest time to commit grave desecration. Raki took out her phone and checked the local funeral home website. "No burials scheduled today." A gigantic floral spray was purchased to disguise their crime. "A parting gift for our friend, Dolores," Margaret told the florist. "You can put some lavender in it," said Raki. "And balloons," added Joey.

They drove to the Voll mansion, the heavy scent of the flowers mixing with the aroma of nervous sweat. "We smell guilty," said Joey as they got out of the car.

From the third story servant's quarters, down the hall from Joey's old nursery, they surveilled the cemetery. Deserted.

"There used to be people there all the time," said Raki. "Live ones I mean, visiting graves, watering the flowers."

"Just for today I'm glad so many moved away," said Margaret. "Live ones, I mean."

At three-thirty they drove into the cemetery, not another car anywhere in sight. They parked on the backside of the metal water trough.

Raki looked around as they climbed out of the car. "Coast is clear." She looked up at the lone cloud scudding across the sky. "God help us."

Joey used the spade. It dug as easily as they had hoped.

Raki hovered over Joey. "Only as big as we need, no bigger, but deep."

Raki opened a Bible and began reading. "Jesus called the children to him and said, 'Let the little children come to me, and do not hinder them, for the kingdom of . . .'"

"God!" Margaret interrupted. "Oh, my God. The caretaker!"

Joey spun, turning her back to the man striding toward them. He was still a dozen rows away. She stuffed the dirty spade in a guitar case they had found in Margaret's attic. Margaret placed the floral spray over the fresh dirt, quickly, but with a devout flourish meant for the caretaker's notice.

"Sir!" Raki called out, waving. "Join us for the hymn. We need a man's voice."

It took him a minute to reach them. "Thought you already had a service."

"Just paying last respects. Again," said Margaret.

"Not many do it again." The caretaker looked at the suitcase on the ground, scrunching his brows together.

"Stopped at the antique store," lied Raki. "An old suitcase in such good shape is quite a find."

"My wife appreciated your business, I'm sure. I'll tell her I saw you."

Margaret rushed to the rescue. "Oh, dear, we're so sorry. She meant the shop in Winton."

The caretaker looked disappointed. "Gonna play that thing for the hymn?" He pointed to the guitar case.

"'What A Friend We Have in Jesus' needs no accompaniment, don't you agree?" said Joey. "*A capella* is the way to go."

"I'm no good at singing *a capella*." He stumped away.

They sang all the verses. When the caretaker was far out of sight, Raki pulled the spray of flowers away from the grave. Joey slid the suitcase into the hole. Margaret spaded the dirt back over it and tamped it down. Together they covered it with the flowers again.

They all breathed heavily, in unison. Raki folded her hands and bowed her head. Joey placed her hands around her mother's and Margaret piled on, too. They prayed a prayer of relief and thanks.

Dolores's secret was buried again. Close to her heart.

Did you enjoy this story?

Help other readers like you find this book. Post a review on Amazon.com and Goodreads.com or your favorite book review site.

Discussion Questions

1. How do you feel about the author using a biblical tale as the basis for her plot? Did you look up Genesis 29? Was her updating of the story for modern times appropriate?

2. Yearning for a simpler time is a preoccupation of all generations. Did this book make a convincing argument that the past was more complex than sometimes believed?

3. Did you believe Margaret when she said her sister wasn't really pregnant? If so, why did her sister do what she did? If not, why did Margaret tell the story that way?

4. Sending disabled children and unwed mothers out of the community was a common practice in the past. How do you feel about the author equating the two?

5. The author goes to some length to show that Raki seduced Luke and not the other way around. Who do you think was the seducer in the Raki/James encounter? Does it matter?

6. The Clergy Consultation Service was a real organization (since evolved into The Religious Coalition for Reproductive Choice). Were you surprised to learn that clergy helped women find abortion providers? How have circumstances and attitudes toward abortion changed since legalization? What caused the attitudes to change?

7. Do you agree with the women's decision to bury the suitcase with Dolores? Are secrets ever really buried?

Did your book group enjoy this discussion?

Help other groups find this book by recommending it on Amazon.com or Goodreads.com or your favorite book review site. Post a review using the words "book group" or "book club" and mention your discussion.

ACKNOWLEDGMENTS
In Chronological Order

I am forever grateful to my mom, who instilled in me her love of books, my dad who loved me unconditionally, and to both for reading all my little stories when I was a girl. Hugs to both of you in heaven.

To the English teachers of St. James Minnesota Public Schools, especially Mrs. Helen Hake and Mrs. Mary Otto. I once told Mrs. Otto I would write a novel with no symbols, to which she replied, "No you won't. There will be symbols." In spite of my best effort, she is proven right.

To my husband, Don Rosenberry, for believing in me, providing the freedom for me to write, and for patiently watching me labor over these pages for years without asking for a sneak peek.

To my sister Mary Jacobson Evers and sister-in-law Barb Markos for graciously hosting me during my research. My descriptions of the Dels, Nicollet Island and Dinky Town are more vivid than faded memory, thanks to you.

To the Denver Public Library Western History Department and the Martin County (Minnesota) Historical Society for preserving and sharing your newspaper archives. This story is richer, truer and funnier thanks to you.

To the Rocky Mountain Fiction Writers and especially the writers of the Belmar Critique Group. Every one of you made this story more readable.

To my beta readers for your constructive criticism, which made the story richer, and affirmation, which gave me the courage to keep going. To my husband for his careful editing (yes, I finally let him read it), Lisa French for her 'writerly' advice, Carrie Makenna for her artistic sense, Mary Jacobson Evers for making sure the time and place (though fictitious) rang true, and Pr. Brigette Weier and Pr. Caitlin Trussell for making sure I didn't stray too far into theological heresy.

Thanks to my editor, Dona Chilcoat, and my proofreader Carolyn Reed, for your generous offering of time and wisdom, and to my designer, Susan Tyler, for your cover advice and artistry.

And thanks to all the women who have persevered against an unfair world and to all people who have forgiven and been forgiven.

Speaking of which, to anyone I've failed to mention, please forgive me. Everyone I've ever met is a part of me and a part of this book. Thank you all.

ABOUT THE AUTHOR

Joan Jacobson began writing at age eight. Her professional career began as a reporter for the *Albert Lea Tribune* in rural southern Minnesota. She lives and works in Lakewood, Colorado.